TONY HOGAN BOUGHT ME AN ICE-CREAM FLOAT
BEFORE HE STOLE MY MA

Tony Hogan bought me an Ice Cream Float before he Stole my Ma

Kerry Hudson

Chatto & Windus

LONDON

To the three best women I know: Susanna, Maria, Levia.

Published by Chatto & Windus 2012

2 4 6 8 10 9 7 5 3 1

Copyright © Kerry Hudson 2012

Kerry Hudson has asserted her right under the Copyright, Designs
and Patents Act 1988 to be identified as the author of this work

First published in Great Britain in 2012 by
Chatto & Windus
Random House, 20 Vauxhall Bridge Road,
London SW1V 2SA
www.randomhouse.co.uk

Addresses for companies within The Random House Group Limited can be found at:
www.randomhouse.co.uk/offices.htm

The Random House Group Limited Reg. No. 954009

A CIP catalogue record for this book
is available from the British Library

ISBN 9780701186395

The Random House Group Limited supports The Forest Stewardship Council (FSC®),
the leading international forest certification organisation. Our books carrying the FSC
label are printed on FSC® certified paper. FSC is the only forest certification scheme
endorsed by the leading environmental organisations, including Greenpeace.
Our paper procurement policy can be found at
www.randomhouse.co.uk/environment

Typeset in Goudy by Palimpsest Book Production Limited,
Falkirk, Stirlingshire

Printed and bound by
CPI Group (UK) Ltd, Croydon, CR0 4YY

1

'Get out, you cunting, shitting, little fucking fucker!' were the first words I ever heard. The midwife, a shiny-faced woman who learned entirely new turns of phrase that night, smoothed Ma's hair.

'Yer both fine. We'll have tae give yeh a quick stitch-up later, but – baby girl just ripped you a wee bit coming out.'

Ma laid me, sticky and slack-limbed, on her chest and wondered how something so pink, puckered and fragile could be so vicious as to tear the person who was meant to love her most in the world. But that was the Ryan Women: fishwives to the marrow, they were always ready to fight and knew the places that would cut deepest.

I was not vicious, though. No one could tell if I was clever, or sly as my grandma had predicted while blowing Benson & Hedges smoke rings over my ma's swollen belly. I was a 'bad baby', forever gurning and spitting out my ma's nipple. My delicate skin had mottled with the indignation of being ripped by forceps from a warm, cosy spot where I was perfectly happy.

For all my fretful kicking at the air and scratching at my own face, my saving grace was beauty. Everyone said so; a golden baby with extra-blue eyes, the slope of my nose and forehead just so.

'She'll be a wee heartbreaker,' Grandma said, smoothing down her mint-green nylon trousers. 'But she'll have a lot o' jealousy. An' I know wha' a burden it is tae be born with beauty.'

Grandma's violet eyes filled and the tears seeped through her pale powder into the wrinkles underneath.

Ma held me to her bony chest, resting my bum on the roll of flesh under her sharp ribs, which was all that remained of my home.

'Aye, she takes after her daddy. He was gorgeous. Those American blue eyes. She's the spit of him.'

Ma's face crumpled, her mouth sagged in a whine and her face turned pink. I wondered what I'd been born into.

Other mas in the ward came over and eyed me suspiciously, checking I wasn't heavier, livelier or prettier than their babies. Ma's – my – family came and held their faces so close to mine I could smell whether they'd had booze or food for breakfast. It was mostly booze.

Uncle Frankie, who had a scatter of freckles across his face, eyes the colour of Aberdeen skies and hair like silky copper, picked me up and held me above his head like a football trophy.

'Yeh did it, sis! An' what a little beauty an' all!'

Even though he was as short as Ma and a bit chubby around the edges he made the other mas laugh and tuck wisps of hair behind their ears and the nurses raise their eyebrows and lower their chins; a very nurse thing to do, I'd noticed.

My Great Auntie Aggie came, wearing saucer-sized glasses and carrying a half-eaten bag of sherbet lemons. She said I was the image of Rodney Boyle, her first love who broke her heart, and went to sit at the end of the bed, with an unlit fag in her hand, to update Grandma on the 'Andy Maguinness fiasco'. My ears, no bigger than a slice of button mushroom, told me the young one 'was begging for it'. After they'd sucked and crunched their way through the sherbet lemons and the juicier details, 'standing up in the bus station toilet, Aggie. Imagine, the filth! I won't be using them again, I'll tell yeh that,' they hoisted their handbags onto their shoulders and marched off in their matching beige high heels to the bingo.

The flickering light was switched off and the nurse put me in the plastic box of a cot. When the squeaks of her shoes were far enough away Ma picked me up and tucked my head in the crook of her shoulder. I allowed her one minute of peace and curled my lips, so small and sweet that they asked to be bitten like jelly sweets, into what my ma joyfully thought was my first smile. It was, in fact, the beginnings of wind. As I felt her arms slacken with the possibility of sleep, I filled my lungs and screamed like only a Ryan Woman can.

The crabbit woman opposite sat up and snapped her bedside light on.

'For goodness' sake, lassie –' her gold cross glinted as she leaned forward – 'see to your child and give the rest of us some peace. She'll be spoilt before she leaves the crib.'

My ma, Iris Ryan as they knew and loved her, sat up and declared with as much dignity as a woman who has two milky wet patches on the front of her nightie can, 'My lassie can cry as long as she wants tae, an' anyway, it was probably yer ugly mug that set her off!'

She swung her heavy legs to the floor and took me out to walk the green, gleaming corridors. I stopped crying, gave her the gift of another woozy, windy smile, and understood for the first time that she was my ma and it was us against the world from that night on.

Uncle Frankie borrowed a red car from his pal Meathead and I was swaddled in my basket on Ma's knee in the front seat, sucking on two fingers, my feet cushioned on the stringy wet tissues that Ma kept stuffing there. She'd cried for the last twenty-four hours, the sobs getting quieter and her eyes puffier with each hour. She'd cried so much there wasn't a clump or speck of mascara to be seen; Frankie said he hardly recognised her. In those hours Ma undid years of indelible mascara residue.

'Come on, sis, yer going home. Ma'll look after the wee un and yeh can have a rest.'

Ma bit the inside of her cheeks, stared straight ahead and let tears stream and soak into the neckline of her T-shirt.

'Just start the car, Frankie.'

But he didn't; instead he reached to the back seat for a plastic bag.

'An' look what I got yeh. A wee pressie!'

Ma took it, sandwiched it between her stomach and the end of my basket, then waited for the car to move.

'Look inside then.'

She pushed down the sides of the bag and produced a thin black bottle of vodka and a lurid pink miniskirt, which even in her pre-pregnancy days my skinny ma couldn't have got herself into. She stared at the pink skirt as though deciphering a code, turned it over in her hands.

'What's this?' she demanded, her temper stopping the tears. 'Is this some kind of joke? Taking the piss out of yer sister's fat arse?'

Frankie's blue eyes were wide in confusion, a blush spread behind his freckles. 'What? Reenie, naw, I –'

'For the last time it's fuckin' Iris! I didnae go all the way to fuckin' London to come back an' be the same old Irene!' A fleck of spit landed on my cheek, my engine revved, I gave a few hiccups and started up crying.

'Iris. Sorry. But honest, it's no' a joke. I just wanted tae remind yeh there'll be lots more nights out tae be had. Now yer no preggers any more. Yeh can hit the town. An' Shelley, she's my new girl, she was meant tae come an' help me choose an outfit fer yeh but then she had tae babysit an', I just . . .'

Even with my eyes closed to summon my loudest wails I could tell Frankie was close to tears himself.

'Forget it, Frankie. Let's just go.'

'See, Reenie, I mean Iris. I just got this wee thing until yeh could come with me an' pick somethin' proper.' The last sentence was barely audible over the rain smashing down on the windscreen and my tantrum.

Tears gathered on Ma's lowered lashes. 'Sorry, Frankie. It's a lovely thought. I'm just tired, will yeh start the car now?'

Frankie looked at Ma, her eyes closed, head back against the seat, then at my legs and fists beating in rhythm with my screams, and shook his head.

'An' another thing,' said Ma, eyes still closed, 'what's so important that Ma couldn't come?'

A bead of sweat popped on Frankie's forehead and rolled into the auburn thicket of his eyebrow. His eyes roamed but found nothing to rest on.

'Aw, ehm, bingo.'

Colour rose in my ma's face for the first time that day, her eyes snapped open. 'Bingo? Yer telling me the two fat ladies and legs eleven is why she's no here tae collect her first grandchild?'

Frankie turned off the heater, wiped the back of his neck with the palm of his hand. 'Aye, but it's –' he looked over at Ma then directed the rest of his sentence in a whisper to his knees – 'Triple Jackpot on Thursdays.'

'The fucking bitch.'

As we pulled out of the car park, Ma stared straight ahead,

glitter-eyed and tearless, and I let sleep seep into my exhausted wee body.

We drove through the grey estate and Frankie helped us to the door, carrying me with the bottle of vodka under one armpit and a teddy with a pink bow under the other. Ma said he could keep the skirt to clean his windows with and followed behind dragging her string bag that held a nightie, a Harold Robbins novel, a few grubby sanitary towels.

At the doorstep Ma gave a twitch of her lips that might have been a smile.

'Thanks fer getting us. An' sorry fer earlier, I'm a hormonal monster. I just can't believe I'm back at this dump.'

Frankie leaned over to give her a kiss, their close-together heads putting me in shadow until the blue sky and smoke-puff clouds opened up between them again.

'Listen, yer going tae be a great ma. Member how yeh looked after me?'

'Aye, well our darling ma was always half pissed or down the bingo so . . . no' much has changed, has it? Will yeh come up an' have a drink of that fancy vodka? Wet the bairn's head?'

'Sorry, sis, Shelley promised tae make it up tae me fer no coming shopping.'

'Well, Romeo, yeh'd best not keep her waiting.'

Frankie's grin dropped. 'There's another thing.' He passed me to Ma, put the vodka and teddy on the doorstep and pulled out a brown envelope from his back pocket. 'Now don't get pissed off. It's just a wee bit of cash in case anything comes up an' yer no' wanting tae go back to McHennessy's.'

Ma's eyes filled as he slid the envelope into my basket. 'Frankie . . .'

'It's no much because of the rent going up and that new telly, just a few hunner in case.'

'Yer too good, an' that's the truth.' They stood and looked at each other. 'Now, are yeh going tae keep yer hot date waiting?'

Frankie gave Ma another quick kiss and squeezed my hand between forefinger and thumb – 'She's gorgeous –' and bounded down the steps.

'An' Frankie?' Ma shouted to his back. 'Fer fuck's sake use some protection! You don't want tae end up with one of these!' But he was already inside the car, the Specials' 'Too Much Too Young' vibrating through the windows.

Ma wrestled, vodka under one arm and me balanced on her knee, to unlock the door. The little flat smelt of fag ash and stale dinner dishes. In the bedroom Ma sat on the rumpled bed, putting me behind her, and reached for a note on the bedside table that said 'IRENE' in big block capitals, a circular scribble where the pen wouldn't work above the R. Ma leaned forward and I saw the bumps of her spine through her T-shirt, the sag of her shoulders once she'd finished reading.

'Well, my wee one, Granny wants us tae run out fer some milk an' twenty Benson & Hedges. Welcome fuckin' home.'

She put me in the cot and through its slats I saw the glint of the slim bottle as she tipped it towards her lips.

It was half empty when she staggered from the room and came back with the pink teddy, sodden and grimy from its hours discarded on the doorstep, and put it into my cot. Then, she lay down and fell into a sleep so deep that even my screaming for dinner wouldn't break it.

2

Grandma had cooked mince, tatties and skirlie. It was pension day. Ma sat in a nylon nightie, one with scratchy lace around the sleeves, stirring the oatmeal-and-onion slop into her tatties.

'Aye, well, it just wasnae what I was expectin', that's all. I've only been home a few days.'

'I just thought, since she isnae taking the breast, it wouldnae make a difference if it was me or you. An' McHennessy's will bring in more than the dole.'

'But I'm sick of it, Ma. The white boots that reek of other women's feet an' the buckets of bloody water an' fuckin' stink of fish guts. I'm no' a fishwife, I don't want tae be one.'

'No' good enough fer yeh, is that it? Miss High an' Bloody Mighty thinks she's too fancy fer the fishhouse now she's been tae London and got herself preggers by a Yank? Well, what an affront. It was good enough tae put food on the table fer my ma and her ma before her.'

Ma stirred her tatties slower, twitched her left foot.

'Naw, Ma, it's no' that. I just want tae get tae know my bairn. An' what about when you're at the bingo or want tae go down the Black Dog?'

'I'll just take her with me of course.'

Ma stared down at her muddy plate of mixed food her lips set firm. 'Well, I'm not doing it and yeh can't make me.'

Grandma put down her knife and fork, food half finished, and reached for her fags. 'While you're in my house yeh bloody well will. Yeh'd think yeh've forgotten that it was you who turned up on my doorstep, without a penny to yer name or a father fer yer bairn.' Grandma didn't raise her voice, though there was steel there: cold, sharp and ready to cut. But Ma wasn't afraid, she was used to her own ma's slicing words.

'What? An' have her dragged about from pub tae pub like we all were?'

'An' what's that supposed tae mean? At least I could keep a man, someone fer yeh all to call yer da.'

'But it wasnae one man, was it? It was three, an' what a fuckin' bunch of charmers an' all!'

Grandma took a puff of her fag and stubbed it out. 'At least they stuck around an' helped tae bring some money in. And yours hasnae. That is why, my ungrateful wee daughter, you've got tae work.'

From my cocoon of pillows on the sofa I saw the gleam of the knife and fork in my ma's tight white knuckles.

'An' where are they now, Ma, yer army men? Are you keeping them under the sink, eh? Maybe you rush off tae a penthouse at the Palace Hotel when I'm at the fishhouse? Because the last time I looked it was just you, by yourself, in this wee flat.'

She put her knife and fork on the plate. Grandma's face crumpled, like air had been sucked from her lips and cheeks, but she rallied, raised her chin, pointed a polished nail at Ma.

'Yeh ungrateful bitch. Tae make fun of a poor pensioner who's taken yeh in, out of the kindness of her heart, offering tae look after yer wee bastard.'

'Aye, cause yeh did such a good job of that on our first day back from the hospital.'

'Still the same old Irene Ryan, yeh'll never change. Runt of the litter, a black sheep. Runnin' off tae London and getting intae

God knows what. Runnin' around wi' a Yank that couldn't get shot of yeh quick enough. You always were a nut job but I ignored the gossip, held my head high an' I never loved yeh any less.' Grandma's teeth slipped out and she snapped them back in. 'Yeh've never been a proper Ryan, yer nothin' better than a cuckoo in the nest.'

I felt myself roll sideways, watching Ma's stunned face upside down before I saw a rush of velour and my arm and shoulder exploded with a thump, my cheek scraping itself across the sour-smelling brown carpet.

Silence, a stilling of six lungs, as Ma and Grandma stared in horror until I screamed. I felt the burn on my silky cheek, the burst of pain in my shoulder no stronger than pipe cleaners and Play-Doh.

Ma grabbed me. 'Are yeh alright?' She picked up my limbs and shook each one. 'Is she alright?' She turned to Grandma who took me in her rough grip.

'Ach, it's nothing. Look, she's kicking away an' that's just a wee carpet burn, but this is proof, yeh can't look after her yerself.'

Ma looked over, lips tightening into a line of skin, and put her arms out to take me back. 'I see what yer trying tae do. Yer trying tae take my bairn but yeh can't take this away. She's mine an' yeh won't keep me here by stealing her.'

Ma had her hands around Grandma's wrists trying to wrench them from my middle. My head waggled back and forth in the struggle.

'Yer not a fit mother an' anyone would tell yeh the same.'

'Aye? Well, look in the mirror, Mother.'

In a burst of mad genius, Ma lifted her hands to Grandma's damp armpits, gave them a tickle then grabbed me, my neck snapping backwards with the force of it.

'Yer nothing but a bitter old bitch, an' yeh'll not see her or me again. I'm her ma, fit or otherwise, an' that's not fer you or anyone else in this town tae judge.'

Grandma pulled back her hand and delivered a slap that echoed from her fox-hunting decorative plates and rang in my ears like a scream.

'Get out o' my fuckin' house then.'

'Don't you worry, we're going.'

Grandma sat back in her chair, turned up the TV and didn't look round as Ma left, holding me with one arm and fingering the burning red blotch on her cheek with a shaky hand.

So we trundled through the rainy streets; Ma in her nightie, winter coat and grubby plimsolls and me in a Moses basket propped on my pram. Underneath me was a tumble of knickers tangling with rattles and leaky shampoo bottles.

Ma had stuffed me into my snowsuit, letting out a growl each time my slithery legs escaped. We left in a frenzy of clothes-throwing and screaming and, finally, the slamming of Uncle Frankie's note-stuffed envelope through the letter box. The scatter of notes a reminder to her ma: she was no one's Charity Case. The weather girl told us it would be 'rain, rain and more rain again' at high volume, as if the volume itself was proof enough of how little Grandma was reacting.

The rain beat down; I imagined drops sliding down the inches of bare flesh between Ma's coat and plimsolls, slicking her bony ankles. At the phone box Ma wedged the pram half in half out and rummaged till she found a 10p piece. She tried two times before she got the right number.

'Frankie? No, she's alright, but me and Ma had a massive screaming match an' she's chucked us out. We've nowhere tae go. Come an' get us? It's pissing down.'

The rain covered my blanket with sparkling wet diamonds.

'What? What do yeh mean yeh don't want tae take sides? Fuck's sake! What do yeh mean go back? She threw me out an' then she slapped me, while I was holding the wee one an' all . . . I shoved it back through the letter box, I'll not have her saying I was sponging . . . Aye? Well, fuck you then!'

She slammed down the receiver, banged the window with the palm of her hand, looked at me with pity, maybe a little hate, picked up the receiver again and punched in three sharp numbers.

'Hello?' She spoke in a posh, softer voice. 'No, not the fire service an' not the ambulance either. Maybe the police? Aye, well, I'm out in the rain with my two-week-old baby an' we've nowhere tae go.' She listened, whispered 'bitch' under her breath.

By the time Ma had spun half-truths (a slap, a baby, no place for the night) and half-lies (there was no storming out, no Postman Pat with twenty-pound notes, no telling Frankie to fuck himself) we had an address.

I was wet, crying the fat, futile tears of a baby who thinks she is owed something. We walked for twenty minutes, past warm squares of window and sprinkles of laughter from pub doorways left ajar. Ma cried the whole way too, her salty tears mixing with the rain and glossing her cheeks. The family that cries together stays together. Aberdeen, as cold, hard and grey as you would expect from a town carved from granite.

A woman wearing a plastic headscarf, anorak and wellies stopped us.

'You alright, love?' She looked at the bluish stretch of skin where Ma's coat fell open. 'Yeh shouldnae be out in this weather.' She peered into the pram at my pink screaming face and the pile of sodden clothes. 'An' with a baby. Do yeh have somewhere tae go, lassie?'

'We're going somewhere now. Thanks though.'

'Where to, love? Would yeh not catch a bus?' She looked at the pile of clothes, the huge showpiece pram that Frankie had bought. 'No. Maybe a taxi would be better for yeh?'

Ma's exhalations came out in low sobs.

'No, honest, we're just ten minutes away now. Don't worry, we are going somewhere.'

The woman, cheeks ruddy and rounded, took Ma's elbow. 'Then yeh'll let me put yeh in a taxi, aye?' She looked closely at Ma's face. 'For the baby, if no' for you.'

Ma nodded. And so we three waited for a taxi to splash along the shining street. The taxi that would take us somewhere warm, after the cab driver had bundled our knickers, shampoo bottles and pram into the boot and the woman pressed five pounds into Ma's hand and made the sign of the cross when she heard the street number and name, though you couldn't have known it if you hadn't been there yourself. Ma took the note in her wet, limp hand and forgot to say thank you when the taxi pulled away.

That's how we found ourselves at the Grafton Women's Shelter, a house so inoffensive you'd never guess how many bruised faces and hopes were sheltered inside.

Years later I'm told this story, as a humorous cautionary tale about the famous Ryan Women's temper, but as Ma summoned the strength to ring the bell there was nothing funny, nothing funny at all, about a shivering twenty-year-old in her nightie and winter coat, with a screaming baby in the pram beside her.

A circle of light, a shiny star, flashed in the centre of the door and darkened just as quickly.

The door opened ajar showing a mousy fringe and a nose

that dipped up and down assessing us. Then it opened and flooded our miserable bodies in syrupy golden light and I heard Ma exhale; breathing out the cold, horrifying afternoon.

The woman in the doorway smiled, looked closely at Ma's face, and seeing me, smiled wider. She had short hair, a haircut that made you think of a bathroom sink and a pair of kitchen scissors. Her square, short frame was covered with a green, bobbled sweatshirt and she had the kindest face I had seen in my two short weeks of life.

The hallway was heavy with the sweet smell of tomatoes and garlic.

'Iris, is it? I'm Jane the Centre Manager.' She gave a short light laugh and smiled at Ma's expression. 'They called and let us know to expect you. You're safe.'

Her accent was different, the *rrs* sliding like soft butter into your ears.

It was so quiet I wondered if the people who lived there ever turned up the telly or stitched their sentences with shouted swear words aimed to wound.

'Now I'll just take you into the Welcome Room and get you set up. I'm sure you're exhausted, cold too.

We left the pram in the hallway and in Ma's arms I was ushered into a hot room with pink floral wallpaper and fat orange armchairs. There was an electric fire in the corner, yellow light dancing behind the dusty plastic coals.

In one of the armchairs, a dirty-blonde head stooped; she turned and I saw two wide blue eyes full of fright and a face like a stamped-on overripe fruit: yellow and purple, split with gashes, swollen and sunken in the wrong places.

'Oh, Sandra. You're still waiting for the doctor? Sorry, I'll just get Iris settled and I'll see where she is.'

Ma looked at the girl in the chair, who was maybe younger than her, with her mouth open.

'OK, Iris, we'll have a chat about everything tomorrow. In the meantime I'll –'

'There's nothing tae talk about.'

'Well, we won't make you talk about anything you don't want. There's time, please don't worry about anything right now.'

Ma's head shot from side to side, looking for an escape route. 'No, what I mean is I, I'm no' like her.' She jerked her head to the girl who gave a derisive, flat 'Ha' in response.

Ma bit her lip. 'Sorry, I didnae mean . . . No, I just mean I think there's been a mistake. I didn't know this is where they were sending us.'

Jane placed her hand on Ma's shoulder. 'Listen, whatever the case is with you, and everyone is different here I promise, there's a place for you and . . . what's your little girl's name? Can I?'

She opened her green sweatshirted arms and Ma settled me in. Jane smelt of vanilla and newspapers.

'Oh, I've not decided. But listen, I don't belong here.'

The girl in the chair let out an exasperated sound, turned round and said in a hard, child's voice, 'Listen, none of us want tae come here. Just be fuckin' grateful. Do yeh have anywhere else?'

Ma's arms hung at her sides, a shamed look on her face, and Jane looked up from me.

'Come on, Iris. Have a shower and warm yourself up. I'll look out some clothes for you. We'll talk about how to move on after you've had a sleep.'

Ma nodded dumbly and Jane's arms loosened from around me.

'You don't mind, Sandra? I'll just show Iris the shower room and then come back and find out where that doctor is.'

Transported from the warm sureness of Jane's embrace to Sandra's tentative arms, I felt her holding her breath, then exhale as she looked down towards me, my own little battle scar still on my cheek.

In the corridor I heard Jane tell Ma that the house was completely secure. I looked up at Sandra's big blue eyes and thought how beautiful all those beaten-up colours were.

3

A moderately stained mattress was brought in from the hallway into a room three others shared.

Two of them only left their beds for their meals. They sat silently, spooning in mouthfuls, gulping them down at Jane's insistence, before retreating to their duvets. One had the jutting body of a little boy and the other heavy drooping breasts and they were known, in plural, as 'the Sleepers'. It was Jodie, our third room-mate, who first called them that and it stuck like pillow creases on their cheeks.

Jodie had a body that dipped and oozed with the suggestion of sex and dressed to show it off in sleeveless, plunging blouses and denim minis, though her skin was greying and puckered from the cold climbing all over.

Her face was generous too; she had a round lopsided nose, a blob of pallid pastry squashed there in a hurry, her teeth protruded from loose lips and her eyes bulged inside the stumpy prickles of ginger hair that circled them. The same coarse orange colour stuck up from her head in an unruly pelt, no two sections going the same way.

The first night in the Grafton Hilton, as the guests liked to call it, Jodie and Ma swapped stories in whispers, fat velvet caterpillars curling into each other's ears.

'. . . ended up in topless bar, Mayfair though. I didnae care – before I had this one I had a lovely pair. I was chuffed tae show them off.'

'They're still nice, Iris, I noticed right away. I bet yer heart goes out tae me, blessed with a body like this an' cursed with a mug like this. One of my boyfriends, and not the one who landed me here either, would only do me from behind. Did me like a dog so he didnae have tae see my face. An' I liked him that much that I didnae really mind. An' then he borrowed forty quid an' stopped coming round anyway.'

'Jesus.'

'Aye, an' he was a fat fucker an' all. Talk about the pot calling the kettle black.'

Smiles lingered in the dark. Shared secrets, warmer than five blankets and a radiator.

Jodie turned on her side. 'I'm chuffed yer here, Iris. It's good tae have someone tae talk to who isnae writing it all down and nodding in sympathy or dozing off like them two. How long will yeh stay?'

'No idea, but not long cause of the bairn. I didnae plan any of this, Jodie.' Ma stopped, as though those fat velvety caterpillars had started crawling down her throat.

'Well, none of us did, Iris, that's for sure.'

'I know, an' I'm much better off than some, but the last time things weren't spinning I was in a squat in London an' planning tae catch the Victoria Line tae a clinic tae get rid. I don't know why I changed my mind and I don't think I can do it.'

Ma's voice was thick, the words rushed out in a panic. Jodie climbed from her bed; the light from the hall warming the edges of her wild hair and neat curves.

'None of us think we can, Iris. But we do, an' you will too. Spinning or not you'll find your way.'

She brushed Ma's hair with her fingers.

'Now get up an' share with me cause yeh'll be hot as fuck by that radiator an' I can't sleep by myself anyway.'

So we lay, two Ss and a comma tucked together, surrounded in a blanket of each other's heat.

We stayed at the Grafton Hilton for three weeks. In that time I saw tears fall into spaghetti-hoop dinners and spines jolt at the sound of drunken passers-by.

There were fourteen of us in total but only two kids; me and Mark. Mark was a fat four-year-old famous for putting things down the back of the nappies he still wore. A fried egg from breakfast or Jane's mini-stapler; he wasn't fussy.

Within two days, with Jodie as her sidekick, Ma was holding court at mealtimes talking loudly about her psychedelic trip to London and my da.

'Yank. Loaded he was, but I said, "It doesnae matter tae me. Yer just no man enough for a good Scottish woman."' Chuckles rose and fell around the table. '"Please!" he begs me. "I've taken eight Valium." Eight? "Well," I said to him, "yeh'll have a nice afternoon sleep. Now ta-ta!"'

The women laughed so loud that Jane stuck her head in to see what the commotion was. Shepherd's pie sat forgotten on plates except for the Sleepers who grudgingly ploughed through theirs, eager to get back to their beds. Jane gave them an ignored thumbs up and my ma a lingering look.

Since the only things I stowed away in my nappy were what nature intended I was the favourite, passed from woman to woman 'for a hold', like a coveted toy in a poor family. Sometimes Ma would come in, smelling of outdoors and fags, and shout, 'Where's the bairn? Jodie, if yeh've painted her nails again I'll murder yeh!'

Jodie and Ma shared mascara wands and blow-job tips and

planned nights out down the Roxy, for when they had some cash and no curfew.

'I've a suit from Selfridges in London. It cost a bomb but the Yank bought it when he was trying tae win me back. I wear it with nothing on underneath, it's dead sexy.'

Every few days Jane took Ma and, if I wasn't being petted by one battered wife or another, me into her office to discuss Options for Moving On.

'Well, we have the house in Monarch Avenue and –'

'I'm not moving tae Monarch Avenue, I've told yeh. What sort of area is that for a bairn? I might as well start shooting her up on smack now since that's what'll happen.'

Jane took a deep breath, nodded.

'Or, the other option –' Jane lingered for a moment, lowered her voice as though to protect me – 'is temporary state care; just until you get yourself sorted out? We have some really good foster-parents and it is very temporary.'

'No, I'm not having her taken intae care. I know how it works; yeh get her an' then some posh woman with dried-up ovaries takes a fancy tae her an' I'll never see her again. No fuckin' way.'

Jane looked above Ma's head at the clock.

'OK.' She met Ma's eye. 'Iris, everyone here is very . . . fond of you. I especially am very fond of you indeed. But four weeks is all the relocation time we are given when there's a minor involved.'

Jane took Ma's hand, rubbed the palm with the pad of her thumb.

'There is . . . another way. I've got a –' she gave an uncomfortable cough – 'a spare room in my flat, and as I said I have grown, been growing, very fond of you.'

Ma straightened, her head tilted to one side as if straining to hear, though the message was loud and clear.

'And I know you've become close to Jodie but I thought
. . . well, once you're officially out of my care there's no reason
I shouldn't offer you a place to stay. With me.'

Jane's face was a beacon; red, full of wishing and embarrassment. Ma removed her hand slowly and gave Jane's knee a
stiff pat.

'Jane, you're wonderful, but I'm not that way inclined. I
mean, if I was I wouldnae be in this state! But I'm flattered,
honest. An' I mean, if yeh had a cock, well, then –' a giggle
gurgled up Ma's throat – 'that would be a different matter!'

Jane gave a dry laugh and looked down.

Ma leaned over and gave Jane a soft kiss on her burning
cheek. 'Always worth a try, eh? Now, tell me about the Monarch
Avenue place again.'

Two days later Jane bought us all fish and chips and bottles of
pop. Mark stole a fishcake and put it down his nappy, but no
one paid any attention, it was mine and Ma's night. They said
how much they would miss us and smeared my face with fish-
and-chip kisses. The rustle of hot newspaper filled the room as
greasy raspberries vibrated on my stomach.

Ma stood, clinked her Coke bottle with a wooden fish fork.

'Ladies, ladies! I'd like tae make an announcement. As yeh
all know, so far the wee shitting an' eating machine here has
been nameless as well as gormless. But I've decided she should
be called after two of the best women I know.' She held me high,
'Everyone, meet Janie!'

Silence, a few women exchanged confused glances, one
snuck another chip.

'See? It's Jane and Jodie mixed together?'

Jodie piped up. 'All I get is "ie"?'

Ma looked at her, lowered me slightly. 'An' the "J", yeh both get that!'

'Iris, it's an honour, thank you so much.' Jane's eyes shone.

'Aye, ta very much,' Jodie said sulkily, taking a bite of saveloy.

Jane stood. 'Everyone, a toast to Janie and Iris and Monarch Avenue!' Eyes rolled at the words Monarch Avenue but Coke and Irn-Bru bottles were raised. Ma held me above her head, and surrounded by chip wrappers, raised bottles and bruised women with wary eyes and smiling mouths, we celebrated the night I became Janie Ryan.

Dirt caked into every nook and cranny of 125 Monarch Avenue. The blocked coal fire had blackened the surrounding wall and the kitchen had a sweet, bitter smell that Ma couldn't get to the bottom of, but it was our first proper home. It even had two bedrooms and a back garden with a forest of nettles that the late-November weather pummelled.

We were at the end of Monarch Avenue; 'easy escape' is what Ma said.

On the way to buy the moving-in essentials – tea, milk, bread, fags, Jif and a half of vodka – my eyes soaked in our new neighbourhood. Graffiti and scorch marks, echoes of small fires, decorated doorsteps. Golden Special Brew cans and crushed vodka bottles, bright as diamonds, collected in the gutters. Front gardens were filled with mouldy paddling pools and, occasionally, a rust-burnished shell of a car. I had never seen anything so beautiful, so many colours, before in grey Aberdeen.

Ma bought her shopping from a dusty shop with a sign saying 'To avoid embarrassment, please don't ask for credit', and someone had scrawled 'Then we won't have to tell you to go fuck yourself' in blue biro underneath.

Ma walked us home quickly, not stopping to look round. Three teenagers with dark lips and stiff moussed hair walked behind us.

'Look at the state of that fat fuckin' pram,' said one who had dark eyebrows pencilled in above her fluffy pale ones.

'Never mind the pram, look at the fat fuck who's steering it,' a taller girl said, sucking on a blue ice pole, hard enough to ignore the winter cold.

The third girl, who walked behind them, had a roll of fat around her chin and a protruding belly through her T-shirt, no coat. 'Aye!' she added. 'Fat bitch.'

Ma's grip tightened on the pram handles and I saw her flinch at the word fat.

'Haw, bitch! Aye, you, yeh no going tae stop an' have a natter? Too posh fer us, are yeh?' asked Ice Pole Girl crunching at the blue ice with grey teeth.

'Yer no from round here, are yeh? No with a fat fancy fucker of a pram like that one,' shouted Eyebrows, but Ma didn't turn round. 'Haw, yeh stuck-up cunt, I'm talking tae yeh!'

Eyebrows took an extra-long step to catch Ma's heel under her foot. Ma's heart beat so fast I could see the pulse in her neck. Still, we had already made it past the boarded-up window with 'NONSE' sprayed on it and in a few minutes we'd have been home and could have locked the door, maybe boarded up the windows. But Ma had lived in the town too long, established herself in enough squats, to know that closing the door wasn't enough.

Ice Pole Girl spoke up. 'How much do yeh reckon is in tha' purse, Shona?'

They were close enough to smell cloying perfume over grubby skin and the fag breath whistling through craggy teeth.

'Enough for a wee score, I reckon,' replied Eyebrows while Ice Pole Girl sucked the last of the juice from her wrapper and spat it towards Ma. 'Bitch, will yeh loan us yer purse?' Ma walked faster, heels inches in front of their feet. 'Look at that! The fat fucker is ignoring us. Well, Shona, we asked nice, didn't we? We'll just have tae take it.'

Eyebrows and Ice Pole Girl lunged for the pram's handle where Ma's bag swung but Ma pushed in front, her full body leaned forward, she looked capable of murder. She kept her voice low but her face was ferocious. 'Get the fuck away from me and my bairn.'

Eyebrows lifted her hand and Ma jabbed her hard in the chest with two fingers.

'I'm fuckin' warning yeh. This is your chance tae walk away. Take it.'

Ice Pole Girl rolled her eyes but didn't move. Ma gave them a long look.

'Do yeh know my fella? No? Well, my boyfriend is Tony Hogan. Do yeh know the name? No? Well, ask yer brothers or das or yer fuckin' dealer. Now I'm warning yeh, step back or he'll not just have you lot he'll have every bloke yeh gave a blow job tae in the last six months an' all.'

Eyebrows and Chubby took small steps backwards but, credit due, Ice Pole Girl stood her ground for a second before shrugging. 'We were just having a laugh.'

'Aye? Well, fuck off an' have a laugh somewhere else.'

They turned and ran, Chubby tripping over her laces as she went.

Ma walked to our door as slowly as she could manage, shoulders back, looking straight ahead. She lugged the pram up our front steps, unlocked the door with a shaky hand and bolted it again before sliding down the hallway wall. I chewed my pale yellow sock and wondered who this Tony Hogan was and what would happen when Ma's lie was found out.

4

It took over two years for Tony Hogan to show up. Until then I busied myself taking my first steps in a sunny patch of garden cleared of nettles. I learned words: Ma, Frankie, coffee and poo. My favourite word when he walked into our lives was, unsurprisingly and appropriately, a joyful, sometimes frustrated, 'fuck!' I loved the attention that word would bring.

Ma laughed more. Sometimes she laughed so much that tears seeped out and those sparkly little drops became big heaving sobs. I kept an eye on her.

When I turned one, and Ma's friends came over to drink to my birthday, Jodie arrived with a black eye and a limp and Ma wouldn't let her leave again. She stayed in my room and slept under the Danger Mouse duvet that Frankie had bought me.

I had lots of uncles but Uncle Frankie was the one who came every week, brought presents and wanted to play with me and not just Ma. The other uncles picked me up for about three minutes and then put me aside like a fag end, not taking their eyes off Ma or the bedroom door over her shoulder.

Jodie chased Frankie for a whole year, wearing less and less as her lust – and his uninterest – got more and more. I once caught her sitting on my Danger Mouse duvet with her nose buried deep in the collar of his jacket and her hand down her knickers. One day Frankie told her to settle for his pal Meathead instead. Jodie did as she was told.

After a few months living at Monarch Avenue Ma said she

was 'burying the hatchet' and started catching the bus to Grandma's where Ma cleaned and bought shopping and I'd watch *Sesame Street*. Today is brought to you by the letter F and the word 'fuck'.

Sometimes I'd try to spray the foamy polish for Ma when I could see from the slump of her shoulders that she was tired from listening to half-pissed advice on child-rearing while polishing fifty-six decorative plates.

Back at our house it was sometimes so full I couldn't put names to the quick-changing faces, smells and antics. I couldn't tell you who the man with a moustache and torn anorak was who went into the toilets for an hour at a time, or the name of the woman who had bracelets dancing up and down her scratched wrists. If something dodgy happened Ma would say, 'It's just a pal of Frankie's. I'll make him get shot.'

Busy as the house was, Ma always found the time to bathe me in my too-small pink plastic bath in front of the fire. I always got my vitamin drops that tasted of banana and the smell of bleach and she still spent an hour a day encouraging me, unsuccessfully, to 'cack a housey and pee a wallie' on my bright red potty.

The night I was made to remember Ma's lie about Tony Hogan was the night she said I could do without a nappy and babysitter and Jodie, glass in hand and tights already laddered, appealed to Ma.

'Are yeh sure, Iris? Just have some patience, do yeh no remember fat wee Mark from the Grafton Hilton?'

Ma was at the mirror, shaking her hips in time to the Human League, using a needle to separate her clumped mascaraed lashes.

'Aye, I remember, exactly!' She laid down the needle and looked hazily for her fag packet. 'Besides –' her words were oil sliding on her tongue – 'my ma had all of us out of nappies by the time we were two an' I'll be fucked if I'm giving her another thing tae crow over.'

Jodie scooped a handful of blue gel from a tub and slicked it through her hair; the bubblegum smell filled the room.

'You an' yer bloody ma, Iris. Honest, if yeh popped out a solid gold baby yer ma would say that hers was diamond-encrusted and shat pure platinum.'

Ma found her fags and lit one up, the lighter making two passes before finding the tip.

'Aye, aye. More importantly, is Meathead bringing some mates tonight or what?'

'Aye, a new bunch he's in with.'

'Well, I hope one of them is a ride.'

Ma stood by Jodie at the mirror and they turned their hips this way then that; Jodie wedged into a lacy red dress and Ma, with those cheekbones and that rail-thin body, in leather trousers and a black satin blouse.

'Right, are yeh going tae help me with the drawers?' Ma scooped bottles of nail polish, crusty eyeliners and a dirty ashtray off the top of the chest of drawers.

'Iris, seriously, are yeh sure about this? We can just get them tae bring over some booze an' draw and have a wee party here?'

'Not a chance.' Ma fluffed her tight, chemically enhanced curls in the mirror. 'I havnae been out all week. An' it's fine, Denise said she'd nip through every hour or two.'

Ma bent and gave me a boozy smacker on the cheek.

'Alright, Janie-Jane, see yer potty? When yeh want tae go cack a housey or pee a wallie yeh go an' sit on there. Sleep tight, wee one, an' keep that water in the basin!'

She left me with my basin of water and jam jars and I

carried on my endless, joyful cycle of filling and pouring, filling and pouring, while Ma talked about her 'clammy arse in these trousers', and they pulled the chest of drawers across the door.

'Ta-ta!'

In a clatter of heels and one dropped and retrieved handbag they were gone, leaving just the smell of fags and bubblegum hair gel.

For a while I filled and poured and filled again, fascinated with the long arc of water, changing shape as it went from jar to jar, jar to basin. Then, like a sudden blow winding me, I felt it: the quiet. So quiet I could hear the fridge's disgruntled hum and a rubbish bin being kicked over in the street.

'Ma!' But my voice was swallowed into the quiet, 'Ma! Ma! Ma?'

I knew she had gone. I knew it after the first wail but I filled my lungs, it felt better to shout. I threw myself belly down on the bed and screamed, I thought maybe Denise would hear and come and give me a cuddle, take me to her flat to watch some telly.

I cried till my lungs burned and my face was stiff with snot and it wasn't until I felt the familiar clenching in my stomach that I stopped. The potty was in the corner, shiny and red, still smelling of plastic from lack of use but I would not go to it. I would not please my ma by getting up and 'cacking a housey' in that stupid red pot. And so, my first act of rebellion was to shite myself. That'll show her, I thought, as I felt the hot ooze down my legs.

The bangs on the door woke me as Ma tried to get the key in the lock. My bottom half felt sticky and itchy; I started to cry. Ma stumbled along the hallway to our room and stood in front of the chest of drawers.

'Chony, gimme a shand with thish.' Ma's tongue was swollen from the vodka.

'Fuckin' hell, what's the smell?'

The first time Tony saw me I had a red, snot-encrusted face and my own filth sliding down my legs onto Ma's duvet cover. The first time I saw Tony with his sharp nose, slitty eyes and mouth twisted in disgust I knew that, if I hadn't already, I would have shat myself right there and then.

At first Tony bulldozed my days in small ways, with streaky underpants thrown over my Lego, placing a lit joint between Ma's lips as soon as she woke or dumping me at Denise's so he and Ma could go for steak dinners. With him around there was never enough time for baths and the lid of my vitamin bottle stuck shut.

Tony had yellow-blond hair that he dyed once a month leaving the bathroom smelling of pissy ammonia. He spent half an hour, more sometimes, making sure the spikes of his hair were just so. One day he caught me watching him, turned, and gave me my first ever smack. It left a grown-man-shaped handprint on my bum cheek for twenty minutes but Ma never saw it.

He had a complexion the colour of Spam that mixed badly with bleached hair, and an earring with a dangling silver skull. When people first met Tony you could see their eyes dancing over him; their mouths twitching in amusement. Until he met their eye with a dead stare and said: 'Tony. Tony Hogan. Yeh might have heard of me.' And even if they hadn't yet, if they didn't already know he was the Aberdonian King, or at least Duke, of thugs and drugs, they pretended, showing respect by nodding and averting their eyes.

And Ma? Ma loved the power of being connected, truthfully

this time, to that name. She thought she had willed it that first day on Monarch Avenue, told Jodie, 'It was fate,' and hooked her arm through his in ownership, smiling up blindly at his sharp nose and dark eyes.

When he asked her to go to the shop for fags, he took a bum-shaped wad of warm twenties from his back pocket, peeled off two and told her to buy herself some sweeties and Ma giggled. Not a grown-up's laugh but a skittish, excitable noise. Definitely a giggle.

Tony and Jodie didn't get on.

'She's trying tae turn you against me, Iris. Jealousy.' He kissed the inside of Ma's wrist, gave it a bite. 'An' who can blame her, eh?'

Jodie soon left to live with Meathead and his ma in a flat above the chip shop. With Jodie gone Tony moved me back to my bedroom by dumping my toys, clothes and me onto my bed in a pile. When Ma got home from the shops she found us all in a shocked bundle and he grabbed her elbow and told her in the shadow of the hallway, 'This is a suitable place for a bairn, our bed is not.'

Ma squinted and looked at me quietly organising my things by size and colour. 'Aye, I suppose yer right. I couldn't get Tennent's, do yeh want a Skol?'

Frankie was a wee boy trying to impress a teenager, laughing too soon at Tony's patter, rolling up his T-shirt sleeves over his shoulders and calling Ma 'the wee woman', just like Tony.

They sat drinking whisky with Special Brew, Tony setting the world to rights, swaggering his shoulders in his chair. 'I know a bloke, good as gold he is, he has some of the best stuff coming intae Scotland at the mo.'

Frankie nodded his ginger bowl cut slowly, sucked air through his teeth.

Tony took another swig of Special Brew. 'It's uncut like, so yeh can make a tidy profit with a wee bit of home economics,' he snorted, 'but for business or pleasure just say the word an' I can put yeh in touch.'

'Aye, cheers, man. That'd be good.'

Frankie's voice magically deepened, but a giveaway pink blossomed behind his freckles. Tony laughed and ruffled Frankie's mop.

'Just don't fuck it up, eh, son?

Frankie shook his head and gulped his whisky too fast, leaving him coughing long after Tony's thin laughter had stopped dead.

Grandma wasn't sure about Tony or his clothes and she asked Ma, red frosted lips around a fag.

'What's his job again?' but Ma didn't need to answer because, just then, an Interflora bouquet arrived and all Grandma's questions evaporated from her tongue at the sight of a dozen red roses.

So, Tony smothered the life that me and Ma had built, a furry mould growing over a sweating slab of cheese.

It started with an earring; something that small. Insignificant even, unless the earring is a little swastika pinned through an ear.

Ma said she wouldn't go out with him wearing it. They'd been drinking warm cans of lager in the sun, draped across each other on a thick blanket thrown over the regrown nettles. Ma laughed as she said it and he brought his face close to hers and gave her a hard look with those dead eyes.

'Ashamed of me, are yeh?'

'What? No, I just meant –' Ma tried to pull away but Tony held her shoulder, dug a dirty thumbnail into the soft dip above her collarbone. Ma's eyelids fluttered and her heavy gold hoops swayed in sympathy.

'Naw, I'm just saying that I'm not comfy with it. In London I had loads of coloured pals.' Her voice skittered along with her eyelids.

'When I was in London,' Tony mimicked in a squeaky voice and the nail dug in deeper. Even from my place, well in front of them, I could see it cut the flesh.

'Aye? An' did yeh let them fuck yeh? The blackies with their big donkey dicks an' maybe Pakis with their wee chipolatas?'

Ma struggled but he had her wrist, his fist white from holding so tightly. She stopped struggling and lowered her head. 'No as it happens. But your opinion's yours an' mine is mine. Can we just forget about it? Let's just have a nice night. We can leave Janie at Denise's an' –'

Tony took a swig from his lager and spat it in her face. The sweet sticky smell filled the air and I felt my stomach turn.

'Tony! I –'

'Do you, yeh stupid, ignorant bitch, think you can tell me what tae do just cause yeh lived in London? A whore in a squat? Think yeh'll tell me what tae wear?'

I could see her eyes roaming, searching me out. She saw me, knees pulled up, by the back door.

'Janie, get inside right now.' Her voice was steady, she even tried to smile, but I couldn't move, I was glued to the ground with the morbid fascination of a child seeing something too adult.

Tony poked a finger through each of Ma's gold hoops.

''Member I bought these for yeh?'

Her lashes quivered, black blades of grass in the summer heat, and her eyes met Tony's.

'Aye, aye, Tony, they're lovely. Thanks . . . it was –' she hunted for words, took a breath – 'it was good of yeh.'

'Well, I'm taking them back.'

Tony snatched with both hands and ripped the hoops from her soft white lobes, then he stood and pushed Ma to the ground, forced one knee on her chest and held her arms with his free hand.

'Janie,' Ma said, 'go to your bedroom right now and close the door. Fucking now, I said.'

And I did. I turned my back on my ma being pinned to the ground by a known psychopath and then I closed my ears to the screams and thumps by cramming my Penfold pillow around my head.

The next morning Tony took us for breakfast and I was allowed to have a Coke float and a bowl of chips. I was deep into an impressive sulk.

Ma glowed, though she had two bloody lines in her earlobes and a long deep scratch on the inside of her arm. Tony kept giving her little pecking kisses at the side of her neck, his blond spikes brushing the earlobes he'd ripped just the day before.

My Coke float arrived with its vanilla froth spilling over the edges.

'Now, we've something to tell yeh.' Ma stopped and looked to Tony. He rolled his eyes but leaned towards me smiling.

'I'm sorry if we frightened yeh. Sometimes grown-ups row about grown-up stuff but it doesnae mean we don't love each other.'

'Or you,' Ma added. Tony huffed at the interruption.

'As a matter of fact I row with yer ma because I love her
so much. An' because of that I've asked yer ma tae be my wife.'

Ma stretched over the table, a big smile making her split
lip stretch, a mustard-coloured bruise visible under the peach
blusher caked over it. 'Tony's going tae be yer daddy.'

I said nothing, poked my chubby finger at the soft bubbled
surface of my Coke float.

'Well, what do yeh have to say tae that, Janie?' Ma asked.

I shrugged, stirred my float round with my finger. 'Fuck.' It
was sullen, with a sharp 'k'. Ma slumped back in the booth,
disappointment written as clearly as the bruises on her face, and
Tony laughed and opened his fags.

'Well, maybe yeh won't want that nice Coke float then,
Janie?'

I sat forward and sucked up all the Coke through the red
straw, letting the icy bubbles burn the back of my throat and
shoved the vanilla foam into my mouth with the long, thin spoon
in record time. Tony might have been an arsehole, but he wasn't
worth wasting a good Coke float over.

My limbs stretched, lost their baby fat, and I used the toilet like
a good girl. All of a sudden, as though someone had snuck in at
night and placed them on my tongue, I knew lots of words and
how to put them together to hurt, be funny or angry. I thought
I should be the main feature, my cleverness, but it was only the
Tom and Jerry cartoon before the bloody film that became our
day-to-day.

It didn't matter what the reason was. If the toast burned or
her trousers made her look fat, if she spent too much time
'pandering' to me or if she wore red.

His face closed off and in a low, patient voice he explained why what she was doing at that specific moment made her a 'stupid cunt'. Ma would try to duck, weave and lace words of protestation, placation and flattery through the air, though rarely, if ever, did they work. Soon he was firing tiny drops of spittle down on her from his roaring angry mouth as she kept her head low, maybe tried to shuffle away from any sharp corners.

With her head still down, she'd shout at me to go to my room and, with an ever growing ball of shame lodged in my chest, I always did. I got under the covers and turned on my fuzzy, static-filled radio and listened to the thumps and pleading in time to the beat of 'Billie Jean'.

The next day there was Ma, skinnier than ever, making breakfast, 'good as new', with her caked-on 'warpaint', and Tony watching every move she made. The air was punctuated by Ma's thin, wavering laughter, telling Tony with too-wide, watering eyes that it was 'already forgotten'.

Sure as the ice-cream van wailed 'Green Sleeves' on our street just before *Blockbusters* came on telly, it continued. The routine was only broken by the trip to hospital (two broken ribs and a mashed nose that would be bumpy and crooked forever more) and the first, shameful loosening of my warm bladder onto my sheets.

One day I saw Ma bent over the bath cleaning my piss-soaked sheets, her skin grey, face dead under bright streaks of blusher, and I started pulling out my eyelashes for her, one by one, to make up for my cowardly, betraying bladder.

I only managed a few before it hurt too much, but I spread them on Ma's pillow the next morning and made a wish anyway.

I suppose my wish came true. By the time I was four Ma had given up on dreaming of a thin band of gold or even a day wearing a pretty dress with a piss-up at the end. She swallowed those dreams and settled for the sickly morning-after words and the rare days of quiet. Ma let Tony's shiny promises settle on her skin like armour against the next beating.

The end of Tony began with pepperoni pizza, *The Tube* on telly and the June heat. Maybe Ma thought she was safe because this pizza, me being allowed to stay up late and sit with them, was a day-after treat from Tony; just like that Coke float a year and a half before.

Ma sat on the sofa laughing at New Order on the TV, one hand laced through the blonde tangle of my hair and the other holding her slice of pizza. She was in her knickers and a T-shirt that said 'Fanta, Fizz Me Up'. I sat on the carpet below them in my Winnie-the-Pooh pyjamas filling my mouth with the greasy stretchy cheese and salty meat, not wanting the night to end.

Ma was so busy calling New Order stupid fucks that she didn't notice Tony's face harden, and before she did he'd snatched the pizza from her hand.

'Look at the fuckin' state of yeh, eatin' like a fuckin' animal.'

I looked up at them and I thought she must really be relaxed, thinking she had credit from the night before, because of the eight oozing fag burns dancing up her arm like a dot-to-dot puzzle, because she didn't cower or even stop stuffing her pizza in her mouth. Maybe that was the night she'd just finally had enough, enough of flinching when the door went and avoiding everyone's questioning eyes. Enough of biting at her lip till it bled wondering if that night she'd be let off or not.

'Just don't, Tony. We're having a nice night. Let's not spoil it.' Then her slice of pizza was being mashed into the side of her face, while he used his free hand to hold her. It was worse than the slaps and thumps, there was something too awful about the smear of tomato sauce on her pale cheek and the circle of pepperoni that dangled from her chin before plopping onto her bare knee. Ma must've felt it too because I saw the tears and she uttered just one quiet word.

'Tony.'

'Think yeh'll tell me? Look –' he grabbed her chin, forced it up – 'even yer own daughter is disgusted.'

I was standing now, trying to change my face from one of terror, but there was no other face to be had. Even after all these years I hadn't learned how to be brave. Ma's chest shook, her tears running down Tony's wrist where he held her chin, and she looked at me.

'Janie love, go to yer room an' put yer radio on. Go right now.' My half-eaten pizza was still in my hand, and I looked at Tony and Ma and wondered if this was the last time I'd see her with all her teeth or the same shaped face, but I still moved towards the door, my bladder aching.

'No, not tonight yeh don't.' It was Tony.

'Tony, listen. I'm begging yeh. Not her.'

I cried, snot dribbling down to my mouth; I felt bubbles of panic flood my chest. 'Ma?'

Tony tightened his grip as she struggled. 'Janie, yer tae throw yer slice of pizza at yer ma because she's been bad. Make it a good throw an' yeh can run away.'

I looked at Ma sobbing and at Tony's hand forcing her to keep her head lifted. 'I'm warning yeh, throw it.'

I threw it at Ma. Not a good throw, it slid off her bare knee, but still never to be undone.

'Yeh see, bitch. Even yer own flesh an' blood thinks yeh deserve it.'

He raised a hand, the one with the chunky jet and silver

ring and I threw myself at Ma, pushed my face into the wet front of her T-shirt.

'Ganging up, are yeh? Well, two is just as good as one as far as I'm concerned.'

He lifted his hand again, higher this time, and I felt the warmth on the inside of my legs, my bladder giving in. I waited for the sting of a slap but then Ma was dragging me down the hallway until we were out on the dark concrete steps, Ma screaming in her T-shirt and pants to the deaf ears of Monarch Avenue.

'Help, he'll kill us.'

Tony was behind us, had hold of Ma's hand that wasn't clinging to the stair rail, and I swung from their arms trying to break his grip.

Ma broke away, falling down the stairs, dragging me behind her, and then we ran, tripped towards Denise's door.

'Open the fuck up.' Ma banged the door with both hands. 'He'll kill us, Denise, open the fuck up.'

Denise opened the door and closed it again in a flash, latching the Yale and bolting the top and bottom before turning to us with a face that said she wanted nothing to do with this. Ma sunk to the floor, pulled me to her, wrapped her arms around my head, and I felt her hot breath on the back of my neck.

Denise pulled us up and hurried us to the living room and she and Ma dragged a coffee table against the closed door. Then we covered our ears to the sound of Tony's threats and banging.

Forty minutes later the police arrived smelling of coffee and boredom and the next day the social workers came and I could see from Ma's face that she was too tired to fight any more.

5

It should have been a warning that there were two of them, nearly a gang. The woman pallid with bulging grey eyes, peering under her heavy brown fringe and him, looking around at Denise's china dolls. She had a lazy eye that strayed about the nooks and crannies of the room and he wore jeans with a stiff crease down the front and hiking boots meant for somewhere even rougher than Monarch Avenue. She held out her hand.

'Miss Ryan. May I call you Iris? We're the social workers assigned to you and Janie.'

She talked like she'd been practising in the mirror and Ma, wearing a pair of Denise's extra-extra-large jeans with her tomato-stained T-shirt, said nothing, just looked ahead with a lit fag in her hand.

Denise, cider already on her breath, took me by the hand. 'Come on, let's make some tea.'

While fetching milk from the stale-smelling fridge, I heard voices, one posh and prim, the other deep, faltering, bump from wall to wall. I couldn't hear Ma's voice but imagined her, staring hard at them, blowing her smoke upward to shield her face.

I pushed my finger through a sparkle of spilled sugar as I listened until I heard Ma's voice full of panic. 'Over my dead body! I'm the victim here and yeh'll no take her.'

I ran through to the living room and put both arms tight around Ma.

The social workers looked tired or maybe like they were

thinking about their cheese-and-pickle sandwich waiting back at the office.

The man examined his hands, with their neat trimmed nails like a woman's, and Ma held me and murmured into my hair that I wasn't going anywhere. The woman stared at her colleague before tutting and turning to us.

'Miss Ryan, Iris, we have the paperwork here. Bearing in mind this is your second recorded incident of this kind and —'

'Second? Well, if yer talking about that trip tae the hospital, I fell down the stairs an' —'

'No, it's not that, it's your stay at the Grafton Women's Shelter in October 1980? And added to last night's incident, well . . . it's just temporary care. We'll be able to make an assessment and then, all being well, you'll have Janie back at home in no time at all. It's for the best.'

'Don't fuckin' tell me what's best for my kid!'

I clung tighter, my tears cutting through the hardened snot from the night before.

The woman looked over. 'Gerard?'

Finally, he looked up. 'There'll be an assessment, Miss Ryan, and if you are uncooperative, if you make this more difficult than it needs to be, it will most certainly go against you.'

'Please don't do this.'

The woman offered me her hand and I slapped it away, so, with a roll of her eyes, one good, one lazy, she put her hands under my armpits and the man prised my hands away from Ma.

'Ma!' I screamed, kicked and flailed my arms as they carried me away.

Ma stood, holding up Denise's giant jeans with one hand and told me through sobs that it would only be for a wee while, I'd to be good and try to have fun.

Denise put her arm around Ma and helped her follow us out. They wedged me into a too-small baby seat in a too-big black car and I saw Ma sink to the doorstep and Denise bend over, sheltering her with that big soft body.

I was still screaming and kicking when they turned the key in the ignition and left Monarch Avenue. I was planning to scream myself sick.

Three weeks after my bladder had started playing tricks and two months before the night with the pizza, I had started needing to hold Ma's red handbag when we left the house.

If she wouldn't give it to me I would throw myself down and scream until snot bubbles puffed from my nose and pavement grit stuck to my cheeks. After enough of that she would always loop the strap around my neck and tell me to hold on tight.

That is why, in that too big black car that smelt of stale fags and farts, three streets from Monarch Avenue, I stopped shouting for my ma and started screaming for a bag.

'Bag! I want bag.'

'I don't see why I always have to, Gerard. Do you not have any balls yourself?'

'Well, Sarah, I just don't see any point in rushing it. Slow, steady and gentle, that's my approach. Otherwise, we end up with hysterical parents and –' his eyes flicked to me in the mirror – 'screamers.'

'Aye, well, at least she cared enough to get hysterical, I suppose.'

I was light-headed from screaming, static showered in front of my eyes.

'Jesus!' The woman turned in her seat. 'You'll have to be quiet, Janie. You'll make yourself sick.'

'And us while you're at it,' the man quietly added.

'Bag, bag, bag!'

He sighed. 'For God's sake give her yours and see if that'll quiet her down a bit. We've still twenty-five minutes till we get there.'

She tutted and took out her purse, placing it on the dashboard before handing me her lumpy black bag.

It didn't smell like tobacco and dust like Ma's but I tucked the bag under my wet chin, stopped screaming and watched the string of houses passing.

I didn't know where we were or how far we'd gone; I'd never remember the way back to Ma. These bored, crabbit grown-ups were the only ones who knew how to get me home and I realised I'd have to be good if they were ever going to take me back.

I shoved a salty wad of leather into my mouth, bit down and screamed silently until it felt like my eyes would explode. The woman stared, eyebrows knitted, her mouth hardening.

'Well, that's just great. Teeth marks! That's Italian leather.'

They led me into a room where kids shovelled fish-and-chip sandwiches into gap-toothed mouths and nudged each other's elbows away from the blue plastic bowls of crisps placed down the two long tables. The air was thick with the gurgle of Kia-Ora cartons being sucked dry and the rankle of malt vinegar soaking into bread.

I stood in the doorway, flanked by Gerard and Sarah, in one of Denise's grey T-shirts that reached my feet. I felt my face burning, blotchy and pink with shame. A kid at the table clapped eyes on Gerard and Sarah and wailed until one of the grown-ups came and carried him from the room.

The kids were different ages; the older ones looked over at us, but mainly the focus in the room was on getting ketchup swirls perfect or sneaking hands towards the communal crisp bowls before someone said, 'Christ's sake! Leave some for everyone else.'

A woman walked towards me. She was the first black person I had ever seen who wasn't on telly. I loved Arnold from *Diff'rent Strokes*, he was my favourite, though I was only allowed to watch it at Denise's.

This woman looked different from people on TV though. Her skin was darker and shone like a brown, salty pebble held in your mouth for its smoothness before being spat into your palm. She wasn't like Ma; she was rounded and soft, but not like Denise either, because she looked strong, firm. She wore an orange dress and a long necklace of clicking green beads. She bent down to speak to me and I thought her voice would be beautiful because it came from that shining, smiling face.

'You must be Janie? I'm Nell.' She followed my eyes to the older kids whispering and blocked their view. 'Just ignore them. I'll introduce yeh to everyone later.'

'You speak like my ma but you're a blackie!' The social workers stiffened slightly behind me, the kids stopped talking and Nell laughed.

'Aye? Well, that's cause me an' yer ma are both from Aberdeen, I imagine. An' next time yeh'll say black instead of blackie, won't yeh? It's better.'

I thought I'd been bad until she smiled and I slotted my sticky hand into her smooth warm one, but then the picture of Ma crumpled on the stairs stuck in my mind and I pulled my hand back.

She led us to a little room with shelves piled with towels, beaten-up board games and twists of ping-pong nets.

As she reached for a big box on the top shelf I noticed she was barefoot, and that her toenails weren't polished but thick and yellow.

'Now, I want yeh tae have a rummage through here an' pick out anything yeh want tae wear. Just until we get yeh something tae keep. I'm just going outside tae speak to Gerard and Sarah an' then we'll get you dressed an' get you a giant sandwich and some crisps.'

She left the door ajar and I felt a flutter of excitement at the piles of games, giant sandwiches and crisps. I thought maybe this was like a holiday, so Ma could have a good night out, 'a relax', like she called nights when she slurred and swayed, and then she could find another boyfriend who wasn't Tony. She had told me to have fun. Maybe she had just cried because she'd miss me.

I felt fuzzy, a bit sleepy, because my heart had stopped thumping and I didn't have the same twist of lemon curling through my stomach.

Rummaging in the box of clothes of other kids who had moved on from the home, I considered an orange ra-ra skirt, and then I heard my street.

'Monarch Avenue. Single mum, boyfriend, sorry *fiancé*, with a record, abusive.'

'To both?'

'Mother says no but certainly as of last night.'

I heard a sigh.

'Judging from the journey over Janie is very disturbed,' Sarah added.

'The mother definitely wants her but I wouldn't be surprised if she was using. You know, skinny as a rake, not very responsive at first.'

'Yes, well, speculation aside you just need to look at Janie to see she is clearly a troubled little girl.'

'Well, she's just been taken forcibly from her mammy –' there was a sliver of ice in Nell's voice – 'so that's hardly surprising, an' listen . . .' I felt their ears on me, 'she's good as gold now.'

Sarah spoke up, her tone cutting through the warmth of

the little room. 'All the same, don't go making any promises about it being a few days.'

'It's a temporary care institution so I'll tell the kids as I see fit, thank you. An' what about the mother?'

'An assessment and voluntary psychiatric interview.' A pause. 'She's got a history.'

'Right, well, thanks fer filling me in. Let me know what's going on and I'll call tomorrow.'

There were no goodbyes.

Nell opened the door and found me holding a He-Man T-shirt and the orange ra-ra skirt.

'Janie, are you sure this is what you want to wear?'

I nodded, they were the best clothes I'd ever seen. My eyes lingered on one of the boxes. Nell nodded and shifted it from under a pile of other boxes.

'Just until Ma comes tae collect me from her relax. Do you know when she'll come? Cause I'll only play until then an' I want tae be ready.'

Nell rubbed her dry palm against my cheek.

'You can play for as long as you like, Janie, until yer ma is relaxed and happy again. Now do you like fish fingers?'

I left with the clothes and box under my arm and hoped that Ma would wait until I'd had fish fingers and played awhile with Nell to finish her relax.

I hopscotched my way through Nell's gentle questions while colouring in in her office, then spent the rest of the day lying on my tummy on the green carpet of the playroom, my eyes a-blur with red and yellow discs.

The other kids approached me, out of curiosity or sometimes at a grown-up's urging.

'Can I play?'

I was generous. I let them lie down opposite me and squint at the new girl through the empty blue plastic holes. Whenever Tony's face snaked into my head I counted the yellow and red discs and worked out my way to the lucky four. I could count to six now but sometimes I forgot the five.

Mostly the kids were OK, except for one chubby girl who kicked the board over, scattering pieces under the sofa, when I said she couldn't have two goes. None of them seemed to mind my sudden appearance or my sprawling belly down in their playroom.

Dinner was sausage and mash and Nell sat next to me and didn't slap my hand or throw the ketchup bottle against the wall when I made red polka dots on the two scoops of grainy mash. Instead she asked me quiet questions about my dinners at home, was Ma a good cook and did I ever get really hungry? I answered her questions back with some of my own.

'Will we have sausages every day? Is there pudding? Did you cook this, Nell? Are yeh no eatin' yer sausage?'

For pudding there was a wobbling, pink blancmange topped with a blob of red jam; Nell let me eat half of hers.

We got to watch *Tom and Jerry* before bedtime. As Nell turned the video off there was a sudden scramble of legs and arms to leave the room and I knew why when I saw the queues for the bathrooms. Each of the two doors were minded by a grown-up who made kids breathe on them before leaving the bathroom.

I held a pink toothbrush with a duck on the handle and Denise's grey T-shirt for a nightie. The sight of my room with the beds so close you could touch the kids next to you made my tummy upset, making me think of all that red ketchup, jam, blancmange churning together.

I plucked at Nell's dress. 'Can I tell you a secret?'

She crouched. 'You can tell me anything at all. What is it?'

I prayed none of the other kids would hear as I cupped my hands around her ear. 'Sometimes I need tae pee so bad in the night that I dinnae make it to the toilet.'

I pulled my face away but she hadn't flinched or yanked my arm to drag me to the toilet. I tried to make her understand. 'That means sometimes I pee on my sheets. But I'll try really hard not tae on yours, honest.'

Nell nodded. 'Well, yer very grown-up telling me. We'll make sure that yer in a room where no one will mind, even if an accident does happen. Don't yeh worry about anything but having sweet dreams.'

I joined the bathroom queue and saw her exchange a few words with one of the grown-ups. After I'd swallowed a blob of stripy toothpaste, and breathed on a suspicious-looking woman, I found Nell. She took me to a room with just two beds; one for me, and one for Sue, the girl who'd kicked over the Connect 4 board. Nell kissed us goodnight and left a light on. When we tried to get comfy I heard the safe crackle of plastic sheets.

As I drifted off I imagined Ma in the Roxy having vodka on wobbly legs, laughing about Tony and the police and maybe meeting a nice black boyfriend, Nell's brother, who would stop Tony from coming over ever again.

I woke the next morning without clammy, itching thighs or the sheets to hide at the bottom of the washing pile, and when Sue got out of bed with a wet patch across her pyjama bottoms I turned away and pretended not to see.

6

I was reading the *Dandy* in the office for twenty minutes before Ma arrived, panting and explaining about the buses. She wasn't wearing any make-up and her eyes looked small, her mouth thin, wet hair combed backwards. I could tell she'd rushed.

She knelt and put her arms around me then pulled back to look at me. 'Janie? What have they done to yer beautiful curls?'

My hair was cut in a short bob and I wore the red dungarees and yellow T-shirt that Nell had bought for me. Ma stared at me as though I might be an impostor.

'The haircutter said he couldnae get the comb through it at all. I cried, Ma, when he cut it all off, but I like it now.' I raised my hands to the soft blunt edge of my hair and remembered the golden tumbleweed being swept across the linoleum floor; my tears at my 'boy's haircut' and Nell stroking her fingers through it and telling me it was a new beginning and it would grow back 'straight and shiny like a princess's'.

That day Nell bought me my dungarees, four different-coloured T-shirts, a pair of orange plimsolls and a pink brush with sparkles in the handle. In the evening, while we all watched our cartoon, she showed me how to separate my hair into two halves and brush it until it was soft as 'kitten's fur'.

Ma raised my chin with her finger and stared at me, looking for the two weeks of change she'd missed. 'Did anyone hurt yeh, Janie? Did yeh miss me?'

She looked angry, with her thin lips and taut, pale face. I

lowered my thin lashes to cover my eyes. 'No, did anyone hurt you, Ma?'

Sarah stepped from behind her desk. 'I assure you Janie came to no harm, Iris. It's one of the best homes we have. She's been happy, in fact . . . but . . . of course she's missed you very much.'

Ma hugged me to her chest, her collarbone jabbing my cheek. 'Yeh know I never wanted yeh to go? An' it won't happen again. I'm yer ma.'

I nodded, staring at my orange plimsolls, upset that I'd scuffed them already when I wanted to keep them nice, new and bright.

'I missed yeh, Ma.'

Nell had told me that Ma would want to know that.

Once we were outside Ma reached for my hand.

'Are we goin' back tae Monarch Avenue?'

'Aye, of course we are. It's home. An we've a big surprise fer yeh.'

I stopped walking, waited for her to bend down to my level, head inclined to show she was listening. Instead I saw a lick of impatience; harassed and wide-eyed she tried to keep calm and hold back her tears. I thought maybe I'd let her down.

'Will Tony be there? At the house?'

Her face softened and the tears spilled quietly over and down her cheeks. She crouched to look me in the eye.

'No, Janie. Yeh'll never have tae see that man again an' that's my promise. It'll just be the two of us from now on.'

I put my arms around her neck and slid a small kiss along her salty cheek.

We caught the little minibus, the A13, and Ma fired questions at me in an empty, cheery way about the kids, food, the grown-ups, what I did in the daytimes.

'I played Connect 4, it's a game, an' combed my hair in the mornings and at bedtime, an' I didn't need tae pee ever in the night, not once!'

I sat on her flat knee and told her about the black woman who talked just like us and how she'd taught me to comb my hair. Ma's eyes drifted down and then up, her mouth drooped; it was the same face she pulled when Tony surprised her with a slap.

After that I decided to keep Nell a secret, I wouldn't tell Ma that that morning I'd cried on Nell's soft lap because I didn't want to go, fingering her green beads while she told the top of my head that I'd be happy with my ma, that I was lucky to be going home and I should tell my ma I'd missed her.

'Look, Janie, one stop till home an' yer surprise!' Ma's mouth pulled at a smile that wouldn't spread to the rest of her face. Her hair was starting to dry, making curls at strange angles.

I saw the shine of smashed bottles, the scribble of graffiti on a boarded-up window. Yes, we were nearly home.

I tried to pull breath into my tight chest as we walked through the door. I hadn't been away for more than two weeks but already the house felt like a stranger.

I saw for the first time the roughness; the maroon carpet nailed down at the edges, the stained wall where Tony once threw a bottle of whisky and the scorch mark by the kitchen where one of Frankie's pals fell asleep with a lit fag. Our home, made for passing through.

In the living room there were balloons on the floor, the long thin kind that hurt your chest to blow up if you don't give them a good stretch and, over the window frame, a shiny sign saying 'Welcome Home!' stuck up with four grey nuggets of chewing gum. The table had cake, crisps and a bottle of cola on it. On the sofa, Frankie, Denise and Jodie sat in a row. Meathead was in the armchair, his hand stretched across the divide to stroke Jodie's leg. They held mugs of cola and wore limp smiles.

'Surprise!' Ma shouted; it rang around the corners of the quiet room. 'I'll put on some music.'

Frankie opened his arms. 'Come here, kid.'

I ran to him and he hoisted me onto his knee. Jodie beamed at him and Meathead pulled away his hand tutting. Denise brushed her plump fingers through my hair. Blondie, 'Hangin on the Telephone', burst through the room.

Ma sat on the floor between Jodie's legs and Jodie reached down and gave her shoulders a little squeeze. Frankie looked me over.

'You OK, kid?'

I nodded, let my eyes stray to the yellow-and-pink Battenberg cake.

'Yeh'll no' see that man here ever again, right? Yeh believe yer Uncle Frankie?'

'Aye, Ma said. I like Blondie, Uncle Frankie, I'm a blondie too, see?'

Frankie looked at the carpet. 'I just wish I'd known and could've fixed it sooner. Cause yer Uncle Frankie can fix anything, alright, Janie? Remember that.'

His words tore through the air, full of sting and as unwelcome as glass splinters. Even I knew that everyone knew. It was written all over Ma's face, you just had to look under the ton of warpaint plastered over the truth.

Denise shifted. 'Shall we all have a wee bit o' cake?' Her soft voice wavered. 'Yeh all know I can't see cake sitting there an' not eat it. An' the hell with calories; I'm starting the Slimfast Plan the day after tomorrow anyway.'

Jodie got up, maybe so we wouldn't have to watch Denise shifting herself from the low seat, and cut thick slices of the Battenberg for everyone. She gave Ma her piece first, and I saw she was crying again.

'I've made such a fuckin' mess of everything.' Ma poked at her slice of cake.

Jodie gave out the rest of the Battenberg and sat on the carpet by Ma, balancing her piece on her bare knee. 'Come on, Iris.' She spoke in a low voice, as though it would stop the rest of us, in touching distance, from hearing. 'Cheer up fer Janie. Look at all the effort Denise went to an' we've still the presents tae do. Let's save tears fer after someone's bedtime.'

I was only half listening, engrossed in peeling off the sticky marzipan skin and pulling apart the yellow and pink squares.

'Right, let's do presents, eh?' said Frankie, slapping his dirty denim. Everyone nodded, except Meathead who was in a sulk.

Ma went to the kitchen, dragging her feet, and came back and stood with her right arm hidden behind the door frame.

'Now this is just a wee one . . . ta-da!'

If her voice was flat I didn't notice. She held a red see-through plastic umbrella; it went with my new dungarees. I split my face into a grin and everyone caught it on their faces too. If this was the wee one what would the next one be?

Ma bent for a moment then straightened to reveal a giant cloth clown, at least as tall as I was, with flopping long, thin legs and arms. He looked dead; his stitched face had wide, leering eyes and his gaping red mouth had teeth sewn in. His head flopped to one side; he looked like he came alive at night to eat brains. I buried my head in Frankie's chest.

'No! Take it away! I don't like him!' I gathered steam on my tears. I wanted to play Connect 4, watch cartoons and comb my hair. I wanted Nell. 'It's scary, I hate it.'

Ma took the clown and put it back in the kitchen. I peered round to see that the door was shut on the evil toy. She came back and stroked my hair and asked if I liked the umbrella and I nodded sullenly and snatched it from her. Ma sat back on the floor and started picking apart her own yellow and pink squares until the others dredged up some chatter about Blondie splitting and James Bruce being put inside for car fraud and at some point Jodie asked Ma, 'Where's Janie's granny the day?'

Ma rolled her eyes, took a breath. 'The fuckin' bingo.' They shared the tiniest of giggles before Ma saw my narrowed eyes, tucked her knees under her chin and went back to rolling her marzipan into a ball.

I inched forward on Frankie's knee and held my umbrella in front of me. It smelt of chemicals but it was shiny and had a red handle to go with the see-through plastic. I unclicked the popper on the band and watched the plastic spring open, a giant flower blossoming. I slid my hand to pop it open and Denise's own hand shot out, circling the umbrella and trapping mine.

'No, Janie, it's very, very bad luck tae open an umbrella inside.'

Ma let out a short bark of a laugh. 'I think we're well past that, Denise. In this house we've had our fair share. Go ahead, Janie, maybe it'll bring some good luck instead.'

Frankie laughed and Jodie joined in. Denise smiled and I pressed the button on the umbrella and watched the sad party and grubby room fill with colour as it exploded open. I spun the umbrella, watching its ruffles, and let out an excited gurgle, and soon enough we were all of us filling the dusty corners with laughter. Except for Meathead, who was still in a sulk.

Everyone left and Ma took me into the kitchen and made me a mug of tea with two spoons of sugar. We sat at the kitchen table, Ma on a stool and me on the little spin dryer. Ma ripped open a bag of crisps for us to share.

'Now, Janie, do yeh remember the social workers who took yeh?'

My eyes were on the crisps.

'Janie?'

I raised my eyes, nodded, and went back to the crisps.

'Well, the reason you got tae come home was because I told them we'd make some changes. Get organised.'

I reached for the biggest crisp and started licking off the sweet tangy cheese-and-onion flavour making rough, rasping noises.

Ma let out a sigh and picked at one of her bloody cuticles. 'Just eat it for Christ's sake, Janie.'

I put it in my mouth and crunched it into a paste.

'Now the first rule yeh know, and that is that we can't see Tony any more. There's a special sort of law that'll keep him away an' if we see him, even just in the street or a shop, we've tae get away an' then get the police, alright?'

Still crunching I reached for another crisp with a big bubble on it. I nodded.

'Fer God's sake, Janie, this is serious.' She snatched the crisps away and slammed them in a cupboard. 'Please, Janie, try an' listen, this is important. After we're finished talking yeh can have the whole bag tae yerself, OK? Now drink some tea. Alright, so that's the first new rule. The next one is that you need tae go to nursery this summer before going tae proper school. Yer so smart, Janie, that yeh'll be fine just going for a few months an' there'll be lots of kids tae make pals with.'

I put down my mug with both hands. Ma bit her lip.

'What will happen at nursery, Ma? Do you come too? Is it every day?'

'It's a place where I leave yeh for the day an' you play with other kids. An' it's only three days a week an' there'll be nice ladies there tae help an' look after you.'

My heart puttered with excitement and nerves. Ma wouldn't be there. I'd be by myself and there'd be kids to play with.

'So it's like Nell's house then?'

'Not exactly, it's –'

'An' will there be Connect 4? Or will I need to get a set? Could I get it, from Santa early?'

'I'm sure they'll have one.'

'Will there be fish fingers?'

Ma blew the steam from her tea in a short huffy breath. 'Maybe, Janie, I don't know. Now enough questions, I've more news.'

I knitted my pale brows together and nodded along with her but really I was wondering if the other kids would recognise me standing up and without my hard mask of blue holey plastic. I wondered if Nell would comb my hair after lunchtime or maybe take me shopping for some more T-shirts.

'Janie? Janie, did yeh listen to any of that? Stop pulling that stupid face for fuck's sake.' She slammed her mug down. 'I said we're moving. We're moving in four days.' There were tears in her eyes. 'I don't know why I bother.'

She went to the cupboard and threw the opened bag of crisps so they scattered across the table, and walked out. I heard the bedroom door slam. On the spin dryer I tried to think of some more things about nursery and to eat a few crisps but they hurt my throat all of a sudden and I couldn't think about Nell without my lumpy throat making them scratch more.

The next day, our third from last in Monarch Avenue, I got up to make Ma breakfast. She hadn't got out of bed all the night before and made me go to my room when I wanted to climb in with her. Since I'd come home it was her temper and tears I saw mostly. I thought she might be sick. How else could all the laughs, cuddles and the soft parts of a ma disappear? Now Tony was gone she was meant to be better.

I went to the kitchen and took the Flora margarine out of the fridge and dragged Ma's stool across to climb up to the cupboard for the coffee and bread. The bread was a bit hard at the edges but it softened up with an extra thick layer of marge. When I'd finished the bread was covered with fingerprints through a soft, greasy yellow sea. They looked like tiny elephant footprints so I made some more.

I needed to make Ma coffee to go with her cold toast. She always said, 'Janie, don't say a word until I've had my cuppa.' I couldn't touch the kettle though, because once I pulled the cable, trying to see the steam, and Ma pulled down my tights there and then and gave me a smack. But I knew coffee had to be hot, so I climbed onto the stool again and sprinkled the Mellow Bird's powder into the toaster's holes. After just half a jar, I added, just like I'd seen Ma do, a drop of milk. When Ma went to Grandma's she'd say, 'Just a dot o' milk in mine, Ma.' I pushed the lever and climbed down.

I ran through to the bedroom and threw myself on the lump under the sheet. Ma had been sleeping a long time.

'Ma! I made yeh a breakfast.'

I heard a sound under the covers like a kicked dog swearing then her face poked out and I was so close I could smell her sweaty hair and her smoky and savoury breath. Her face was already wet.

'What? What did yeh make? I'm warning yeh, if you've touched the hob or the kettle I'll –'

'No, Ma, I didnae! I made yeh some toast but not hot cause I had tae heat up yer coffee in the toaster.'

In the kitchen there was a loud popping sound. Ma sat straight up, jumped out of bed in her vest and pants, and shoved a pair of Tony's old boots on her bare feet.

'Fer fuck's sake! Stay here.'

When she came back into the room she looked at me through her little, naked eyes like I'd done something to hurt her. She looked at my face for a long time like she was trying to recognise me and I looked at her thin legs sticking out of the big black boots and tried to muffle a snort of laughter.

'Ma, was it not good? Breakfast tae cheer yeh up?'

Her face was sharp and I felt a seeping black feeling that maybe I hadn't done something I should have. Did she want jam? A fag lit to have with it?

She bent down so we were nose to nose, her smoky breath covering my face.

'You, Janie Ryan –' I quaked at the use of my surname – 'are a naughty wee beastie an' an awful chef!'

Then she threw me on the bed and tickled me with expert Ma tickly fingers. I wriggled, my arms flailed, but while I screamed for her to stop I was really begging her for more.

7

Buchanan Terrace was part of a big concrete estate. You could walk ten minutes in any direction and it would look like someone had been at work with grey blocks of Lego, a someone who liked clean lines and order and who probably didn't care too much about the families who'd have less space than battery hens.

They weren't tower blocks though; each building was U-shaped, with four levels of ten flats. We even had an upstairs and a downstairs and Ma said that made it a proper home. Buchanan Terrace was squeezed between two grim blocks. Ours was the red door on the fourth floor.

We didn't take much from Monarch Avenue, Uncle Frankie couldn't fit much into the boot of his tiny, fancy black car.

The estate was ugly but there wasn't the same threat in the air. Instead of broken bottles and petrol cans there were ice-pole wrappers and shitty nappies spilling out of ripped bin liners.

'This is a place fer families, Janie.'

There were gangs of kids who ran the streets, the youngest ones with heavy, sodden nappies under their short T-shirts, and when the ice-cream man came, chiming out 'Teddy Bears' Picnic', they would run after it, banging their grubby fists against the side of the van whether they had a shiny coin clenched inside or not.

Frankie said that business was good. He bought me a My Little Pony duvet and a grey rocking horse with stiff, shiny hair. Ma got a Breville toastie maker and a record player with a dead spider in the radio tuning strip. The best gift, for both of us, was a big colour telly with a remote control. Its colour and sound fell across the room in the evening and pushed away all the dark spaces like a rainbow.

Even Grandma brought something for us.

'Yeh wouldnae believe the journey on that bus. I hope yeh appreciate this. Of course, if yeh'd not got involved with a thug I wouldnae have tae be bringing yeh my neighbour's cast-offs.' She'd brought thick orange curtains that I wrapped myself up in, swanning through the house like a princess. Later Ma found me asleep at the foot of my bed, my limbs tangled in the tangerine velvet.

Ma decided to 'Get Organised' and each Monday we joined the long, impatient queue at the post office to cash the benefits books before going to Safeway and getting out the List.

'Then we'll last on whatever cash is left for the rest of the week and at least we'll have food in the larder.'

For the first few days we had tinned spaghetti, fish fingers and pink wafers, but by Sunday the cupboards were bare and we ate a lot of toast and porridge and talked about what we'd buy the next day in the shining aisles at Safeway. Over toast with a scrape of marge Ma explained she was just getting used to it and she'd find a way to 'make the grub last'.

On Mondays, after I'd helped her carry the bags of shopping and packed away the things in the freezer, Ma gave me a soft pound note; my pocket money.

'Run right there an' back an' don't let anyone take it from yeh, Janie.'

I ran with the note tightly rolled in my sweaty mitt all the way to the shop where I bought a comic and a Cornetto or sometimes a plastic cone of raspberry-swirled ice cream with a cold, crumbling gumball at the bottom.

'Do yeh not want tae save some for the week, so yeh can

go tae the ice-cream van?' she asked while I was astride my rocking horse, a drip of ice cream idling down its grey flank.

'Nope.'

No, I'd watched the kids from the landing that ran outside our door, chasing the red-and-white van, a pack of animals hunting, and I definitely didn't want to go down there with my precious pocket money.

My scalp was tender and my hair fluffy from brushing that I had started at six thirty and had finished after eight. I was dressed in my red dungarees, blue T-shirt and orange plimsolls.

'So they'll recognise me, Ma.'

She stared, shrugged, pushed my vitamin dropper to me and continued buttering toast. 'Put yer vitamins in yer milk.'

I squeezed the dropper, watching the oily yellow drops drift over the white surface. My hands were jerky, my head fizzing; today was the day.

'An' will there be Connect 4? For me tae play with the kids?'

Ma shrugged, her face pinched, she never wore make-up any more or went anywhere except for Mondays. I thought that 'Getting Organised' must have made her tired. She had bitten her nails to swollen, scabby stubs and I worried my pound-note pocket money was making us very poor.

I sat and watched *Sesame Street* and tried to swallow down the toast that stuck in my throat while Ma was getting dressed. She came back in a pair of stained jeans, a big black T-shirt with a panther on it that used to be Tony's, and a pair of white high heels. Her tight curls had become flat on top and frizzy at the ends. I looked at her smoking a roll-up.

'You look nice, Ma. You're beautiful.' She grabbed my arm

and pulled my face close to hers, her brown eyes hard. 'Don't bullshit, Janie, do yeh hear me? Never to please anyone. Even yer pathetic ma.'

Her voice was level but there was no hint of a smile. She dropped my arm and gave my forehead a quick kiss. 'OK?'

'OK, Ma . . . I think yer hair is a wee bit messy. Will I get my brush?'

'Aye, Janie, but be quick, we can't be late.'

I got my brush and followed the path of the bristles through Ma's hair with my chubby fingers while she had another roll-up and sat still for me.

When I finished and she stood, her face was wet from tears and her hair was double the size, soft and full of air as candyfloss. She put her hands to her head and gave a short laugh.

'Well, this feels like an improvement alright, Janie.'

She took my hand and we left for my first day at nursery.

It was a low building with barbed wire on the roof and wind-scorched, flaking cartoon characters on the walls. I told myself that it didn't matter that it was a different place.

Ma gave me a winding, rib-crushing cuddle before pushing me into the legs of a barrel-chested old woman wearing round pink-framed glasses.

'Be good and I'll be back later.'

She left quickly with her head down and didn't turn to look again.

'Janie, I'm Mrs Walker. Are you excited about your first day?'

I didn't answer the woman. I was too shocked by Ma's quick exit; she couldn't wait to get away.

She took my hand and led me through to a room scattered

with toys and pictures, all fighting for eye space. The only colours
and shapes that weren't crowding my vision were the ones I
wanted. My eyes didn't rest on Nell's shining skin or clicking
green beads. The collection of upturned noses, freckles and shin
bruises on the red carpet did not belong to any of the kids I knew
and I couldn't see a Connect 4 box anywhere.

I bit into my top lip with my bottom teeth. Ma had said
so, she'd promised. I felt the prickle behind my eyes, the swelling
inside my chest. I tugged Mrs Walker's sleeve.

'Do you have Connect 4 for me tae play with?' I asked in
a low whisper.

Kids froze with fingers up noses, they pulled their hands
from inside their shorts, a sea of squirming limbs on the carpet
stilled; these kids knew the build-up to a tantrum when they saw
one. At the front of the carpet a boy with dark shadows under
his eyes breathed noisily though his mouth.

'Oh, well, I'm not sure. Connect 4 you say?' She rolled the
name around her tongue. She'd never even heard of it. 'Anyway,
we play together here, Janie, in a nice big group.'

I began to match the boy's noisy breaths with my own until
the tight pain in my chest exploded and I started to howl. The
kids watched me as my mouth gaped with strings of saliva and
rivulets of snot pooled above my upper lip. They watched, wide-
eyed, as I turned pinker and pinker and I threw myself down into
a ball on the floor. Mrs Walker clucked around me, first trying
to calm me and then eventually trying to pull me away from my
audience, some of whom were threatening their own tears. As
she lifted me I shouted: 'Get off me, yeh . . . yeh fuckin' fat old
bitch.'

The whole carpet gasped. The boy with the dark circles
under his eyes started to cry.

'Don't hit her!' I never knew if he was worried about me or Mrs Walker because she was pulling me across the room, my plimsolls squeaking against the yellow lino.

I spent the rest of the day in 'the quiet room', taking out my temper on innocent crayons. I scratched scribbles onto sugar paper and made sure that every crayon in the box was snapped and crushed. If I saw a bit of crayon on the floor, I stamped my heel on it to make bright waxy streaks.

By the time Ma arrived there was a firework explosion of colour on the floor and I was sleeping on a stuffed monkey. She bent down and shook me gently.

'Janie?'

From her crouched position she looked up at Mrs Walker and then down at the crayon hate on the floor.

'Did she have a nice time? I mean, was she good?'

Mrs Walker pursed her lips and sighed through her flat nose. 'Well, to be honest we've had smoother starts, but I'm sure things will be better tomorrow.'

But Ma was already hoisting me up distractedly and I breathed in her roll-ups and coffee smell. 'Aye, well, see yeh tomorrow then.'

Mrs Walker reached out her hand and touched Ma's arm. 'A few other things; children pick up all sorts of things these days. Will you have a word to Janie about swearing? Maybe explain why we don't swear, especially at nursery?'

Ma looked at me and then Mrs Walker with a squint expression.

'And does Janie have the game Connect 4 at home? Is she particularly fond of it?'

Ma's squint deepened, her expression vague. 'Connect wha'? No, Mrs Walker, not that I can think of. I've never heard her talk about it even, but I'll ask her the night. I've just got tae get home right now though.'

We left the nursery in silence, Ma smoking a roll-up, looking like she hadn't slept for a week or maybe like she had slept for a whole week. When the nursery was just a grubby finger smudge behind us Ma looked down at me and said, in her poshed-up telephone voice: 'Will you speak to Janie about swearing? Fuckin' busybody.'

I laughed and swung our linked hands. 'Aye, fuckin' busybody!'

Peals of laughter escaped us and spiralled up into the hot, blue Scottish sky. We laughed all the way home and that night Ma didn't speak to me about swearing, but she didn't ask me about Connect 4 either.

The rest of summer the kids at nursery watched me carefully. I could take their toy or steal half their chocolate biscuit but when we had to walk with partners I would always be left with Davey, the boy with dark circles under his eyes and hands thick with flaky eczema. With no one else to walk with I happily chattered away as he looked wide-eyed and interested and said nothing; though I pulled my jumper sleeve over my hand before I held his.

Davey lived on the next terrace along from us. Above those dark shadows he had milky-blue eyes that made him look like he was waiting for a beating. His sister, Leanne, was six and went to proper school already. She had a skinny body and straight dark hair framing her hard face, narrow brown eyes and dusty skin that looked like it needed some rough treatment from a wet flannel.

I attached myself to them and held on tightly as though I

expected to be thrown off. Leanne was my best friend at home and we left Davey to trail silently behind, scratching his hands and taking the parts we didn't want in our games.

Leanne was brave and loud; she shouted a lot and broke rules. She also shat herself. We would be playing shopping or hairdressers and Leanne's face would become serious as the smell washed over us. She never said a word, just carefully stood up and ran, bow-legged, back to her house. I still had my own shameful days of waking to sticky legs and an acrid smell and I never said a word either.

Davey and Leanne's parents liked a drink. That's what Ma said when I asked her why they sometimes couldn't walk. It was true; whether I called for Leanne morning or night there would be a sweating can of lager and a plastic bottle of cider on the table and her ma and da would be lounging on the sofa watching the one channel they could get with the help of a bent coat hanger.

Ma called them Jack Sprat and wife because Leanne's da was so skinny you could see his bones and her ma's big arse spilled right over the sofa's edge. They both had blurry sea-green tattoos up their arms and if you stared long enough you could make out the dragons and lions and words crawling up their skin and under their T-shirt sleeves. The only thing I ever heard Leanne's da say was, 'Leanne love, fix us a snakebite.'

Us kids could do what we wanted, which normally meant taking our clothes off and chasing each other through the reeking dirty clothes and greasy plates in the bedrooms and jumping on the beds until something underneath snapped. I often stayed for tea at theirs though Ma didn't like it. 'They've enough on their plate, Janie, without another mouth tae feed.'

But Leanne's ma was organised too and on Mondays we would often bump into her in the booze aisle at Safeway with four big sacks of frozen chips thawing in her trolley. There was always a mouth-watering, fatty smell in the air at Leanne's and at the beginning of the week there would be red sauce too.

After enough visits to fetch me home for dinner or bed Ma gave in and said yes to 'A cider and a plate of chips, Iris?' After that she started joining them with her bottle of cider in front of the telly, on an armchair cleared of their crushed beer cans.

When Ma wouldn't let me stop for tea Leanne and Davey came over to mine and listened wide-eyed while I described the Fray Bentos pie and peas or Findus Crispy Pancakes I'd just eaten. I'd tell them I'd ask Ma if they could come to tea soon but I never did for fear of missing my plate of chips at theirs.

One night we heard the grown-ups laughing so loud that we ran downstairs. Leanne's ma was holding an empty chip bag.

'Call the police!' Ma slurred. 'No, the newspapers! Mary Dunne is out of chips.'

On the sofa Leanne's ma held the chip bag upside down and cried from laughter.

After the tears were wiped and the laughter died, Ma held out our door key to Leanne. 'Now bring back three eggs an' three slices of bread.'

Leanne looked at Ma and frowned, stuck out her chin. 'An' why do I have tae do that then?'

Ma sipped from her glass, her eyelids half lowered. 'Cause I'm making you kids eggs an' soldiers!'

Leanne grabbed the key and raced through the door, me and Davey trailing behind.

I sat on the doorstep and mourned my plate of chips while Leanne skipped down the street shouting for all to hear, 'We're havin' boiled eggs an' soldiers! Boiled eggs an' soldiers fer dinner!'

*

When January came with its winter winds biting through to our bones things had changed; I'd started proper school and hadn't gotten into trouble, except when Mrs Brown, our teacher, caught Davey humping on top of me and I said we were playing mammies and uncles. Ma was called to the school and nodded and looked concerned, then we'd laughed all the way home.

Ma'd cut off her hair so it stood from her head like the soft black feathers of a baby bird and started painting thick eyeliner around her eyes. Sometimes she even borrowed Jodie's pretty clothes. She looked nice again.

We started going to Grandma's every Sunday and Ma and her would cook the food while me and Uncle Frankie watched telly in the living room.

One Sunday he swore me off salt. I was sitting with him in my pink pants and blue vest, on the checkered bag of dirty washing he brought over to Grandma, digging into roast chicken and chips.

'Don't eat salt, Janie.' Frankie pulled the brown china shaker from my chubby fingers. 'It'll kill yer heart.' He put his rough hand just under my neck. 'The thing that pumps all the blood?' He shoved a piece of chicken skin into his mouth. 'It'll kill yeh, Janie, eatin' salt, like.'

I picked up a fat golden chip, brushed off the oily granules and wiped my greasy mitts on my thighs. Ma laughed from the kitchen doorway. 'My wee brother, the fuckin' loon. Janie, take what yer cracked uncle says with a pinch of salt.' And, laughing at her own joke, she turned back towards the kitchen and Grandma, who was shouting for help with the dishes.

The colour rose in Frankie's face; he slammed his plate to one side and tilted his head back. 'Yeh don't know everythin', yeh know, sis.'

Ma came back and leaned on the kitchen door frame, smiling. 'Yer right enough, Frankie, but I knew enough tae run away to London and no' tae bloody Blackpool.'

Grandma came through holding a pair of pants in one hand and a bar of black soap in the other. 'Aye, but unlike some he came back with a wad o' cash an' a bottle fer his ma. You just turned up with trouble an' a bun in the oven.'

Frankie snorted, picked up his plate and nodded down to me in agreement.

Ma's face dropped. 'Well, Ma, he's over twenty now, do yeh no' think he's old enough tae take a bar of soap to his own skidders?'

Grandma raised her pencilled eyebrows and twirled the white cotton pants on her forefinger. 'No' skidders like these. They're boskers, they need a ma's touch.'

On the bus home Ma huffed and dug her hands deep in her coat pockets. 'Even his fuckin' skidders are better than mine.'

Frankie would sometimes drive us home on a Sunday after using Grandma's phone to call some pals round to ours. All the estate kids would crowd the car and Frankie would give one of them a pound to mind it even though I always said I'd do it.

'Needs tae be a boy, Janie. Sides, I'll give yeh a pound anyway.'

Buchanan Terrace, like Ma, was starting to look better. Frankie had sent round paint the colour of vanilla ice cream and a brown sofa that left a flower pattern on your bare legs if you could sit still long enough.

We hung the curtains Grandma brought and it was a favourite game of mine to tangle myself up in one of them, wrapping it around my body and twisting until it swallowed my hair and pulled me into the Irn-bru cloth, then, eyes closed, I'd let the fizzy sunlight seep through my eyelids, warming my brain. That's how Ma would find me, still in my velvet chrysalis, ankle-socked feet sticking out.

For all our time in Buchanan Terrace one curtain was always happily crinkled while the other hung stiff, straight and unloved.

Frankie always came over Thursdays. He had to come once a week to collect the little bags of white powder that Ma measured from a bigger bag on scales with numbers like Frankie's digital watch. Ma did the measuring on Saturday mornings and the little spoons and jumping red numbers always stole my attention, even from *Fraggle Rock*.

'Can I have a go?' My eyes were fixed on the shiny spoons, the soft white powder.

'No, Janie, how many times do I have tae say? Watch the telly.'

'Just tell me what it is though?'

Ma gave me a look and then sighed. 'It's special flour. An' I have tae measure wee bags so that people's cakes come out just right. Now watch the telly. If I can't concentrate the cakes'll be shite and then we'll not have chocolate biscuits or cola this week an' yer Uncle Frankie won't come over.'

I still loved Frankie, especially now he came over every week, so I let her concentrate.

Once, he gave me, Davey and Leanne two pounds each and we ran with the ice-cream van and bought something on every street of the estate. We managed ten stops, to Arbroath Street, before our puff and the money ran out on us.

When Frankie came over, especially on Thursdays, he went to the toilet for a long time. Ma always said he was just having a shite and he came out eventually, just a bit sleepy and pale.

'Frankie, did you have a big poo?'

He gave his lazy laugh and looked over at Ma. 'Fuckin' hell Iris, what are yeh like?' He'd watch telly with us till it got dark then he always had to go.

On school nights me and Ma would watch the Terry Wogan show, dinner on our laps. Ma had stopped me from staying at Leanne's for dinner because she'd rowed with Leanne's ma, so she gave me the chips I'd come to love and 'something with some vitamins' to stop my sulks. Sometimes it was sausage and egg and chips, sometimes egg, chips and beans. Eggs and our evenings with the cheeky Irish host went together.

I didn't want to eat eggs; eggs came from chicken's bums and they were really baby chicks. Having one given to me from the frying pan made me panicked, reckless. I did not want an egg in my tummy.

The first time I hid an egg Ma was in the kitchen getting us Jaffa Cakes and tea for afters. I turned my knife on its side, lifted the egg and slid it under the sofa. But guilt festered in my stomach, a slimy green thing under my scratchy school jumper; the egg was there, waiting in the dark, to expose me as naughty Janie who didn't deserve her Jaffa Cakes at all.

The Sunday after I hid the egg, Frankie came over with some pals. Ma put on Madness, pencilled around her eyes and drank brandy. They stayed for a long time and Frankie's pals kept grabbing at Ma when she tried to get up and she'd flutter and giggle, like she was being tickled, before falling over on wobbly brandy legs.

I sat in my vest and pants and watched the spider dance on stiff dead legs in the record player, worried about the egg sitting under Ma and Frankie's pals' bums, before falling asleep in front of our two-bar electric fire. When I woke up, my face bumpy from the carpet and my skin blotchy from the fire, there was no one there but I heard voices in the kitchen.

Through the door frame I saw Frankie standing at the kitchen counter, his sleeve rolled up and arm held tight with a shoelace. I smelt matches and something sweet and he had a needle, like for getting jabs, in his hand.

'Fuckin' hell! Mate, mate, it's the wee un,' said Frankie's pal slouched against the kitchen sink, not Meathead who never came over any more.

'Frankie? Are yeh sick? Will I get Ma?'

'Get the fuck out, Janie!' He started towards me, arm raised and ready to hit, the shoelace waving like a ribbon in the wind.

I ran to Ma's room; her door was blocked from the inside and I banged my fist on it. I could hear noises, I knew she was there but she wouldn't come out, I knew that as well. So I made myself small in the corner between my bed and the wall, my favourite nook since I had fallen asleep there in my tangerine curtain nest.

It was my fault Ma was ignoring me. She must know about the egg. In my mind, full of the teachings of Bert and Ernie, I made a deal: I would tell the truth. Be a good girl and maybe she would talk to me again and Uncle Frankie would get better. With this promise made I wedged myself deeper into my nook and cried until sleep lapped at the sharp edges of that night. I waited two days before I told Ma, with tears in my eyes, a black bat's wings beating against my ribcage.

'Ma, I'm sorry.' Her tight face turned the pale, sickly colour I remembered from the days before Tony went away. I couldn't talk, my chest heaved. 'I'm sorry.'

Ma grabbed me.

'What? Tell me fuckin' what?'

I got down on my knees in front of the sofa and Ma followed. She lifted the sofa a few inches with both hands and there was my monster, gleaming in the half-light, winking with his orange eye, promising revenge. She rescued it, hard at the edges with congealed grease, its yolk cracked down the middle.

Ma stood, egg in her hand, silent. I was sorry I told her. I explained, about chickens' bums and baby chicks in tearful, half-gulped-down breaths. She bent down and stared at me. I waited for her to 'blow'. That was always the warning. 'Janie, I'm warning yeh, I'm about tae blow.' I held my breath, closed my eyes and prepared for the famous Ryan temper to fall down on me. I held my breath until sparkles appeared then opened my eyes to the silence. Ma looked at my face, her shoulders fell and she tutted. Shook her head and put her hand to my face. 'Janie yeh know yeh don't ever have tae be afraid of me? I'm yer ma, Janie.'

'I know, Ma.' Then, as though pressing a bruise, I said it quickly. 'Ma? Is Frankie sick? Cause he has tae give himself jabs?'

Ma sat on the sofa's edge and said to the split orange eye in her palm, 'Out of the mouth of babes.' She looked up. 'Aye, Janie, I do think he's sick but he doesnae want anyone knowing so yer not tae talk about it, OK? Promise?'

'Aye, I promise.'

And so that first promise of silence shattered inside of me like the twist of a kaleidoscope; to be joined by so many more jagged secrets, pushed into a little body for safe keeping until they threatened to cut their way out.

The summer I was six it was so hot that the gold of the sun turned the windows of the estate into shiny new pennies that winked and glinted around us. I spent all my time at the swings, waiting for the highest point, that split second when it felt like floating and then jumping off to land on feet that fizzed in shock when they hit the concrete.

That day I didn't land on my feet and ran up the stairs with a grit-filled scrape biting with every step. Our front door was wide open. I saw shapes moving through the frosted glass of the living-room door, people trapped under a layer of ice, then I heard Ma laughing in a way that made me think of her head thrown back and that made me forget about the sting of my knee.

'Ma?'

The laughter stopped and she opened the door, just enough to squeeze her body through sideways. 'Janie, yer finished playing already?'

'Aye. I hurt my knee.' I stared past her, 'Who's in there?'

'Come into the kitchen, Janie, I'll get yeh some juice and fix yer knee up. An' take off yer jumper, yeh've a face on yeh like a beetroot.'

She sat me on the sink draining board and I tugged off my squeaky wool jumper while she made me a Vimto.

'Do yeh remember yer Uncle Tony?'

She wet the dishes sponge and pressed it against my knee. I stopped drinking but kept the glass to my face. I frowned behind the sticky rim as the sponge soaked my raw skin.

'Come on, Janie, it's just a wee scrape. An' of course yeh remember Tony . . . silly question. Well, he hasnae been tae see us in ages, has he?'

'It's against the law. You said. You said if he did the police would come and I'd get taken away.' My words smacked against the bottom of the glass and echoed back out.

'Shh! Janie, not so loud.' She ran her fingers across her scalp. 'Janie, he's all better now. He was . . . sick, like yer Uncle Frankie, but he's feeling better.'

I stuck the glass over my chin and mouth and gulped the air out of it so it stuck to the bottom of my face.

'Iris?' The familiar shout from the living room. Ma pulled the glass off my chin and it gave a loud fart.

'It's just a visit. Will yeh come through?'

Would I? I wasn't leaving him alone with my ma again. She lifted me down from the sink, and though my legs dangled down to her knees, she hoisted me onto her hip to carry me through.

Tony was sprawled across the rug in front of the fire, though it wasn't on. He was the same; he didn't look any better to me. Same dirty denim and spiked hair and chunky, silver rings. The only change was that he'd shaved and had the first of the year's sunburn that made a T-shape across his face.

'Janie my wee petal, look how big yeh got.'

He straightened and opened his arms to me and I moved behind Ma who placed her splayed fingers and palm on the crown of my head and said in a quiet voice, 'We'll just give her time. She'll come round. She's too young tae understand.'

'Can I watch the telly?'

'Aye, go on.'

I heard their laughter behind me and drinks pouring and I knew that Ma wanted to get shot of me and that it might be a long visit.

It was the chimes of the ice-cream van that cut through my sullen channel flicking. Ma came over.

'Janie do yeh want an ice cream or not?'

I stood by the sofa, smelling Ma's breath like pink nail-varnish remover, on the table I saw the bottle of vodka and carton of pineapple juice.

Tony had 50p held between his forefinger and thumb, a magician about to do a trick. I stared at it shining in the light and thought it over. It might be a trick; to get me out of the room and away from Ma or it might just be a free ice cream. The best thing to do was to get an ice cream but make it fast. A free cone was a free cone after all.

Ma reached forward and took the coin from him, placing it in my hand.

'Are yeh going tae say thank you, Janie?'

I started running for the door.

'Ta.'

Before the door slammed I heard Ma shout, 'Don't forget tae bring some change back.'

I was down the stairs and elbowing my way through the crowd of kids before Tony would have had time to pick up his drink again or Ma could apologise for me.

I got the biggest ice cream, a giant soft whorl with a flake, drenched with glossy raspberry sauce, and ran back up the stairs taking bites of it, licking drips of sticky sauce off my wrists and cramming the flake into my mouth sideways before it softened and burst in an explosion of chocolate crumbs.

I ran back into the living room and gave Ma back the 5p change.

'Janie, yeh cheeky thing. That's a giant ice cream.'

Tony shrugged, sipped his drink. 'Come on, Iris, it's a treat.'

Ma smiled at him and patted the sofa between them.

'Sit here, just while yeh finish it, I'm not having yeh get raspberry juice on the remote again.'

Ma's words blurred at the edges and Tony had a dopey smile on his face; the bottle on the table was almost empty. I sat on the edge of the sofa between them, filling my mouth with ice cream as fast as I could.

'Can I have a drink of yer pineapple juice?'

'Course yeh can,' Tony replied, shaking the empty carton. 'There's more in the fridge.' And he went through to the kitchen like he owned the place.

'Janie, when he comes back put a bit of ice cream on his nose.' Ma's whisper was warm, ticklish in my ear.

'What?' I looked at Ma grinning and open-faced, her eyes urging me.

'Fer a laugh. Go on, it'll be a laugh.'

Tony came back with my chewed-up baby cup that I hadn't used since before he went away. He held it out, face full of pride.

'Nice an' cold from the fridge an' all.'

I looked round to Ma grinning and nodding me on. I did it for Ma and the pizza. Tony turned to speak and I took one final lick of my ice cream and mashed it onto his nose so the cone pointed out like a snowman's carrot from his sunburned face.

'Janie! I said a wee bit not the whole cone.'

Ma's smile was fixed but her eyes were wide as we watched the pink in Tony's face deepen, a drop of ice cream roll down his face. He lifted his hand and I grabbed a handful of Ma's T-shirt, but he just pulled the cone off his nose with a slurp and laughed, cleaning his face with the hem of his T-shirt.

'Were you playing a trick on me? Yeh monkeys!'

Beside me Ma collapsed into the sofa. She bent double as though her mouth wasn't big enough to let out all the laughter contained inside her. In between breaths she kept saying, 'Yeh should have seen yer face! Fuck's sake, Janie, I meant a wee bit not the whole fuckin' cone!'

While she laughed I watched Tony's flat, unsmiling eyes above his wide grin and my lovely ice cream melt into a sad pool around the almost empty vodka bottle. Once Ma had caught her breath she said, 'Janie it's time fer yer bed.'

But she wasn't looking at me when she said it.

'Are yeh going tae come up and see I've brushed my teeth?'

'No, not tonight, yer a big girl, Janie. Now tae bed with yeh.'

'Could I not stay up a bit later till Tony goes?'

'Aw, Janie, I'm sure yeh'll see Tony in the morning. Now, bed.' As I left I heard her say to my back, 'I love yeh, yeh wee beastie. Night-night.' And the gurgle of another drink being poured.

That night I tucked my duvet into my dark nook and kept my eyes open till they burned waiting for thuds and screams, but that was one night they didn't come.

'Yer new da's hair's funny.'

'He's not my da, he's not even an uncle. It's just stupid Tony.' Pop, pop, pop.

'My da says he's a hard man about town an' if he gets married tae yer ma yeh'll have someone to look out fer yeh like me an' Davey.' Pop, pop.

'They won't ever have a wedding. He was meant tae ages ago but he never did. He'll just stay for a while smashing stuff up an' then he'll go away again an' I'll help get Ma better.' I felt a sharp set of kneecaps in my tummy. 'Leanne, shift yer legs they're digging intae me.'

There was a flurry of 'pops' as Leanne adjusted herself. We were in an empty cardboard box that a neighbour's twin tub had come in. It was filled with bubble wrap and as soon as we saw it we turned it upside down and climbed in, filling the dark space with popping and giggles as we got comfy in our new den.

'Besides, my Uncle Frankie, the one with the fancy car, can fix him any time. He told me.'

'What's he smashed up?'

'Just stuff. Ma says it's secret anyway.'

'Does he hit yeh?'

'It's a secret, Leanne, I crossed my heart an' hoped tae die.'

I picked up a hand of bubble wrap and squeezed it in my fist. It was hot but I crossed my legs tighter as I felt the usual heavy feeling in my tummy.

'But we're best friends so yer allowed. Everyone knows that.'

'Really?'

'Aye, that means we tell each other.'

My heart beat so loud I thought the cardboard walls would shake but I lifted my hands up and cupped them around the hot skin of Leanne's ear anyway. She stopped popping, held her breath, leaned towards me and I said in a whisper, 'He doesnae hit me but he hits Ma, he hits her an' she even bleeds.'

'That tickles.' She shook me off and said in a normal voice, 'Is that all? That's what das do. So Tony must be going tae be yer da then.'

I kicked the plastic off my sweaty legs, 'How's that then? Your da doesnae hurt yer ma, does he? Not so she bleeds an' cries?'

I thought maybe Leanne had nodded in the darkness. Instead she said, 'I'm roasting in here, let's get out.'

We pushed the cardboard box so it fell backwards then stretched out our legs to get the air on them and blinked some sunshine into our light-thirsty eyes.

'Leanne, does your da hurt your ma?'

'Just when there's no' enough booze. Or too much. That's what Ma says.'

I flapped my skirt to get some breeze up there and looked at my best friend.

'But yeh stop him, don't yeh? From hitting yer ma?'

'I would, I'd kick him in the balls when he hits her, but she told me the hits hurt more if there's someone watching. An' the bruises are bigger.'

She shrugged and started ripping off a piece of cardboard. It made sense; every time I ran to my room I was helping Ma to hurt less and making her bruises smaller so she wouldn't have to use up so much blusher. Leanne put back her head, put a scrap of cardboard on her pursed lips and blew it high into the air.

'Does he hit you?'

'Naw. Just Davey, but only sometimes, and Davey can run faster than him if it's the days when it's too much booze.'

'Well, my Uncle Frankie can sort anything an' he'll come an' sort your da as well as Tony. I'll ask him.'

Leanne tore the pieces of cardboard into brown confetti. 'Naw, don't bother. He doesnae mean it. Ma's always saying how much he loves her an' us.'

'That's what my ma says about my da.'

'That Tony?'

'Naw, I've said, he no' my real one. My real da is American like a film star. Ma says he's a big house in England. She says she might take me to stay with him, like when I went tae Nell's house.'

'Who's Nell?'

I shrugged and put a bit of cardboard on her upturned lips; she smelt sweet and dusty like a wine gum from the bottom of Grandma's bag. She blew and we watched the card fly.

'Just someone nice. My real da is maybe going to look after me for a while Ma says, while Frankie's fixing things.'

She shrugged, poked a finger into her ear and had a gouge. 'Do yeh want tae go?'

I shrugged back, pulled my knickers out of my sweaty bum crack. 'Ma would come an' get me she said.'

'Davey would cry. He cries when Ma locks the door fer a bath even.'

'Where is Davey?'

She turned to me, a big grin on her grimy face. 'Getting nit shampoo with Ma.'

'Ugh! Davey's got nits?'

She stood up and started dancing around the box.

'Aye, Davey's got nits but I havnae. Davey's got nits! Davey's got nits!'

I chased her doing my own stomping, Red Indian dance.

'Nits! Nits! Nits!'

Our sandals slapped against the dirty paving slabs, our arms and hair flew wildly about us.

'Let's wreck it!' Leanne said, aiming a kick with her pink jelly sandal at the side of the box.

'Aye! Let's smash it up! Nits! Nits! Nits!'

And we jumped on our cardboard home and kicked and ripped it to shreds with our bare sweaty hands.

'Nits! Nits! Nits!'

Pop. Pop. Pop.

It had only taken two weeks for him to start again. The coffee table had gone first, its smooth glass top broken cleanly into three pieces, then the grate on the front of the fire was kicked in, the dented wires touched the electric bars so we couldn't turn it on. 'Well, it's summer now,' Ma said, looking at the floor. The top of the record player got smashed in and I wondered if the spider had been scared, it seemed deader. Next the frosted pane of glass in the living-room door was shattered by the silhouette of a wrangling man and woman. Ma gaffer-taped over the hole with a cornflakes packet. 'There, good as new.'

Then it was Ma's wrist that was broken, from a boot brought down on it, and her nose, for the second time, by Tony's forehead.

Tony slammed the door as he left and Ma called for a taxi, repeating the words over and over until they understood her blood-slippery lips. The driver made Ma sit on a bin liner from the boot and looked straight ahead. He didn't ask if she wanted to go to the hospital even though Ma had blood all over the bottom of her face like a winter scarf pulled up high.

When we got to Frankie's flat, the first time I'd ever been, he locked the door behind us and called another taxi for Ma. After she went he took me for fish and chips and when we came back Jodie was sitting on the doorstep goosebumped and full of temper. She gave me a hard hug and I let myself be cradled in her soft curves that smelt like Charlie perfume and Silk Cut.

Ma got back after I'd fallen asleep and must have wrapped herself around me on the sofa because I woke to Ma's staring, bruised eyes and her taped-up nose.

That morning Jodie washed my hair in Frankie's big round bath but I could still hear the row in the next room.

'You said, you said yeh could fix it. Before, when Janie came home an' . . . yeh know I can't go tae the pigs. They'll take her into care.'

'Aye, but it's not the same now, sis,' Frankie was pleading, 'I can't piss off my suppliers an' Tony's connected. He's the one got me into this.'

'So it's about money then, is it? Over me an' Janie?'

'No, it's . . . I mean . . . yeh know it's not just fer selling that I need a supply. Please.'

'Oh, I understand alright, first Ma an' now you, it's like we've no flesh an' blood tae depend on.'

I looked up at Jodie.

'Lie back now, Janie, get all the soap out.' Still Ma's anger moved through the water, a slow sea creature, reaching my ears in time.

In the days that followed Ma's mood could turn on you as quickly as a Scottish summer day, leaving you chilled, bewildered and running from a storm in your flimsy dress.

When Frankie took us back to Buchanan Terrace the telly had been kicked in and the sofa cushions slashed, but it was my bedroom that smelt like the payphone by the shops from the stale piss soaked into the mattress and made Frankie's face twist. 'Fuckin' hell.'

Ma pulled my burning face to her flat belly. 'Shut it, Frankie, just shut it right now. Alright, Janie, yeh've tae pack yer school uniform, jammies, an' two changes of playing-out clothes.'

'What about my toys?' I asked, breathing through my mouth, my eyes on my rocking horse with its sticky sides and plastic hair.

Ma let an exasperated breath from between her lips. 'Don't make this harder, Janie. One – fuck it, two toys but small ones.'

I chose my red umbrella and my Glow Worm, that had stopped glowing after the first week, stuffed my lunch box with anything else I could fit and then piled my arms with toys and got Frankie to carry my rocking horse to Leanne's. Ma stood by the car waiting for us smoking a roll-up.

Leanne and Davey were at school but their ma let us in with a shrug. Once we'd left the toys in a pile on a bed I went into the living room while Frankie waited outside.

'Will yeh tell them it's just fer a wee while? I'm coming back but they can play with them until then?'

Leanne's ma put down her glass and gave me a kiss on the cheek. 'Aye, Janie, I will. An' you tell yer ma from me she's well out of it. Well out. Are yeh off tae stay with family fer a while?

She looked tired and maybe worried about us so I gave a big smile. 'Aye, don't worry, we're going tae stay with my da in London. He's from America!' But that just seemed to make her sagging face even sadder.

Frankie drove us to Grandma's and we said our goodbyes with the motor running.

'Sorry, Ma, we've tae catch the overnight coach.' Ma looked at her feet. 'Save on a night in a B&B, yeh know.'

Grandma's violet eyes were blue behind a film of tears. She touched Ma's face, the bruises green and brown now, the tape over her nose gone, leaving grubby marks.

'Do yeh have to go straight away though? An' looking like that.'

'Aw, don't worry; down there they'll just think I had a nose job.' Ma gave a hard laugh. 'An' yer right enough, if we stay he'll find us an' the wee madam here is better off away, just fer a while.'

I circled my arms around Ma's legs, I said nothing though I was fairly sure who 'the wee madam' was.

'Yeh know if it wasnae fer my hip I would've minded her for yeh? Don't yeh?'

Ma didn't reply, just bent down to me and gave me a shove towards the door. 'Say bye tae Grandma, Janie, yeh won't see her for a wee while.'

Grandma bent down and tears splashed onto the concrete between our feet. 'My darlin', you be good, alright?' She puckered her shimmery lips and gave me a wet kiss that left me wiping my mouth with the hem of my skirt.

Ma rolled her eyes.

'Ignore her, Ma, thinks she's too big fer kisses nowadays. She'll . . . we'll be home fer Christmas anyway, once it's died down, or yeh could come tae where we are?'

'Well, let's see where yeh end up, I can't take travelling like I used tae.' She looked behind us at Frankie. 'Well, enough of making a show of myself on the doorstep. Get off or yeh'll miss yer bus.'

Her door was closed by the time we had walked back to the car. No backward glances on either side.

'Was she alright?' Frankie asked, his eyes on the road.

'Aye, she just loves a bit of drama, even at her own kid's expense. Mark my words, tonight she'll be off having a laugh with Aggie at bingo and she'll barely remember she has a daughter.' Ma looked in the rear-view mirror, prodding at her bruises. 'Frankie, do yeh think I could tell people this is a nose job?'

He turned his head. 'Not with the nose on you, sis. Sorry, but not a chance.'

8

The filthy coach station was full of the noise of people leaving. A hen party filled up most of the waiting room with their shrieks, criss-crossing arms passing bottles, their breasts bursting from the tops of dresses.

Ma looked over. 'I hope to God they're not on with us.'

'No, Ma, they're just here fer a bevvy.' My eyes were on the black-and-white departures board, waiting for the next change. 'They just came here cause it was the first place the bride got a ride off her husband.'

'What?'

The times changed and the slats on the board rolled over, making the sound of hand claps, black and white flashing like a swarm of insects' wings until the board lay flat again.

'I heard them say just now.'

Frankie was laughing and craning his neck at the women, but Ma looked sad. 'Right, well, let's get some sweets fer the journey.'

'Why don't you go, sis? Yeh know some people's eyes are bigger than their bellies. I'll stay here an' mind her.'

She pulled a face at him but went off to the kiosk. As soon as she started walking Frankie pulled two twenty-pound notes from his jeans pocket. I tore my eyes from the board and started jumping to get them as he held the notes just out of reach.

'Now, Janie, keep those safe. It's no tae buy toys or sweeties with, do yeh understand?' I nodded, though a second ago I was planning to run to the kiosk and buy every packet of Jelly

Tots they had. 'If you an' yer ma get stuck an yeh need a taxi or maybe a proper dinner then yeh can use it. Now put it somewhere safe.' He watched me fold the money into soft squares and tuck it in the empty Velcroed slot in my Glow Worm that should have held batteries.

'An' it's our secret, aye? Don't tell yer ma until yeh need tae, when yeh get really skint.'

I grabbed his forearm and got him to swing me. My Glow Worm and I had a secret but I thought maybe I'd be allowed to tell my da.

With every turn of the wheel my throat closed and my stomach flipped. Ma had made us queue for twenty minutes outside the coach so we could get the three back seats by the toilet; she said it was for space but I had a growing doubt about that. I lay on Ma's lap, tasting the sweet, bitter taste of my own bile.

'Can I have a sweetie? Tae take away the taste?'

'No, Janie, yer better off with an empty stomach. We're not out of town yet an' there's a long way tae go.'

The bus rocked from side to side and in the dim of the robot-eye ceiling lights I saw the man who was sitting in the seat in front of the toilets watching us. He was old, maybe fifty, with shiny eyes under long scratchy-looking eyebrows; I named him Mr Badger. I felt his eyes whisker over our bodies, fall on Ma's bruised face and spiky hair, then scurry across the fringe that I'd cut myself with kitchen scissors behind Frankie's sofa. I felt the shiny dots of his eyes land on my grey socks with holes and I tucked the worst one under the other and turned my face towards Ma's belly.

'Come on, Janie,' she said, stroking my head, 'yer just a wee bit travel-sick. We'll stop soon an' yeh can have a bit of juice an' we'll tidy you up.'

I pulled my knees in tighter, to squeeze out the sick feeling and forget the smell of the plastic toilet bowl with petal-shaped fag burns around the rim and thought my da had better be really special. I thought he would be. Ma didn't used to like speaking about him but suddenly she wanted to tell me how funny he was, that he played tricks and was always nice to cats and children.

At Newcastle we got off and I walked with Ma through the bright service station like the marrow had been sucked from my shin bones. She said this was the latest I had ever stayed up and that it was a special treat, but when I saw people spearing coils of pale bacon and greasy slabs of fried egg into their mouths I was sick on the floor in front of the cafe. It didn't feel like a treat.

Outside the air dried the sweat on my forehead and Ma held a Ribena carton, telling me to take little sips, but each drop of sweet purple juice made my tummy twist.

'Will I smell like sick fer meeting Da?'

'Ach, Janie, no.' Ma gave a smile and ruffled my fringe. 'We'll tidy yeh up. Besides, it's probably him yeh get it from. He used tae have tae get steaming before a big journey. Absolutely blotto.'

I pushed the carton away and stared at her from under lowered eyebrows. 'Well, yeh could've got me steaming an' all then, Ma!'

We were second back on the bus, after Mr Badger and his big eyebrows.

'Excuse me, miss?'

He stood in the aisle. Ma stopped a step away from him. 'Aye?' Her voice was cold.

'I hope you don't mind but I thought you and the kiddie could use this?'

In his hands was a tartan blanket, the white price label still swinging from a corner.

'What for?'

'To keep you both warm.' He smiled. 'These northern summers can turn and it's cold to be travelling in just T-shirts. I've daughters of my own and –'

'We've jumpers.'

'And . . . it's a gift . . . to keep.' He extended the blanket. 'Please.'

Ma's hand got hotter in mine. 'Thank you,' she said taking it, 'it's really decent of you.'

He said nothing but sat down and allowed us to pass. Back at our seats I lay down and let the soft blanket, smelling of nothing but new, wrap itself over me, and behind my head felt Ma's stomach soften as though she was letting go of a long breath. I whispered, 'Is my da as nice as him?'

'In a different way, aye. Yer da's less . . . traditional.'

I felt Ma move before I saw him.

'You don't mind if I sit here, petal?' A fat belly in a yellow T-shirt and a hand with ginger hairs on the knuckles holding a can of lager. 'Can I offer you a tinny? Help you sleep?'

Ma stiffened. 'No thanks.'

'Suit yerself, love. Just bein' friendly.'

The engine started, the lights went down.

'Ma, I feel sick, I think it was the Ribena.'

'Shh, Janie, try tae think of something else. Listen, mister, my wee girl's sick . . . it's her first time on a coach an' I really think she'll feel better if she can sleep. Would you mind moving so she can stretch out?'

There was a long silence, the can disappeared and then appeared again. 'There's no seats.'

'There's one right there, look.'

'Yeah,' he said in a loud whisper like Grandma's, 'but I'm no sittin' next to a Paki.'

Ma's hand clenched her knee. 'Right. Fine.'

She tried to move me into a better position but the tipping of my head brought up the rush of warm, sweet sick collecting in my throat and I bent my head over Ma's lap and let it out. When I opened my eyes his trainers were covered with pink watery vomit.

'Bloody hell!' He went into the toilet, slamming the door after him. I cried as the smell spread like a pink mist through the air.

'I'm sorry, Ma, I couldnae hold it.'

Ma kissed my sweaty face and shifted into his seat, putting her feet to the side of my sick. 'It's all right, Janie, really. Now stretch yer legs all the way out, there's a good girl.'

As soon as I got off the coach I saw Nell. Except of course it wasn't, neither were any of the other round-hipped, dark-skinned women who made my heart soar and dip, a bird in the wind, while we waited for the bus.

We caught a red double-decker and Ma squeezed us to the front so we could sit on the seat diagonal to the driver and look straight out. They had a special man who came and took our money and gave us bus tickets.

'Well, what do yeh think, Janie? This is London.'

I thought London seemed like smears of colour through the window and that the people were worms twisting blindly in dirt, moving around each other as though they each knew where the other would step before they'd decided themselves.

'Ma? What's wrong with her?'

Ma followed my finger to a woman swathed in black with just a letter box of space for her eyes, then smiled around the bus apologetically.

'It's cause she's a different religion an' her husband doesn't want anyone but him tae see her body.'

'Like Tony then.'

She gave me a hard look. 'Aye, I guess a wee bit like Tony, but Janie, yer not to mention all that when we see yer da, alright?'

I breathed and misted the window and revealed London again stripe by stripe with my fingertips.

'Will Da be happy tae see me? He won't mind babysitting? Yeh do like him again now?'

Ma pulled me from the window seat up onto her lap. 'Aye, Janie. I was just upset cause he went on such a long holiday an' when yeh miss someone yeh get sad sometimes.'

I thought about Nell and decided this made sense while Ma cleared the window with a zigzag of her palm.

'But now it's fine cause, after all –' she reached up and straightened my fringe with her fingers – 'he's yer da and deserves some time with yeh too. And that's why I need tae look fer the stop.' She crouched over me and cupped her hand to the window-pane. 'I'll know it when I see it alright.'

But she didn't know and in the end we got off our bus and caught another back to Victoria Station and started again from the same bus stop.

Ma wouldn't answer any more of my questions and back at the bus stop I looked at her, marching ahead, with her sticking-out bones, stained jeans and sad bruised face and I didn't want to be with her. I wanted to be with my da in his nice big house. When I looked at Ma I got a temper snake in my belly eating through anything nice. I threw down my lunch box with a slam and refused to let go of the bus stop when another bus eventually came and Ma lifted my skirt and gave me a burning slap across the back of my legs before shouting at the people getting on the bus, the bus we should have caught. 'What are yeh all looking at? Mind yer fuckin' business!'

When the bus pulled away I couldn't tell if the sardine-tight passengers thought me or Ma had had the worst tantrum.

We made up over a fluffy slice of lemon meringue pie in a cafe with tall stools and glass tables. Ma said it was worth it for the treat even though she counted the money in her purse twice after she paid the bill and left a few coins under the plate.

On our last bus I felt shame, the sticky material of the seat and Ma's slap prickling at the back of my knees as I stood wedged behind her fluffing her hair with my fingers. Ma's nose touched the window as she tried to see something but I didn't know what and she wouldn't tell me.

'Come on, Janie, get yer stuff, this is us!'

Ma took our case and we stumbled out onto the almost dark street. My job was to carry my lunch box, Glow Worm and umbrella but I'd broken the catch of the lunch box and every few steps it would come apart and Ma would have to watch me, with her fingers jerking, put it all back: my brush, swimming costume, pink plastic cup, colouring pencils, all in their places.

'Just shove it in, come on.'

It took us ages to find the right house. Ma stamped along the pavements like they might be tricking her and when we got to the house she spent a long time looking at the street and doors as though that might be a trick too.

The house was tall and white, like one off a fancy TV programme, with a door that shone in the orange street light and a big blank window at the front. There wasn't a sound on the curved street, just rows of silent white houses staring at us.

'OK Janie, you stay right here with the bags.'

Ma clawed her lower lip with a sharp white tooth and climbed the six steps. Reminded, I licked my own crusty meringue moustache and started to brush my fringe. I was sure I smelt of sick and wished I had some of Jodie's Charlie perfume. Ma told me that Da looked just like me, 'you're the spit of him', and I imagined him taller and in boys' clothes but with my wonky fringe, eyes that turned to a line of blondie lashes when he did a big smile, a dot of a nose in his round face; just like me.

My arms felt all twitchy, stuck on the wrong way, and my knees made little wobbles under me. I'd never really missed not having a da, lots of kids didn't have one on the estate, but now I couldn't wait to fill the gap I hadn't even known I had with a da like one from the TV, who would buy me presents, play games with me and eat Sunday roasts that Ma would cook and drench in gravy like that advert.

I didn't realise that the door had opened until I heard Ma's voice and turned to see a tall shadow in a thin column of light.

'Please, Jennifer. Listen, I know this is a bit much but –'

I couldn't hear what this Jennifer was saying but I saw Ma's shoulders sag in the light. She raised her voice.

'Of course she is. An' I'll tell yeh what else, it was him who wanted rid, not me!'

The chink of light got thinner. I tried to breathe quieter and heard a few words, the tone cold enough to make your teeth sting just from listening.

'Steal . . . affair . . . drag him –'

'Oh, an' yeh think that was stealing, do yeh? Well, since

that's all he's ever given fer her upkeep I'd say he's the thief. An'
he knew where we were. Now it's his turn tae –'

The door slammed, sharp and final as a slap. But clearly
the door and this Jennifer didn't know what they were dealing
with. No door was big enough to shut the Ryan Temper out.

'Janie! Come on.' Ma came down and yanked my arm so
the contents of the lunch box scattered. She started pulling our
suitcase up the stairs. 'Come on! Pick it up and get up here.'

I piled everything into my arms and climbed the steps. 'Ma?
Is this Da's house? An' that woman, is she angry with us fer
coming at night-time? Was she watching *Corrie*?'

Ma kicked over the suitcase with her heel and it fell with
a thud on the doorstep. 'Be quiet an' sit down, Janie.' She bent
to the letter box and shouted through the flap, 'An' if yeh don't
believe me come an' take a look at her face! One look. Don't
think I want anything from you but an address or a number. An'
if we've tae stay here all night I'll get one.'

'Ma, is this where Da is? Will he no' babysit me now?'

The sky was indigo and birds fell across it like scraps of
black paper. The white houses curved over our heads.

'Yeh think I'm trash, do yeh? Well, it's on yer doorstep.
We'll stay here all fuckin' night.'

Ma unzipped a side of the suitcase, rummaged underneath
me and found the tartan blanket to put around my shoulders.

'Ma, if Da's not here can we not just go home?'

In the distance someone gave a short, sharp scream.

'No, it's not that simple.' She tilted her head back. 'WE'LL
STAY HERE ALL NIGHT IF WE HAVE TAE.'

'I don't want tae sleep here, Ma.'

She had her head down and knocked her knuckles together;
I could hear her breathing.

'Ma?' I hated the weakling in my voice, I wanted to be brave and grown up, but my throat swelled with the tears to come.

Ma's head fell in a heavy movement from the base of her neck down and her hands drooped as though she'd had the batteries taken out. I tried to stop my sniffs and shudders.

'No, Janie.' She stroked my fringe. 'No, we won't sleep here. Are yeh hungry? I'll find us somewhere tae stay an' then we can find yer da in the mornin', OK?'

I threw my body against hers and gave her bones and skin a hard hug. Her arms were limp around mine and I wondered how badly she had wanted my da to look after me. I didn't want to stay with that witch, like in *Cinderella*, but I did want to be braver.

'We can come tomorrow, Ma, and speak tae the lady when it's no night-time an' then maybe –'

I never finished because there was a click and pale light from the door flooded us then a cold, calm American voice said, 'Well, are you coming in or waking the whole neighbourhood?'

Jennifer had eyes with almost no colour and hair that was probably brown but that didn't seem like a colour on her either. She was as skinny as Ma but her body was straight up and down, a right knitting needle Grandma would've said. Her face was as blank as her appearance except for the slight twitch her lips made when I walked in. I thought it was because she could smell the sick on me.

Ma tugged the suitcase through the door and I held my breath for the dirty mark along the cream carpet. The hallway had a heavy wooden cabinet in it and dark red walls. The air was so empty it made me want to shrink words in my mouth before letting them go.

Jennifer and Ma stood facing each other. Though Ma's head only came to the tip of Jennifer's nose she seemed to win because Jennifer looked away first.

'Stay here tonight.' She looked at Ma and then down at me and said in a softer voice, 'But I'm genuine when I say I haven't the faintest idea.'

Ma pursed her lips and nodded. 'Listen, I know this is a bit out of the blue.' She stuffed her hands into her jeans pockets and pulled them out again. 'But, well, as yeh can probably see we havnae a lot of choices.'

Jennifer looked away. 'I'll show you the guest room and get some linen. It's en suite, you'll be comfortable.'

Jennifer carefully took my lunch box from me and led the way to a room that was as soft, warm and boring as porridge. Ma took one look at all the cream and white and said, 'Janie, everything off and into the bath.'

Ma started the water running and went off to another room with Jennifer. The bathroom was all white and blue without any sticky shampoo spills or toothpaste-spit splashes on the mirror. I took off all my clothes and sat on the edge of the bath, afraid to put my feet on the floor.

'Knock, knock?'

Jennifer came in and I crossed my arms over my chest. She gave a little smile and held out a little purple bottle. My arms stayed crossed against me but she didn't seem so bad so I gave her a very little smile, the one where I don't show any of my teeth. She poured a long thin purple line of the liquid into the bath, stopped when the bottle was half empty, looked at me and squeezed the last in.

'Let's make it a really big bubble bath.'

She stayed until the bubbles threatened to spill over the

edge and then swirled her hand around the water and motioned for me to get in. I plunged into the mattress of popping bubbles and sank through the softness into the scorching water below. I gave a little gasp and then saw her anxious face and turned it into a grin.

'So do yeh know when my da will be home?'

She turned, looked at the floor and then at me. 'I'm pretty sure not tonight, Janie. Your mom's just fixing you some supper and then you can have some rest. I'm sure your mommy will explain to you if you ask her.'

She seemed to be trying so hard that I didn't ask any more questions or turn on the cold tap until she'd left the room and my body below the bubbles was a stinging pink.

I didn't see Jennifer again that night and Ma only came and got me into my pyjamas, spread the tartan blanket on the floor and begged me not to get crumbs on the carpet.

'Why do I hav'tae eat on the floor though?'

''Cause it's a bedroom picnic of course. Did I not tell yeh that's all the rage down here?'

'Is Da coming home tomorrow?'

'Eat yer tea, Janie. I've adult things tae talk about with Jennifer.'

She left me happily munching my marmalade soldier picnic, whispering away to a fat, grey cat who snuck in with my supper. I named the cat Rainbow and asked if he knew my da before brushing the crumbs off me and getting into the soft bed where I fell asleep to the subdued voices in the next room and the heavy purr of Rainbow on my chest.

Words and timid smiles scattered over the wide wooden table the next morning. Standing at the wide cooker Ma looked almost normal and Jennifer, across from me, seemed more solid as the sunshine hit her shoulders and lit up her eyes.

Below the ping-pong of their morning chatter I spread raspberry jam on my toast, trying to get a perfect layer right to the edges of the crusts. Every time I'd almost done it my hand would give a jerk or a clumsy push of the knife and I'd have to scrape the jam to one side and start again. I had my tongue stuck out trying to do a particularly difficult corner, where the toast had a bump, when I saw Jennifer watching me with the whisper of a smile on her lips. 'It'll still taste the same, honey.'

She was smiling but I felt caught out, and though I knew different, it certainly would not taste the same, I took a wide bite anyway but I put her straight in a spray of crumbs. 'It's jam actually.'

Ma came over with a steaming pot and dished soft yellow scrambled eggs onto Jennifer's plate then her own.

'There yeh go, Jen, try these.' She sat down and took a forkful of the eggs, 'Proper Scottish eggs the way my ma taught me tae make them.'

I looked from Ma to Jennifer, twisting my sticky-jam clown mouth. Jen? Grandma taught her to make them that way? Not for the first time I wondered what grown-ups did while I slept.

'Oh my gosh, Iris, these are sublime, seriously.' Jennifer raised her bony fingers to her lips and wiped them. 'How much butter do they have in them?'

Ma wagged her fork, shrugged and carried on eating with a smile on her face. Jennifer stared down as though it were a plate of drain cleaner and then took a breath and started eating again, making little moans with each forkful. 'Extra callisthenics for me today then.'

I looked at both of them above the rim of my orange juice

and thought I should just stay quiet; even if Da didn't show up for a bit, there were bubble baths, and Rainbow the cat and Ma was laughing. Maybe we would stay.

After I gulped down my third glass of orange juice and gave a forceful acidic burp Ma rolled her eyes and told me I should go and watch some telly. I lay on my stomach in what Jen called 'the den' that the kitchen opened into and flicked the channels until I found *Dogtanian and the Three Muskehounds*.

It was my favourite because the pretty girl dog who Dogtanian loves was blonde, like me, and because I knew all the words to the song, 'One for all and all for one . . .' I'd missed the start but still thought that this could be the best morning ever. In the background bits of their conversation sprinkled in my ears.

'If he could look after . . . just for a while . . . I could get myself sorted.'

'Sure but . . . abandoned little boy . . . you know?'

I tried to remember if I'd seen this one, where Dogtanian was going to meet Juliet, the pretty blonde dog, but she'd been kidnapped. I wished they'd stop talking.

'No . . . went a bit nuts . . . just temporary . . . I probably wouldn't have really.'

'Better off without him.'

Something shifted behind me, like there was a lot being said without any words. It was distracting.

Juliet was using a mirror to send a message from the cottage where she was trapped while Dogtanian was fighting now. More natter drifted over. What was Juliet's message though?

I sighed and turned my head. 'Maybe the telly should be somewhere nice and quiet, Jennifer?'

There was a shared laugh as I pressed the little liquorice bump that jumped the green volume notches higher.

'Still married . . . even if I wanted one I probably couldn't find him . . . turns up every few months . . . cash sometimes jewellery . . . I hide it now.'

I gave another heavy sigh.

'Janie – sorry, Jen, one minute – turn that down we can't hear ourselves think.'

'At least now you know.'

'Aye, we just need a new plan an' – sorry – Janie, I won't say it again, turn that down.'

'It's OK, Iris, little pitchers, big ears.'

'Especially that wee pitcher, I'll tell yeh. We've got tae go anyway.'

Ma came over and switched the TV off before I could even complain that I'd never know what happened to Juliet.

At the doorstep I decided to ignore Ma and Jennifer, since they were best pals now, and spend my time on the carpet between them pushing my fingers into the purring fur on Rainbow's belly.

'You know you're welcome for –' Jennifer looked away – 'well, a few more nights at the very least.'

'Aye, cheers an' all that, but we've tae get ourselves sorted. We'll be fine.'

'Are we off tae see Da now then?' I looked at Jennifer. 'We'll take my da's address and telephone now like Ma said.'

'Sweetie, I don't know where your daddy is. Truly, I wish I could tell you both.'

I stood and stared at her skinny body and puny half-smile and fidgety hands. I ignored Rainbow curling around my legs.

'How do you even know my da then?'

She placed her right hand over her left and shot Ma a look. I was sick of adults' looks. 'I . . . we were very good friends for a long time. That's why your mommy thought I might know.'

I stared at her and a black feeling started seeping into me like smoke filling a room.

'Well, you're stupid then, an' a liar. How can yeh be Da's friend and not know where he lives? Stupid!'

I threw myself down on the carpet and took Rainbow in both my arms, pulling his fur close to my burning face.

'Janie! I'm so sorry, Jen.' Ma lowered her voice. 'This whole thing's a mess.'

'No, I understand. I really wish I could do more to help. But, Janie?'

I closed my eyes and squeezed Rainbow tighter.

'Janie, enough!' Ma yanked me up by the arm and I stared at stupid Jennifer and gave her my worst face, the one where I made my eyes really small.

'Janie?' Jennifer was still smiling, maybe even more than before. 'Your daddy really loves you, you know? You look so alike and he'll be sorry he wasn't around but he'll have wanted you to have this.'

In her hand was a fold of material and when she opened her fingers a red silk scarf, with golden tassels, spilled to the floor. Rainbow slunk over and lifted a lazy paw towards it.

'This was from my da? Fer me?'

'Yup, your daddy's quite the snappy dresser.'

Ma seemed to be holding a giggle behind her fist as I took the scarf and wound it round my neck three times, a silken neck brace. Jennifer beamed at me and I thought maybe she wasn't stupid, she did have a nice cat, raspberry jam and Ma liked her. I leaned forward and gave her a limp cuddle around her hips.

'Ta.'

'Aye, thank you, Jen, and . . .' Ma picked at a thread on the hem of her T-shirt, 'I really am sorry, yeh know –'

Jennifer put her hand on Ma's arm. 'No apologies. You're sure you won't stay another day?'

'We've tae get ourselves sorted.'

After I gave Rainbow a yelp-inducing hug, me and Ma stepped into the morning sunshine with a suitcase, lunch box, umbrella, glowless Glow Worm and a scarf from my da with tassels that danced in the wind.

'Ma?'

'Aye?'

She was walking wonky because of the case; she wasn't as smiley now her pal Jen wasn't around.

'I'd like to see my da one day.'

She frowned, hoiked the suitcase a bit, the veins popped up in her arm.

'Yeh will one day, he'll visit us. Now shush, I'm thinking.'

She missed her pal. I wondered how I could make her better. 'Aye, Da will visit but you'll be here forever an' ever, won't yeh, Ma?'

She lowered the suitcase, flexed her hand and kissed the parting in my hair. It was a quick kiss but a nice one even if she looked a bit sad. 'Yer right enough, I'll be here forever. Now, let's get going.'

9

Ma said it was an adventure but it just took us back to Victoria Coach Station and on the bus there Ma pointed out Buckingham Palace.

'Maybe next time we'll drop in fer tea,' she said.

I eyeballed the barbed wire around the wall. 'We can't do that, can we?'

'Aye, it's her duty.' Ma's face was serious. 'Any British citizen can come fer tea. Not uninvited, mind, yeh have tae let her know so she can get some good biscuits in and cut the crusts off the sarnies.'

'Can we no' stay for a while? Just tae give her a call an' have tea?'

She stared out the window, shaking her head. 'Nothing's the same as it used tae be.'

And I could tell that was as good an answer as I was going to get.

While Ma counted the money in her purse in the coach-station toilets I thought about our tea with the Queen, the dress I'd wear, and wondered whether she'd let me try on the crown.

'Thirty-six, thirty-eight. Thirty-eight pounds and twenty-six pence. Not bad at all.'

'We're not really skint then?' I asked thinking about my Glow Worm's pregnant secret. Ma swept the money back into her purse.

'We'll be fine, Janie; Monday's dole cheque day so we just need tae get through the weekend.'

Ma kept grabbing onto me, mussing my hair up.

'It's just the two of us, Janie, isn't it? You and yer ma. We're having an adventure, aren't we? That place was too stuffy fer us.'

She didn't wait for answers but said I could pick any place from the boards and I stared at the numbers on the board and tried to spell out the letters and see which places sounded fun.

'That one.'

'York? Aye, that would be nice, but I don't think our cash'll stretch that far.'

'What about that one then?'

'Dundee?' Ma laughed. 'No, I don't think so. Look fer something leaving at eleven.'

I looked for two 1s standing close together, stiff and straight, and pointed them out.

'Canterbury? Good choice.' She hugged me and pulled us towards the ticket booth.

I was sick again that coach journey and Ma got into a mood when I asked if we could telephone Jen and get her to tell Da where we were going. The National Express hostess gave me a head-tilted sympathetic nod and forced a free orange juice on me though it was the last thing I wanted after my guzzling at breakfast.

While going up and down the aisle selling her misshaped, cling-film-wrapped sandwiches, she paused and sat on the empty seat opposite us, her stomach bulging over her navy waistband.

'Sit her on newspaper.' She counted the points off on her red fingernails, her made-up face serious and confident; she was a professional. 'Ginger tea, if you can get it down her. There's pills, but I feel funny giving kiddies pills, don't you?'

Ma said nothing and the hostess carried on, a freight train. 'There's Sea-Bands but I don't believe in them myself. Oh, and make her breathe through her mouth and stare at the horizon.' She looked at me and shook her head, 'Poor little lamb,' then fluttered her blue mascaraed eyelashes in acknowledgement of her good deed and squeezed off down the aisle to deliver a corned beef and pickle bap. I watched her rolling buttocks depart.

'She was pretty, ma, and clever.'

'She –' Ma's face was like thunder – 'was an interfering, know-it-all bitch. Thinks she can tell me how tae raise my own kid.'

I was silent for the rest of the journey except for the retching noises when I ran to the toilet to sick up the orange juice until my greedy belly was finally empty.

Canterbury was a magical old-fashioned land, a bit like where Dogtanian and Juliet lived in the cartoon. I looked at the old buildings and wondered if that was where people lived all together, like at the care home.

Ma liked it. 'Well, it's as good as anywhere an' certainly a lot better than fuckin' Dundee.'

We went to a cafe with scratched yellow Formica tabletops and a metal counter and Ma said I could choose anything that didn't cost more than 50p. It was a choice between toast or chips. I chose chips. The stooped old man who brought them over wore a stained vest with thick grey curly hairs bristling over the top. Ma rolled her eyes.

'Jesus, he's a six-pack down that vest, alright, a six-pack of Brillo Pads.'

While I salted and added enough vinegar to make the chips

steam and my eyes water, Ma asked if they had a phone book she could borrow. He said nothing, walked away and the book thumped down on the table five minutes later.

'Would yeh mind if I took it fer a wee while? Just to a phone box?' Ma asked his back and he shrugged one shoulder. Ma lit a fag and gave it a savage puff and I realised I couldn't finish my chips because I was too scared of finding one of those curly silver chest hairs twisting around my tongue. It didn't matter though because Ma finished her fag, hoisted the phone book under her arm and motioned for me to get my stuff.

The phone box smelt a bit better than the ones at home even if it did have shattered glass panes. Ma wedged the suitcase in the door as a seat for me and flicked through the book. I wondered when we would get really poor so I could tell her about the Glow Worm money.

'Aye, I was wondering if yeh had a room fer me an' my little girl? Oh, aye an' do yeh accept DHSS?' She stiffened. 'The fucker hung up! A "no" would be fine ta very much.'

She lined up all our 10ps on top of the phone, going through them quickly because when she asked if they took kids or DHSS the calls finished quickly.

When Ma got to the second-from-last coin she looked so tired I thought I should tell her about the money and we could go for a proper dinner. Or maybe just go home.

'Aye, an' do yeh accept DHSS?' Her voice was flat. 'No, alright, well, thanks any— Who? An' what's the name again an' street number?' Her finger whizzed down the phone-book page. 'Got it!' The phone started to beep. 'That's my pips, but thanks a million!'

One call and a scribbled note in a purple crayon later and

Ma was walking us towards a bus stop with bright eyes and a wide, stretched smile.

'Hurry up, let's go see our new home!'

Mrs Sleathes said she owned seven bed and breakfasts across Canterbury. Ours, The Lucky B&B, was an old house, filled with grubby furniture and the curtains, sheets and towels were all Germolene pink.

Mrs Sleathes led us to our room. She was beaky, that's what Ma said, with a frizz of black hair, like Ma's bad-perm days, and little shiny eyes as unnerving as two black buttons. Her hands were weighed down with rings, and though she was smaller than Ma she seemed to fill the room with her wild gestures and excited, squeaking voice.

'Rules!' she said to Ma in a bright voice.

I started pacing the room and counting my steps behind her.

'Electricity must be off at 9 p.m. except the overhead light which can stay on until 11 p.m. Showers can be taken in the room down the hall and there's hot water from 7.30 a.m. to 8.30 a.m. There's a communal kitchen downstairs to cook and eat in from 6 p.m. until 8 p.m. No laundry in the rooms, or food, except the breakfast provided.'

She gave a tight smile. I had finished walking the length of the room and had counted that it was eleven of my steps long starting with the sink in the corner and ending with a single chair at the foot of the bunk beds. On the chair was a tray that held neatly arranged mini-packs of cornflakes, two tea bags and two cling-film-covered shortbread fingers, all slotted together like puzzle pieces.

Ma looked around the room and at Mrs Sleathes.

'An' what about lunch, we must be able tae use the kitchen fer tha an' all?'

I walked from the chair to the door. Mrs Sleathes waved her manicured fingers.

'Ah now, we operate a lockout system from 10 a.m. until 5.30 p.m.'

'What?' Ma closed her mouth as quickly as she had opened it and then continued in a softer tone. 'I mean, Mrs Sleathes, what are we meant to do all day?'

Mrs Sleathes gave a hiccup of a laugh. 'Well, enjoy the City of Canterbury, dear, you'll be amazed by how much there is to see and do.'

'Would there not be an exception? I mean, it's not good fer Janie tae be out all day, especially in the sun.'

I had been to the door and back to the chair twice but couldn't decide if the room was five or six steps wide. From the door I saw Mrs Sleathes' face become serious as she tilted her head to the side sympathetically.

'Yes, yes, I do understand . . . but no.' She snapped her head up straight. 'The only exception I make is that I accept DHSS tenants, Miss Ryan. Really, if it wasn't for me I don't know where most of my tenants would go.' Mrs Sleathes paused expectantly but Ma said nothing and stared around the room.

'Right! Well, I'm sure you're keen to get all settled in. It's –' she looked at her little gold watch – '4.45 so just this once let's bend the rules but as of tomorrow you can hand your keys in to Bob on the ground floor when you leave and you can ring to get back in at 5.30. Oh, and I collect the top-up each Monday personally. It's good to have a catch-up with tenants too.'

Mrs Sleathes' hands glittered as she tangled her fingers trying to unhook our key.

'What's the top-up when it's at home?' Ma asked, not taking the time to keep her voice soft.

'Well, even with a child your housing benefit wouldn't cover the cost of the room so all my tenants also pay a fifteen-pound top-up payment, in cash, on Mondays.' She looked up with a key in her hand. 'But of course for that you do get breakfast and you've no bills!'

Ma looked stunned and I looked at the breakfast tray that reminded me of Sundays of Ready Brek and toast and not much else.

'Um, could that not be reduced if we didnae have the breakfast?' Ma looked at the floor biting her lip and that made me want to give Mrs Sleathes a Chinese burn or a sharp kick in her skinny shin. 'You know, Janie is a very fussy eater and –'

'I am not, Ma!' I glared at Mrs Sleathes. 'I'll eat anything yeh want me to, don't you worry about that.'

Mrs Sleathes gave her tinkle of a laugh again and stepped gently towards Ma. 'Now there's no need for embarrassment.' She smiled over at me and I gave her my worst look. 'I do understand your situation but as I've said I make no exceptions.' She spoke slowly like Ma was just learning English. 'Besides,' she finished brightly, wagging her finger, 'it's a bed and *breakfast*, silly!'

She left with a wave of her ringed fingers and a 'Welcome to The Lucky'.

After the door was closed I looked again at the breakfast tray and the little boxes.

'Can I have some cornflakes, Ma?'

But she didn't reply. She was running her finger down the two laminated pages on the back of the door and shaking her head.

*

The day after we moved in Bob, the resident key rattler, invited me and Ma to dinner.

'We can have it in my room if you like?' He leaned his head forward so his stringy, sandy hair fell over his pale face. He was dressed in a thin cream shirt, with the stiff creases of the shop's packaging still wrinkling the wrong parts, and brown trousers.

'No point in not bending the rules if you can.'

Ma gave a tight, small smile and said she'd prefer to eat in the kitchen, maybe get to know some of the other tenants.

He bought a Chinese takeaway and a bottle of Blue Nun. Ma kept taking embarrassed nibbles of her ribs and tried to chat to the other tenants as they shovelled their food down, standing at the counter, staring into space before hurrying back to their rooms.

'Well, that was lovely, thank you.' Ma patted her stomach appreciatively and I tried to quickly spoon in a few more mouth-fuls of fried rice.

'Oh, you won't stay for a while?' His sweating face looked crushed. 'There's still half a bottle of wine left.' He piled her plate with more ribs and filled her Garfield mug to the brim, so tiny bubbles jumped and popped above the surface.

'You know, I've been saying to Mrs Sleathes we needed a woman about the place.'

Ma laughed a stiff laugh and looked across to the round shoulders of a middle-aged woman at the cooker. From my seat I could see her, in the orange light of the grill, cleaning under her nails with her fork.

'Oh, I'm sure this place gets along fine.' She stuffed her spare rib in her mouth, ripping off the sticky meat.

'Still,' Bob reddened, 'I'm glad you, you both, have come to live here.'

'We're not staying in this dump!' I said from behind the
foil tray I was licking the sweet and sour sauce from. 'Just until
I start school after summer and find somewhere else, isn't it, Ma?'

Ma gave a little sigh and pulled the foil tray from my fingers.
'Honest, Janie!' She threw a small smile to Bob who didn't throw
one back. 'Yeh'll cut yer tongue off.'

When Ma quickly finished her plate Bob didn't fill it again.

Ma always sent me to drop off and collect our keys for lockout
after that. Lockout meant that we spent summer days wandering
around Canterbury with packed lunches and one of the pink
sheets from the B&B.

When it was warm enough we went to the park or the
cathedral and Ma would sit on a bench ripping the skin from
around her nails or sometimes plucking out arm hairs when she
thought I wasn't looking. I spent long hours on my stomach,
tongue probing the corner of my mouth as I drew tourists, the
cathedral or the crocuses that popped their heads up and over
the neat flower borders. When I was done I would run over to
Ma, page flapping in the wind for her approval.

'Americans, like yer da, Janie, except he wasnae a tacky
tourist. Yer da had some class.'

'Look at the way yeh got those windows just right!'

'We might as well pick them, Janie, before they go, let's
take them back tae the room an' brighten it up.'

She'd started sounding like her batteries were running down.
One day I saw her crumple the old newspaper in her hand and
throw it across the park with a savage arm. I lowered my own
arm frightened for the picture I was holding.

'Are yeh upset, Ma?'

'No, Janie.' She was biting at the side of her thumbnail.

'I'm just bored. I'm just bored tae fuckin' hell an' it's a bad week.'

I thought good and bad weeks were about money. And that the bad weeks were when it rained and there was only bread and marge sandwiches and a jam jar of milk for our picnics that we ate in the shopping centre. There was no lolly treat for afters and for dinner we only had Smash or packet noodles with a tin of tuna; one at a time because the kettle in our room was the size of a doll's kettle.

I kept asking if we were really poor and Ma would say, 'We're fine. Will yeh stop asking that?' and she always looked so angry that after a while I did.

On good weeks there was Strawberry Angel Delight after the noodles or Smash and we'd take turns whisking the powder and milk with a fork. Sometimes it took all the way through *Crossroads* and *Wogan* to get it thick enough but it tasted so good I didn't mind eating it with a stinging, achey arm.

A good week meant a trip to the swimming baths where we would line up with other mas and kids holding fat towel sausages under their arms, goggles hanging from their necks.

'Now if anyone asks yeh, yer five.'

'But, Ma! I'm SIX.' I held my right hand and an extra thumb up to make sure she understood and the queue went quiet. Ma rolled her eyes and stared at the floor and I jutted my chin out, stood tall and dared anyone to tell me I wasn't six.

Bad weeks were called bad by Ma but for me they were worth no jam in the sandwiches or Angel Delight puddings. They were even worth Ma's silences that made my belly hurt, because rainy weeks meant the library.

Running to sit at the little plastic chairs I felt the library's warm, still air push inside me to slow my thumping heart and the second-hand-shop smell snake up my nostrils, winding itself snug around my insides. When I opened the books, and I could open as many as I liked because it cost us nothing, the pictures lay on my eyes like oil on water and the dancing letters settled on my tongue with the smell and the taste of black-jack sweeties. While Ma bit at her lips, ripped at her cuticles and read old magazines, I was learning how stories could make me feel safe.

In August, after five weeks at Mrs Sleathes', Ma found us a new place to live.

'It's a B&B but not like this. It's going tae be like lots of people living together.' Even with her sick-looking bald eyes she looked happy. 'An' there's a garden.'

Afterwards I felt a hard twist of guilt at all the things I hadn't noticed while I had my face in books and bowls of Angel Delight. I hadn't noticed the gaping space at the back of her jeans when she bent over or the way her hands shook when she turned the page of the newspaper. I looked but didn't really see the endless counting out of her purse or the panicked snap as she closed it again.

The day she told me about us moving seemed like a good day for it because I'd wondered if we'd ever be skint enough for me to tell her and I was afraid to ask if we already were.

She held the twenty-pound notes in her fingers and I grinned, squeezing my Glowless Worm to my chest.

'Where did yeh get this from, Janie? An' I want the truth.'

Her voice was low and I thought she must be really surprised and laughed. 'From Frankie. It was a secret fer when we need it an' now we're moving we'll need it to buy furniture! He told me not tae tell yeh. Until we were skint.'

Ma's face went pale and she bit her top lip with her bottom

teeth, pushed me on the bed and pulled down my shorts as far as they'd go.

'You never, ever lie tae me. Do. Yeh. Understand? Never, ever!'

With each word she brought her palm stinging down on my lower back and I screamed and tried to explain, through the snot and tears and shock, that it wasn't a lie, it was just a secret.

We left Mrs Sleathes really early that Sunday, earlier than lockout or breakfast; as early as the birds woke up. Ma said we had to be quiet, especially outside Bob's room, it was a game. I tiptoed holding giggles in my chest, through the soft darkness of the landing and out into the pink-streaked dawn.

Our new place was called Burton House B&B but it didn't have a sign outside which was one of the reasons Ma liked it. It was on a street just off a traffic-filled road that led all the way to the city. The road was squeezed tight with off-licences, betting shops and kebab houses, and I never found out where the road would lead if you slithered far enough away from town. The furthest down we ever got was the 'park' that was really a square of tree-lined grass with a lonely, tall slide in the centre.

Burton House was a twenty-minute grown-up walk or thirty minutes my walk from town. The morning we left Mrs Sleathes' we walked the fifteen minutes to town and Ma stopped at the bus stop.

'Hold on, Janie, I've a stitch.' She set the suitcase down and squeezed her side. After a few minutes she looked at the empty road and then the bakery. 'Alright, we can wait fer the bus tae come or hoof it an yeh can use the bus fare for an iced bun fer breakfast.'

I arrived at Burton House, as at so many places, smiling from behind the sticky crust of my last meal.

Ma said the manager, Majid, was Indian and warned me I shouldn't say anything about him being a different colour or talking different. I wondered what colour he would be and was sad when I saw he just had a bit of a suntan.

'I like yer hat, Mr Majid. I've a crayon that same colour.' I bent my head to my lunch box to show him.

'Just Majid is fine.' He raised his slim hands and straightened the red turban then carried on up the stairs.

We were five floors up, the 'penthouse' Majid said with a gentle laugh, and then saw Ma's face and said more seriously but with the same gentle voice, 'I've made sure it's a nice one for you and your little girl, a bit of space and privacy for our new family.'

The roof slanted down from the ceiling with two small square windows; there was a single bed, a table with two chairs on each side and a big double bed pushed against the back wall. At the foot of the single bed there was a big wardrobe. Even if everything did look a bit squeezed in, I didn't need to count my steps to see it was twice the size of our last room though I felt a pop of grief at the loss of our bunk beds and the packets of doll-sized food. Ma nodded.

'This is great. Thanks a mill, Majid.'

'Good, I'm glad you like it. Do you want me to show you the kitchen and garden?'

But Ma was already pulling the suitcase over to the wardrobe and I had turned away to set things out on my little bed, the ceiling a few inches above me.

'Well, maybe later. You know where I am if you need anything at all.'

After he'd gone Ma kept walking around, opening and closing the wardrobe and bouncing on the mattress like it might be a *Blue Peter* room, all glued together from washing-up bottles, cereal packets and egg cartons. She kept pinning questions on me without waiting for the answer.

'Do yeh like it, Janie? It's big, isn't it? I bet yeh can't wait tae see the garden?'

I stopped trying to answer her and lined all my crayons on top of my lunch-box and stood my umbrella against the bed and when I did turn round again Ma was lying, knees pulled up to her belly, on the bed.

'Ma?'

She kept her eyes closed and pulled her knees up a little more. 'Ma's going tae have a sleep now, Janie. You play fer a while.'

She still had on her thick grey socks and I rolled them over her heels and then pulled them off her hot feet. I laid them, bloated and warm, on the bottom of the bed.

I did some drawing, made up a story with my Glowless Worm where I caught him stealing crayons in his battery pouch and gave him a whispered but ferocious telling-off and spongy spanking until my iced-bun-fullness disappeared.

Ma was still snoring gently, fully clothed, and when I looked at her still face and naked eyelids, gently quivering with dreams, I climbed onto the bed and tucked my knees into the crook of hers and pushed my face into the warm damp of her T-shirt.

When we woke up, the same sweet smell of sleep on the hair plastered to our foreheads and pillow creases on our cheeks, the two windows were black and the house below us still and silent.

Ma hid herself in our room during August, as though having been forced out every day at Mrs Sleathes' made her stubbornly stay inside at Burton House, though some days that room, right at the top of the house, was like an oven. She started taking lots of 'sleeps'.

'Yer ma's having a sleep now. You go play.' She promised that she wasn't sick, 'No' the way yer thinking of, Janie.'

At the end of the day when the air in the room was thick and sweet and I'd milked my imagination dry for games, Ma would stand, tuck her nightie into the waistband of her jeans and throw a jumper over the top and take me to the park with the slide. She'd sit staring at nothing on the bottom until my swooping feet bashed into her and I'd shout, 'Ma, I can't slide with you there!'

On the way home I'd run into the chip shop and ask for a bag of crispies and the red-faced woman behind the counter would scoop all the broken pieces of batter from the bottom of the trays for me for free.

Mondays was the only day Ma took off her nightie and we went to the post office for our dole cheque, joining the queue outside. The queue looked just the same in Canterbury as it did in Aberdeen. Always a long queue, before the post office even opened, as if waiting another fifteen minutes with an empty purse and larder would be fifteen minutes too long.

After the post office, Ma would drop me at the library and I'd read until she came back empty-eyed, weighed down with more than just our week's shopping.

One Monday she told me I could take three books home. I stared at her wide-eyed, wondering if she was really sick after all.

'No, Ma, it's a *library*. Yeh stay here an' be quiet and read them. It's stealing.'

'Janie, I filled out the forms an' we've a card now so it's fine. Just choose yer three books and hurry up before the chips thaw.'

I wasn't sure it was fine but I chose three *Twinkle* annuals,

1975, 1978 and 1979, and spent the rest of the week telling the duvet bump of Ma what Nurse Nancy was doing in her dollies' hospital.

The next Monday while unpacking the shopping Ma pulled out a yellow-and-white teddy bear and a little furry mouse. The teddy's white patches were dusty and the fur was matted in places where I imagined a drip of juice or sucked sweetie dropped from an excited mouth. The mouse's plastic whiskers had been chewed at the end as well but I liked them more for being a bit sad and scruffy; they were better patients for a dollies' hospital.

'Deary me injured whiskers! You need some medicine, Mr Squeak!'

After our busy days of sleeping and nursing we went down to the kitchen to have dinner. We always tried to walk quietly because when she heard our footsteps on the stairs Cathy, from the second floor, would come down and smoke at the table and talk all about her family, her twelve steps and her little boy, 'maybe seven now', who lived with his nana.

She said it was good to have another mother around who understood, though Ma didn't ever seem that friendly while she stirred a pot of boiling water or stood to one side from the fat spitting from our fish fingers.

One night I was looking in the cutlery drawer for a surgical tool to take out Mr Squeak's tonsils, while Cathy, her thin hair pulled back in a face-stretching ponytail, puffed on her fag.

'I'm going for a visit soon –' her boy lived in London – 'and I was thinking since I've been clean for a few months and you've got Janie here now the social services might think about letting him come here for a visit. What do you reckon, Iris?'

Ma turned holding the spatula in her hand. 'I reckon that if you mention me or Janie tae yer probation, social or any other worker, I'll stick this where the sun doesn't shine. Followed by that.' She pointed to the whisk I was holding.

Cathy raised her arms. 'Alright, Jesus! I get it.' She stopped and looked at Ma. 'Iris, is everything OK? You look . . . well, like I used to look like before, well, you know, before. You're not using?'

'No I am bloody not!' Ma looked over at me then turned back to Cathy. 'I mean, no offence, Cathy, but where would I find the cash? I had to skip my Monday drink this week tae buy her a few cheap toys. No, I'm just tired. Yeh wouldnae believe the last few months.'

Cathy stubbed out her fag and kicked out the chair in front of her. 'Then dish out and sit down, I've nothing but time.'

Ma shrugged and slapped my hamburgers over the waiting toast and I cut them into ever smaller triangles as Cathy's stringy ponytail swished in anger or sympathy and Ma stumbled through the last two months.

I was turned to the wall pulling woodchips through the wallpaper and dropping them down the side of the bed; I imagined Ma finding a little mountain of discarded chips under there, the freckled wallpaper giving the game away, but I'd already decided I'd say that a beastie had done it. And then the room went black, a dark so sudden and thick I felt I was being drowned.

'Ma! Ma!'

The wind buffered against the roof, shook the skylights; there was a groan from the bed.

'Fuck. It's alright, Janie, it's just a power cut. Feel yer way over here an' get in.'

But even laying next to my ma the darkness lay on me heavy as wet sand and the angry wind made my limbs twitch.

'Janie, stop it.'

'But I cannae sleep, cause, cause I need a pee.'

She yanked me out of bed and together we felt along the wall down to the hallway toilet, and while I sat in the black box, trying to squeeze out a few drops, I heard another someone join her. Outside, I could tell the shadow, even narrower than Ma's, was Cathy's.

'Come on, we're having midnight munchies.'

Downstairs the shapes of Majid and Beardy No Name, as Ma called him, sat at the table and bread rolls, butter and a block of cheese were all laid out under the light stuttering from four white candles.

'Iris! Sit down, have some food, it's going to spoil. And, Janie, we've kept three choc ices for you – dig in.' Majid waved his hand over the table making the flames flutter.

We sat silently at the table with the oven door open, the gas flame throwing a timid warmth and pale blue light across the floor. The wind pummelled angry fists against the windows and threw its weight against the walls and the oven burner jumped and sighed, like a scared girlfriend.

I crunched through the waxy shell of my choc ice and wondered how it could be so still and cosy inside while things were being thrown around in a tantrum outside.

'Hurricane,' said Beardy No Name, his mouth full of bread.

'What's one of them then?' I asked, dribbling a thin line of yellow down my chin.

'It's a big wind, Janie, but we're nice an' safe here in the house with these strong brick walls.' Ma looked at the window behind her where thrown-up leaves and grit cracked against the glass as if asking for shelter.

I shrugged. I didn't think we wouldn't be safe. 'He's just

angry,' I said, tipping the choc-ice wrapper to my open mouth to get the melted ice cream.

'Who?'

'The wind, he wants tae come in an' have midnight munchies is all.'

'Aye, well, he's not coming in,' Ma replied with another backward glance at the window.

Majid fetched a bottle of wine from his room. 'This is turning into a party.' He shook the dark bottle.

'Ma, am I staying up all night?'

'Just the night, Janie, treat because of the big wind.'

'Can I have some wine? Now I'm seven years old an' three days?'

'Like fuck yeh can, come back in another eight years, fraggle. Eat yer last choc ice.'

They sipped from mugs. 'No point getting out the glasses,' Majid said with a guilty smile and I sat on Ma's lap and listened; it turned out that Beardy No Name's name was Mark and he was writing a script about 'the smarties scene in Manchester', but didn't want to live there so he wouldn't get 'too close to my subject . . . know what I mean?' and Cathy nodded and took another gulp of her tea. Majid told everyone he was going to wait till it was official but that he was going to live with his partner Peter in Brighton and he prayed to God that was far enough away to avoid his parents and Whitechapel for another seven years.

I pushed my finger into the melted wax at the top of a candle, let it flash with heat then dry smooth over my fingertips and wondered how many secrets adults could hold. Ma didn't say much. She held me tightly on her lap, stroking my hair and sipping her wine from her mug. Occasionally Cathy would smile and wink across the table and I would feel Ma's grip loosen.

It was only when Cathy said, 'You should see the new fella in Steve's old room, Iris. Moved in yesterday, very tasty. If I wasn't off men with my twelve steps I'd be in there like a shot.'

Ma didn't say a word for the rest of the night, just listened and laughed along, her bluish teeth and wine-stained lips lit up by candlelight.

Ma said Douglas or 'call me Doug' looked fit from all the jogging he did. I thought it just looked that way from all the sitting around the kitchen he did in his black jogging bottoms and vest, smoking fat, loose roll-ups. He was Scottish too but 'from outside Glasgow' and he had a job, an actual, proper job, delivering meat. He kept making jokes about it to Ma.

He had curly blond hair that would fall over his eyes and a huge nose that he let me grab between two fingers and shout, 'Honk! Honk!' to anyone around who would listen and indulge me with a laugh.

He filled up the house with his army jokes and Drum tobacco roll-up smell and was always in the kitchen trying to get people to stop for a hand of gin rummy or to have 'a jar' with him as they passed through. Everyone did, lost stars circling a steady moon, thrilled to be smiled at or teased for being a shite card player by the new big man of the house.

He reminded me of Uncle Frankie but he was more grown up, so maybe it was Tony who he was like, Tony but without the beatings or 'business'; without the money but without that sour streak too.

Ma got fluttery when she played cards with him, slapping his hand when he let her win and sending me up to bed alone while she poured them both another drink.

I'll say one thing, Doug brought my ma back. She was less

tired, and instead of my flat, pinched, quiet ma I'd gotten used to, she was her old, wild self; full of noise, temper and laughs.

Ma's duvet was in the same rumpled peak that it had been in the night before when I finally gave up waiting for her and fell asleep. Solid fear filled my chest at the sight of the empty bed then melted to a burning temper, pumping through my arms and legs. A temper so savage it threatened to dislodge the crumbs of sleep from the corners of my eyes.

I stomped down the stairs.

'Ma! Where are yeh? Ma!'

I shouted on each landing red-faced and indignant; I wanted the whole house to know my ma had abandoned me for gin rummy and Doug.

I found her at the kitchen table with him. Their hands wrapped around mugs of tea above the table and their feet twined around each other underneath.

'Janie, my gorgeous, come here!' Her voice was too loud.

I stood where I was, unsmiling.

'Aw, out of the wrong side of bed? I've some good news fer yeh though. Yer getting a new daddy!'

Still I didn't move. I just stared at them, though, to my shame, I felt hot tears burning behind my eyes.

'It's Doug,' she added as if there might be another possible da lurking in the fridge. 'Come on, come an' have a cuddle with yer ma and yer new daddy.'

I wanted to say that I had a real da but I scuffed my bare feet across the tiles as I walked, stood behind them and felt left out as they breathed the same morning bad-breath on me. Ma showed me her thin ring with a big sparkly bit of glass that she said was just like a diamond and I shrugged.

'It's just till I save up. Then I'll get yeh a proper ring.'

He kissed Ma on the side of the head and I was nudged out by the side of his face. He turned to me with a sloppy grin and I raised my hand and squeezed his big, oily nose, giving it a good twist while I shouted 'Honk! Honk!' right into his stupid face.

I was thinking that at least Tony Hogan bought me an ice-cream float before he stole my ma.

It was a week and a half after the hurricane blew through that Doug proposed to Ma and a month after that they married in a Canterbury registry office. Everyone from Burton House came and instead of presents Ma asked if they could chip in a bit to the registrar and bring a bottle to the reception.

Grandma came down on the coach and arrived in a taxi carrying her big wide wedding hat, borrowed from Aggie. For the few nights before the wedding Grandma shared the upstairs room with me and would come up late from drinking downstairs, waking me with her boozy belches and static crackling poly-mix slacks.

'Poor as a pauper but a good fella, a good daddy for yeh finally, Janie.'

I told everyone at my new school that my Ma was going to be a bride; even though I hated it there. Ma had found out about clothing vouchers from the social and I had a squeaky navy jumper and pleated skirt to wear but then I saw everyone else wore maroon and I thought of Ma's shy face when she handed over the vouchers at the cash desk and wanted to burn the stupid jumper and skirt.

Every morning, after the register, Miss Addle would make us put our hand up if we were 'school, packed or free' lunches and my heart would pummel as me and Toby, who picked his nose and ate it and who had a hole the size of a digestive in his navy jumper, went and collected our green dinner tickets that said FREE in big black letters across the front.

I had one friend. Molly was round-faced with Barbie hair but because she had thick-framed red glasses and a round plaster that covered one eye no one would be her friend. Even though I was free dinners and didn't have the right coloured uniform I still got to be boss because I didn't have glasses or a plaster over one eye; so I bossed her all over the playground playing bride and bridesmaids, but in a quiet voice because my voice always betrayed me as being different.

Sometimes having a green dinner ticket, navy jumper and a funny voice, would make me make myself as small as possible in a toilet cubicle, swollen-eyed and rageful, until a teacher would come and get me and take me back to class. So for me the best thing about Ma's wedding was getting a day off school.

There is one picture from the wedding day, taken by Sheila Burton, the owner of Burton House. In the photo Beardy Mark and Cathy stand to one side looking at the pavement or maybe their shoes, while Doug, Ma, Grandma and me stand in the middle. Doug has a beige checked jacket on and his wild hair shines with Brylcreem, Grandma is in her big borrowed hat and a pastel suit pouting into the camera and Ma stands between them in a pale blue dress ordered from a catalogue. In the photo you can't see the safety pins at the back of her dress; 'Fuckin' catalogue sizes,' she'd shouted when it finally arrived. Ma is offering up a relaxed smile to Doug and, in front, in my pink summer dress, too thin for almost-Christmas, I stare stubbornly into the camera with my grubby teddy squeezed tightly under one arm.

The reception was held between the kitchen and Madjid's room. There was a leg of lamb, chipolata sausages, roast chicken and bread rolls that Doug said he 'dropped' delivering and everyone laughed but no one ate any of it except for me and Beardy Mark. Instead, everyone sat around on the bed and sofa in Majid's room and got smashed making cocktails from the collection of bottles on top of the chest of drawers. Everyone except for Sheila Burton, who sat straight-backed on the sofa, taking little sips of her glass of fizzy wine.

Fights sparked and petered out, drowned in booze and back-slaps, and at one point Ma went and cried in the downstairs toilet over something Doug had said until he coaxed her out and they went upstairs to bed.

After everyone had drunk everything, even the sticky yellow Italian stuff that Sheila Burton had brought along, I carried two slices of the wedding cake, Victoria sponge with a silver plastic blob that might or might not have been a bride and groom, to Ma and Doug. I left it outside the door and went to cosy up with Grandma who was gummy and snoring in bed; her teeth beside her on the pillow.

In the morning everyone was quiet, the wedding food and empty bottles already thrown in the bin. Ma and Doug sat at the table and, after making me get two big glasses of water, Ma told me the news.

'We're going home to Scotland, but to where Doug's from.'

'Fer Christmas?'

'To live, Janie.'

I said nothing until Ma said that meant I wouldn't have to go back to school until the new year and then I leapt on them shouting that they were the best ma and da ever and they gave grim smiles and said, 'Ta, but be a bit quieter about it fer Christ's sake.'

*

We were doing a moonlit flit. It meant I wasn't allowed to talk about the move and when I asked if I could say goodbye to one-eyed Molly and give her the felt-tipped note I'd written, Ma took it instead, saying she'd send it on.

We left past midnight on a Thursday in a blue Transit van that had patches of rust like a mangy dog, with sad gaffer-taped headlights for eyes. We all had winter coats and shoes ordered express delivery from the catalogue addressed to Mrs Pettigrew but Ma said they were definitely ours for going to Scotland.

Doug ordered tapes from the back of a magazine for Mr Pettigrew and he gave the Madonna to Cathy and the Smiths to Beardy Mark and then Ma shouted at him for only leaving us with Meat Loaf and *War of the Worlds, the Musical* for the long ride.

I watched Beardy Mark and Doug quickly load the van with the chest of drawers and table from mine and Ma's room, the desk from his own, plus both the lamps.

'Are we taking them then?' I asked as their heads swivelled, checking the coast was clear before loading the wardrobe.

'Aye, we bought them from Mrs Burton so we'll have some furniture fer our new house.' Doug turned and raised his eyebrows to Ma who was laughing. 'Jesus, she's worse than the polis.'

We drove off, after a few gruff splutters from the engine, under the black night sky with 'Bat Out of Hell' blasting from the open windows and Ma and Doug laughing so hard they had to wipe away tears to see the long road ahead. In a huff, I didn't laugh at all. Maybe I could see it would be a very long road indeed.

10

I was told to call her Gran, a woman who seemed older than anyone I'd ever met, with tufts of sofa stuffing for hair and big white teeth smiling in her wrinkled face.

'Ma? Do I need tae? She's no my real gran anyway,' I asked while water thundered into the bathtub that had a film of grey halfway up it even after a going-over with a Brillo pad and Jif.

'Just do as Doug says an' stop bothering me with it. I've enough tae be thinking about.'

Ma and Doug's laughter didn't even last till the end of our Canterbury road. It stopped the minute the engine was rumbling and the exhaust started farting out its oily innards.

'What the fuck is this? This won't get us out of the town never mind tae fuckin' Scotland.'

'No need to swear, Iris.' Doug gave a tight smile and peered through the smog. 'Here, Janie, we're goin' back in disguise.'

He chuckled and looked in my direction but there was no chance of us being pals while I was squeezed between Ma and him, them shouting over the top of my head, trying to drown out Meat Loaf and the greasy farts of the engine. I kicked at the dashboard and turned Meat Loaf up.

Ma was sick the whole way and, because Doug took the 'scenic route', we had to sleep a night in the back of the freezing van. In the morning Ma ordered him to stop the van and she screamed at him in the field saying it was all off because if he couldn't even get us to Scotland what sort of man was he? And then she had to be sick again.

Doug did what he always did in the face of Ma's temper, he stood tall and stared into the distance, working away with his jaw and not saying a word except, 'No need to swear.'

I watched from the van, using a wetted finger to get into the corner of my crisp packet and wondered why Ma would marry someone who didn't like swearing and why I hadn't got sick at all but Ma was on her hands and her knees vomiting into the grass.

By the time we pulled into Airdrie our van was on its last legs and Ma, Doug and me sat in a thick silence with the *War of the Worlds* raging on the tape player and inside the van.

Ma scrubbed my scalp raw getting the shampoo to lather and muttered under her breath, 'If he thinks I've come up here tae look after his mother he's another think coming. And what a fuckin' hole; he said Airdrie was a lovely wee town, a good place fer kids. Do yeh think this is a good place fer kids, eh, Janie?'

I couldn't answer because she was pouring a measuring jug of bathwater over my head.

'Not a penny to our names an' stuck here in this place. Fuckin' cheek of him promising the fuckin' world and giving us Airdrie.'

Doug said it was only until the social sorted us out with a nice council place and until then his ma would kindly let us stay in the bedroom she didn't sleep in anyway.

Her bungalow was full of hanging cords and panic buttons. Every shiny red button had a sign saying 'Emergency button. Do not press unless in Emergency.' They looked like they tasted of sour cherry and when Gran caught me licking one she didn't say anything, just wafted her digestive-biscuit smell past and wandered into another room.

The back living-room wall was entirely covered with a wallpaper picture of a tropical sunset complete with palm trees and beach. When we arrived Ma looked at the wall and smirked and Doug said, 'My brother Sammy got it fer her to brighten the place up. It cost a bomb.' His face said there was nothing funny about his ma's tropical wall. 'He's one of a log cabin in his lounge, an' it's very peaceful to look on.'

Gran was thrilled to see her 'wee boy' and me, and even though she smelt of digestives, her big white smile, mad-professor hair and generosity with the TV remote won me over. I even ate the oatmeal she gave me when she mixed up the salt and sugar so I had to stuff my cheeks with it, like a hamster, and go for a pee to spit it out.

Gran didn't seem to be so happy to see Ma. Her teeth disappeared and she kept saying, 'I'm glad tae see he's found a good woman at last.' With a face not glad at all and then she'd look at the floor and make a sound like 'Hmm'.

Ma wrapped a towel around me. 'An' don't be fooled by her old-lady act. She's smart as yeh like an' no pleased tae see us, I'll tell yeh that. She wants her wee Douglas all tae herself.' She rubbed my arms so hard they burned. 'Not that he'd see it. The sooner the better fer that council place – Janie, stop bein' awkward an' just stand still.' She gave my backside a hard slap.

It turned out that it wouldn't be better any sooner though, because the social said we'd made ourselves 'voluntarily homeless', and when Doug explained that he came home to look after his ma they just said we had somewhere to stay then.

'But there's four of us in a one-bedroom place! Did yeh tell them? I should've gone myself instead of staying here cooped up till I'm going mental.'

I looked round from my spot on the floor and Doug was standing above her, taking deep breaths from those wide nostrils, so I collected my crayons in both hands and sat up beside Ma on the bed giving Doug my worst look.

'Are yeh saying I can't be trusted with something as simple as a housing appointment, Iris?'

I didn't look up, I kept colouring, my crayon making a darker and darker green.

'No, I'm saying that maybe yer not as interested in being away from yer ma an' yer brother an' that fuckin' Sheenie's as yeh pretend. But then, yer not the one stuck in here cooking an' cleaning and explaining tae Janie why yer ma smells funny.'

I dropped my crayon. 'Ma!'

Doug shot me a look of disgust and Ma put her head in her hands.

'There's no need to swear.'

Bad feelings flooded the room and I added mine, though I wasn't sure who they were for, and then Gran knocked at the door and stuck her big teeth in the crack and said, '*Emmerdale*'s on, Janie, the one wi' the sheep tha' yeh like. I'll make yeh a piece an' jam tae have while yeh watch it.' Then she shuffled off again.

Ma scratched her fingers across her scalp. 'Fuck it. We'll just have tae say I'm pregnant. I'm fairly sure anyway. I'm late.'

'Yer sure?'

'Fairly, I said.'

Doug walked around the bed, smiling a sappy grin, kissed Ma and then started looking at her belly like it might be see-through and I gave them both my worst look, jumped off the bed and went to watch *Emmerdale*, slamming the door behind me.

*

Pregnant and full of pent-up temper or not Ma couldn't get the social to rehouse us before Christmas. The atmosphere became so bad that Gran's red strings and buttons didn't seem so silly any more. I started walking to the deserted Buckfast-bottle-strewn square of concrete where someone had stuck a swing set but nothing else; maybe the same person who put just a slide in my Canterbury park.

I sat on the one swing that hadn't been twisted over the top of the metal frame, though it swung in a diagonal line and if you went too high you got bashed on your side. In Airdrie, in December, the wind felt cold enough to strip off the top layer of your skin, and I swung as high as I dared and let it bite at my face and lips while I thought about what I could do to make Ma love me and not the new baby. Pooing in a corner and blaming it on the baby was the only plan I had.

Doug went to Sheenies, a rough, one-room bar down the road, with his brother Sammy a few nights a week. On those nights Ma would lie in bed with two hot-water bottles and work her way through the yellowing pages of Gran's Mills & Boon collection, though Gran, mindful of her unborn grandchild's comfort if not Ma's, disturbed her every five minutes to see if she wanted 'a wee drop of tea, Iris?'

On Mondays the four of us went to queue at the post office and Gran had whispered conversations with the old biddies at the front, who then stared at Ma like she might knife them once they'd cashed their pension books. Doug went to the jobcentre to sign on and Ma to the supermarket with a list for Gran (lemon sole, bread, milk, eggs, rich tea biscuits, PG Tips) and a list with normal food for us (burgers, fish fingers, chocolate biscuits, potato waffles, cheese triangles, oven chips).

I was left at the library which had the same quiet and the

same smell as Canterbury Library even if the books were sometimes ripped and there weren't as many. As soon as we got home I'd eat my Monday Treat Smarties, cooking myself in front of the gas fire with my books, turning, a roasting pig, when one side of my face blotched up from being too hot.

Eventually Doug would always say it wasn't good to be cooped up reading all the time and I would be sent out to have a swing on my own in the littered, cracked concrete square and think about ways to make Ma love me more than Doug. Somehow blaming poo in the corner on him wasn't good enough.

Ma said Christmas, death and moving were the three most stressful things in the world. She said that we'd been through two and no wonder she was a nervous wreck.

In the days before Christmas, just like I knew I'd eat my chocolate from the Advent calendar that Doug had drunkenly pinched for me from the Shell garage first thing in the morning, I knew there'd be a whispered argument about one thing or another.

'. . . Fer god's sake, woman, just let her cook. It's her house after all. Are yeh no glad of the rest?'

'No I will fuckin' not and don't call me woman! I've seen what she does tae a nice fillet o' lemon sole so I'm not letting her near our turkey dinner.'

Each argument ended with the door slamming as Doug went to stand in the patch of grass outside the bungalow and have a roll-up with his angry back to the house.

'. . . Off tae Sheenies again?'

'Aye, an' what of it? Sammy's paying.'

'I'll come an' all then. Yer ma can look after Janie.'

'I've told yeh before, Sheenies is no place fer a pregnant woman, an' like I just said, Sammy's paying.'

'Well, maybe yer wee brother knows how to look after a woman a bit better than you.'

Slam.

'. . . Listen, she's just worried about the bill.'

'Doug, it's fuckin' freezing. We're already wearing two jumpers an' carrying hot-water bottles around. Have yeh forgotten I'm preggers?'

'It's just in the night-time she wants it off. She's worried sick about it. She's not sleeping.'

'Over my dead body is the heating going off, end of.'

'Aye, well, I hope it's no over hers that it's staying on.'

Slam.

There were no slammed doors on Christmas Day; instead there was a tense sprinkle of pleases and thank yous, if you wouldn't minds and you're more than welcomes, which were worse.

I opened my colouring book and pens that wasn't a shell suit, with the grown-ups' eyes and still smiles heavy on me and was just ripping into my selection box when Ma ruined it by saying, 'Next year yeh'll have a wee brother or sister to open yer presents with.'

I didn't eat my Mars bar for another whole ten minutes to teach her not to speak about the baby on my special days.

Ma decided all the women would cook, and the kitchen was so silent you could count how many drips the tap made over the sound of 'The Snowman' playing in the living room. Ma made the chicken.

'Just as good as turkey,' she'd said to the checkout girl, clicking and unclicking her purse, though the girl looked like she didn't care if we had bread and water for Christmas dinner.

Once the chicken was in Ma helped me make the Bird's Trifle and when Gran made our sprouts by giving them a sprinkling of bicarb soda and pouring the boiled kettle over Ma told me under her breath, 'Not a word, Janie. You concentrate on yer trifle.'

We ate dinner on the lounge table covered with one of Gran's good white sheets, with *Top of the Pops* on one side and the tropical wall on the other. Ma had to fight Doug to keep *Top of the Pops* on, but since there was just the sound of scraping cutlery on plates and the occasional 'Mmm, lovely', I was even glad when Status Quo came on.

Finally Ma put down her fork and stared around the table with a cheery smile that didn't reach the top half of her face. 'Right, time fer some news!'

I tore my eyes away from the telly. 'My trifle?'

'Aye, the first bit of good news is that Janie made delicious trifle fer afters.'

I nodded.

'The second bit of good news is that we'll have a new place tae live before the new year!'

Doug put his knife and fork down. 'What? An' when were yeh planning on telling this tae me?'

'Now. It's a Christmas surprise. No – a miracle!'

'When did yeh find out?'

'A few days ago. The social called but you were having an early one at Sheenies.'

She forked a sprout and it fell from the prongs landing with a snotty splat.

'Oh, yeh'll be off before New Year's even?' said Gran, who

stared at Doug and then the abandoned sprouts on our plates. Doug ignored her.

'So when are we seeing it? Where is it?'

'Oh, we're not looking at it. I just said yes. We can't stay here another week. I'll go mental if I don't get out.' She smiled at Gran who was staring at Doug with a vague expression. 'No offence. It's a two bedroom in Balfour Court, they've even put us in a new kitchen. Have yeh heard of it?'

Gran put down her cutlery and made her 'Mmm' sound and Doug pushed his chair away from the table and stood.

'You took a flat fer us without speaking tae me about it? In Balfour fuckin' Court? Are yeh fuckin' mad, woman?'

'You shouldnae have been at Sheenies then,' Ma replied with a hard smile and a shrug of her shoulders. Doug started for the door with long strides. 'Oh, an' Douglas? I'm not yer woman and there's no need tae swear, alright?'

Slam.

Doug stood with his back to the house and didn't come in until there were fag ends like confetti on the little patch of grass and the Queen had done her speech. Ma sat smiling at Gran who fiddled with her medallion of the Virgin Mary and looked so winded by the news that I scooped up the mash of sprouts, so like bogeys, and shoved them into my mouth.

'Mmm, these are the best sprouts ever!'

But Gran was already walking through to the kitchen so I spat them onto my plate again and waited for the telling-off that never came because Ma was staring at Doug's back and sawing through her chicken thigh.

The communal bin area right outside Balfour Court was called the Bin House but was just a rectangular low-roofed shed full of giant iron bins, holding rank sacks of shitty nappies, leftover dinners and whatever else no one wanted.

Ma said by the summer the stench would be lethal and Doug said, 'Happy New Year,' in a flat, hard voice. I looked at the dark cloud of flies buzzing above the bins, felt itchy and went to wait outside.

Craigneuk was one of the worst parts of Airdrie, full of 'crims, junkies an' neds', and Balfour Court the worst high-rise because it was so close to the Bin House. Our flat, on the top floor, was the worst in any tower block because even if the lift was working, and it usually wasn't, you had to get into the piss-stinking metal box full of shattered glass and baggy, milky condoms, trying to hold your breath until the nineteenth floor.

The flat had no furniture except for a cooker, two beds and a sofa. Ma said we'd need to ask for a community grant or some vouchers from the social to make it homely.

Like Ma said, the kitchen was brand new but you could still see the pale brown scorch on the ceiling where a chip-pan fire had started, and that scared Ma so much Doug went out and got a thick coil of orange rope from a skip.

'What'll we do with that then? Tie the fire up?'

'I'll tie yis to it and I'll lower yeh down.'

'Twenty fuckin' floors with a fire raging behind. *Really?*'

'Aye, *really*. Unless yeh'd rather depend on the lift?'

But from our balcony you could see the other blocks, grey-gloved fingers stretching for the winter sky, and when it snowed, a few days after New Year's, I tilted my face, stuck out my tongue and truly believed I was getting every snowflake first.

In Craigneuk you had to be Catholic or a Proddy. The first time someone asked me I didn't know what to say. Ma said I should say I was waiting till I was a grown-up to decide, but Doug had a word later.

'Tell them yer a Catholic, Janie, an' a Celtic supporter, an' so is all yer family who're here in Airdrie.'

The next time I was standing watching a group of girls play and they asked me, I did as he said. In no time we were running about the estate shouting, 'Yeh're all just Huns an' yeh can lick our bums. Celtic fer champions – that's right! Rangers and Proddies go eat shite!' Then climbing into skips and bringing home sodden teddies and one-eyed dolls.

Ma was raging. 'I'm not having my daughter turn into some bigot just tae fit in. Some things are more important than fitting in.'

Doug took a sip of Buckfast. 'On this estate there's nothin' more important than not standin' out. An' you're the one that landed us here, 'member.'

Ma could never bear to admit she'd been wrong about Craignuek so let me run around shouting that Proddies could eat shite until one morning, when my pals had gone to Mass and I was bent over a rusty bike Doug had 'found' for me, getting my fingers blackened with chain oil trying to get it back on, a boy, maybe fourteen or so, picked up half a paving slab and dropped it on my head.

Later Ma said I must have a strong head because I heard the thud but didn't cry until I felt the blood trickling into my ear, sticky as golden syrup. I left my bike where it fell and ran home crying while the boy laughed behind me.

'That'll teach yeh, yeh fuckin' wee Fenian.'

Ma washed the cut, said I didn't need stitches but I'd have a big bump, and made me tea with sugar in. News must have spread from one of the glinting square windows because the boy's ma came to the door and I heard her from the sofa saying, out of breath from climbing the nineteen flights of stairs, how embarrassed she was by her Peter, and that he'd have a hot arse when he got home that night. And Ma replied, 'Embarrassed, are yeh? Well, yeh should be – yer boy's a wee fuckin' animal!' and slammed the door.

When she came in she threw a box of jelly babies to me and suddenly it all seemed worth the headache and bump. Doug looked up from the *Daily Record* crossword. 'Iris, yeh've no idea how tae deal with people here. Yeh can't just slam doors in faces, especially well-meaning ones like hers.'

Ma clanked dishes in the sink. 'Well, I survived Monarch Aveue by myself so I'll have no bother taking on Balfour Court without your help thank you very fuckin' much.'

I felt a row brewing. 'Ma? Did that boy's ma bring me these then? That was nice.'

'Oh, jelly babies, big fuckin' deal! They only cost her a pound.'

I looked at the shiny yellow box. 'Maybe she didnae have much money, an' it's a Sunday an' all.'

'Janie –' Ma came through wiping her wet hands on her jeans – 'when will you learn when it's a good time tae shut up!' She slammed the door and I looked over at Doug who kept on chewing his betting-shop pen and filling in the little squares with all the answers.

Nearly everyone was school dinners at my new school, so I was just one of the gang who jealously watched the few packed-lunch kids sit at their separate table with their Penguins, KitKats and bags of crisps with little blue sachets of salt to shake in.

I hung around with the same girls from the estate, practising dance routines from *Grease* and doing each other's hair. The school was Roman Catholic but Ma told the teacher we weren't Catholic and had no intention of converting. The teacher said I'd still have to do my prayers with the rest of the class. And so I did my Hail Marys and Our Fathers in the morning, before and after playtime, lunchtime and hometime, and more if we were naughty or talked back. By the second week they tripped from my lips as easily as 'Humpty Dumpty' while I wondered what the pudding would be at lunchtime.

Ma let me walk home with my pals after school if I promised not to climb into any skips or go to the garages where the glue sniffers went. One evening, when I was almost at the door and hurrying to try and see *Simon and the Witch*, I heard shouts coming from the Bin House. I poked my head into the thick dark air and I saw four boys, three with planks of wood and the fourth, the boy who had dropped the slab on my head, holding a taped-up tennis racket. The littlest boy's job was to bang the bin with his stick and drive out all the brown birds who, for want of nooks and crannies on tower blocks or any trees, had built their nests in the rafters of the Bin House.

As the birds raced from their hiding places with panicked wings, the boys swung their weapons through the air. Sometimes they'd get lucky and there'd be a sickening thud against the side of a wall or bin and a bird would fall to the floor fluttering its wings pointlessly. Judging from the floor they'd been at it for a while.

My lungs burned by the time I'd run up the stairs and because every lungful of air brought a fresh sob it took a while to get the story out. I kept thinking of the bird's shadowy outline stuttering away on the filthy floor.

'What if they're the ma birds an' they have chicks? How will the babies get worms? You've got tae stop them.'

I didn't even try Doug, halfway down his nightly bottle of Buckfast, and bent over the Betamax video player Sammy had got him off the back of a lorry. He turned to me. 'Janie, yer too sensitive. Toughen up, they're just birds.'

But Ma was already pulling her trainers on, smoothing a jumper over her little bump.

By the time we got downstairs the boys were gone, probably to feed their nicely built-up appetites, and all that was left was seven or eight flickering shadows on the floor.

'Janie, go outside an' wait.'

I watched from the door as Ma, her face grim and turned away, pushed her foot against every bird until there was a crunch under her trainer. She came out breathing hard through her nose, an oily sheen of sweat on her face.

'Janie, always put a dumb animal out of its misery; even if it hurts you more than them.'

Upstairs, Doug was in his armchair and all that was left of the yellow-labelled green bottle were black sticky dregs. He popped a can of lager open – 'Too soft, the both of yeh' – then turned back to his *Rambo* video. The sound buzzed and the screen fizzed with white but after a bottle of Buckfast and his four cans he'd barely notice.

When Ma got really big, and she said the stairs were killing her back, they started rowing every day again. They started because Doug was in charge of getting the shopping, and because he wouldn't wander around the supermarket once a week with a trolley and a list, 'like a woman', he had to go each day to the local Spar. He'd return three hours later covering the smell of beer with a Polo mint like a teenager at a school disco.

The rows would've come sooner if that van hadn't come round the estate. Two men with grim faces stood in the back, giving out free slabs of orange cheese, blocks of finger-dented butter and cans with white labels that just said Stewed Meat. Ma said it was from the farmers' mountains. Doug complained he'd had to queue with our benefit books for half an hour to get it when I spat out the stew as soon as it was in my mouth then took a bite of rubbery cheese to take away the taste.

The afternoon the big rows really started was when he brought back two dented tins with 20p written in marker pen on their tops, a roll of *Woman's Own* magazines from 1981 for Ma and a placepot betting slip. Ma heaved herself from the sofa and stared at the tins.

'What am I meant tae do with these? Where's the wee bit of mince or the cheese? I can't make a spag bol with one tin of tomatoes an' another of peas.'

Doug grinned and waved the placepot slip. 'This ship'll come in an' then we won't need the spag bol. Sure thing, it'll be a takeaways an' piss-ups fer the next week.'

But Doug's ship got lost on the way, so he drank, smoked and watched his fuzzy videos and Ma veered between rattling the dishes in the sink in a fury and crying in the bedroom when she thought I was out playing. When Doug saw Ma crying he would stub out his roll-up and pause his video patiently and go and rub Ma's back telling her everything was going to be fine and that this was just her hormones. But it never was fine because on his way to the Spar he could never resist the off-licence, pub or betting shop.

'Food out of mine, Janie's an' yer unborn child's mouths, yeh selfish fuckin' fuck!'

I couldn't make it better for Ma, she didn't seem to even want to see me, and I thought that once the baby and hormones came out she'd get back to normal. I stayed out as late as I could with my pals and we'd go 'Skip Hunting' or spy on the glue sniffers at the burnt-out garages giggling at their druggy rantings and scabby faces.

A few weeks before Ma's due date she started cleaning and said she was 'nesting'. Money was tighter than ever and she thought of new ways to save a few pounds; bulk-buying bargain washing-up liquid to wash our bodies, hair, dishes and clothes with and making big soup pans of potato curry or vegetable chilli for the week.

One night I got back from Skip Hunting with a few scraps of teddy-bear fur and one brown plastic eye to make something for the baby. As soon as I stepped in the hall I could smell the curry; in the kitchen the huge soup pan was on its side on the green lino, a gash of yellow curry reaching across the carpet and right up the wall.

Ma sat slumped on the floor with her back to the cooker having a cry. I tried to cuddle her but she shrugged me away. There was nothing to do but put down my scraps of fur and start picking up the still hot pieces of potato from the floor until Ma spoke through her gulps of breath.

'Janie, just put them beside the sink. They'll be fine with a wash.'

11

The week of the curry Grandma came down on the National Express and as soon as she was inside the door, complaining about how her ankles had swelled to the size of grapefruits in the heat, Ma clung to her like she was the single piece of driftwood in a wild sea.

After a special dinner of pork chops that Ma had braved the stairs to go and buy, we settled back on the sofa and waited for Grandma to dish out some pearls of wisdom, but she just brought a bottle of sherry out of Aggie's wheelie suitcase and spent the night giggling with Doug and giving him playful smacks on his knee.

When they had finished the bottle and Doug said he'd run out to the 'offie' if someone had some cash, Ma and I went through to the bedroom where I sewed my skip fur into a blob with an eye and Ma paced the room bow-legged and furious.

The next day Grandma was sent back to Aberdeen with a hangover and a put-upon face and Doug spent the whole day at Sammy's. 'Helping him with a job.' Which was the truth if the job was a full bottle of whisky and games of gin rummy.

I was out playing the day that the baby started hammering on Ma's womb. I came back to find Doug's ma, hair wilder than usual, sitting in silence on the sofa. She hadn't even made herself a cup of tea.

'Gran, what are yeh doing here? Where's Ma?'

'Yer wee brother or sister's come, so they've gone off in the ambulance.'

I stomped to the TV and switched it on. How could they just leave me with Gran who wouldn't even turn on the TV or boil a kettle for a cup of tea herself? Who'd make my dinner?

After a while Gran said she would give me 50p for the ice-cream van if I'd make her a cup of tea and say a few Hail Marys with her for the new baby. We sat side by side on the sofa with heads bowed, muttering, and I wondered whether the baby liked lolly pops or Wham bars. It would have to be something it could suck on.

Coming back up the stairs with my Monster Munch and a cherry lolly I saw Mrs Mac on her knees bleaching her landing. She probably spent half her pension and most of her life trying to get rid of the piss smell outside her door and I wished I'd used my Hail Mary to ask for people to hold it. At least until they got to their own floor.

We called her Tiny until a name was given. I stopped thinking I'd have to plant a poo in a corner because even though she was a 'good baby' and had soft, dark hair like fur, she couldn't talk and her face scrunched up when she cried.

Ma was tired when she came back from the hospital and for weeks she said she couldn't think about moving from bed. I would go in and see her and she'd show me Tiny's soft pulsing spot on her head that I should never touch and the way to hold the feeding bottle so she wouldn't get wind.

Because Ma slept a lot Tiny became my little doll. I ran home to feed her and Doug said that I was the nappy-changing monitor. I didn't mind, it made me feel important, running and telling Ma whether the nappy contents were yellow and greasy or more brown, that they smelt like popcorn.

Doug made the dinners, a roll-up sticking out of one side

of his mouth while the other side muttered about women's work. Dinner was always egg, chips and beans when he cooked.

Sometimes Ma came through and ate with us in front of the telly and on the nights she didn't Doug would shrug and say, 'She's just tired. Having a baby's hard work, no need tae worry.'

But when Ma did come out, Doug would stare hard at her over his egg, chips and beans and ask, 'Have yeh any idea when yeh might be up tae getting out of your dressing gown?'

'No, I don't actually. Why? Is deep-frying whatever's in the larder too much trouble fer yeh?'

He speared the yolk of his egg. 'Naw, course not, I'm just wondering. I know Janie misses seeing her ma up and dressed.'

Ma gave me a sharp look. 'What have you been saying?'

'Nothing, Ma, honest, I like visiting you an' Tiny in bed.'

Doug slammed the HP bottle down. 'Fer God's sake, woman, yeh've had a rest but it's time tae get up. I'll have yeh know my mammy had four of us and there was never this kind o' carry-on. My da wouldnae have had it.'

Ma pulled her dressing gown around her. 'Don't think I can't see what yer doing. Both of yeh. Just leave me be an' eat yer fuckin' egg, chips an' beans.

That night Doug caught me hanging out of the window with Tiny squeezed under one arm and puffing talcum powder into the air with my other hand. I felt the hard slap on the back of my legs before I saw him and then he grabbed Tiny.

'Yeh little madam. Have I no' enough tae worry about without you playin' up?'

The talc misted my eyelashes and left a silky layer on my cheeks but all I felt was the burn on the backs of my legs and my temper battering to get out.

'It's snow! I wanted tae show Tiny but it's not snow time fer ages.'

Tiny started bawling in his arms, flailing her arms.

'You stupid wee girl! If it's no' you it's yer bloody lunatic ma.'

He walked towards the kitchen and I followed, fists clenched at my sides. 'Don't you speak about my ma! I hate you. You made Ma sick an' now she won't talk tae me an' yeh can't even change Tiny's nappy.'

'Go to yer room.'

'No. Yer not my da. You drink all the shopping money an' you made Ma sick an' now she's in bed all the time. An' Ma said she only ever loved my da and, and, look, even Tiny hates yeh.'

'Is that so?' He spoke very quietly and handed me Tiny. 'Take her then.'

I followed him, Tiny wailing in my arms, towards the front door. 'Aye! Ma says all the time we'd be better of without you cause . . .' I didn't want to finish, I'd gone too far, but I couldn't stop, 'cause yer a sponger an' a waster, she says.'

Slam.

He didn't come home for three days after that but at least it got Ma out of bed. Even though she did cry a lot.

Two weeks later I came home to find Tiny screaming in her cot and Ma shivering in cold, murky bathwater. In the living room Ma's purse lay emptied and open on the floor. There was no sign of Doug.

I left Ma where she was and tried to remember how to make a bottle for Tiny. Eight and a bit months of marriage, four weeks of fatherhood and seventeen plates of egg, chips and beans later, and Doug had left us all alone in Craigneuk, up shit creek without a paddle. And it was all my fault.

*

Ma walked into town the next morning, with Tiny in the buggy that had never lost the bleach stink from Ma's scrubbing after Doug had found it in the Bin House. She went to the social to ask for a crisis loan because of her purse and they said if she was saying it was theft, and she clearly was, she'd need a crime number.

'As if I'd lie about something like that – bureaucratic fucks!'

At the police station they looked at her and Tiny with pity while she filled out the form.

'An' the last thing, Janie, I'll ever accept is pity.'

She told me over our Campbell's Mushroom Soup dinner, the words rushing out while her soup got a grey skin on it, and her toast lay without a single set of teeth marks. She told me, Tiny's oblivious sleeping head resting on her shoulder, of the shame of walking into town on a hot day with the reek of bleach chasing them down the road. Of all the buses that passed and the way she smiled and waved the driver on as though she loved walking fifty minutes in the blazing sun with a month-old baby.

'I've been in some scrapes but I've never, ever had not a soul tae ask a loan off.'

She didn't tell the police about Doug, she just said someone grabbed her purse while she was getting it out at the shops. When I asked why she didn't tell them, so they could find him and put him in prison, she said, 'There are some things, Janie, yeh've got tae be a grown-up before yeh understand.'

I put my whole spoon into my mouth and bit down on the silvery taste to stop myself from confessing.

'Janie, stop fuckin' around with yer spoon. Yeh've still half a bowl of soup tae finish.'

'Was it on purpose, Ma? That he took the money on a Monday?'

Ma said nothing, poked at the skin on her soup with a corner of toast, and I thought maybe I should learn when to shut up but instead I said, 'I'm sorry. I'll help look after Tiny an' you, Ma, if you need looking after.'

And I meant it.

We informed the social of our 'change in circumstances' and got a few more pounds each week because Ma was now officially a Single Parent like they talked about all the time on TV-am in the mornings.

Two weeks after she reported her change in circumstances, the social sent an inspector to see if Ma was lying about her husband leaving us, because apparently lots of people did for those extra few pounds. The inspector seemed sad Doug wasn't to be found hiding in the toilet or under the bed, that he really had done a runner.

'And I see here, Mrs –'

'It's Miss now, Miss Ryan.'

'Fine. I see, Miss Ryan, you also had to ask for a crisis loan due to yer purse being stolen? Quite a few weeks for you, my love, what with a new baby on top of it all.'

Ma put her hands on her hips and jutted her elbows. 'Aye, actually it has been. But what can I say? The bairn does nuclear shites and he wasnae man enough fer the nappy-changing.'

They shared a laugh and then the room fell silent until he said he should really be going. At the door Ma said she couldn't manage the stairs with a buggy and somehow that inspector, who liked Ma's joke, got us to the top of the housing list for rehoming.

My memory of Ma in those weeks, just before we got our new flat, is of her under the heavy duvet, though it was August and scorching. The duvet fell over her limp body like drifted sand.

The only way I knew it was my ma was because of the dark dimple at the corner of her mouth and a scribble of black eyelashes on the pale peace of her face. The room always smelt sweet and thick and I would open the window a crack, reach under the duvet and take off her socks so her feet wouldn't get too hot.

When I started back at school and she still didn't get up, I wanted to jump on the bed and throw the duvet out the window to watch it sail down to the filth below. I wanted to drag her out of bed by the hair.

One night she wouldn't take even one bite of the cornflake cake I'd made at school though I'd carried them home in my empty Flora tub as carefully as if they had been baby animals.

I pressed one to her clenched lips and when she swatted my hand away I told her she was a rubbish, lazy ma and I wanted to go back to Nell's house where everyone got dressed and no one slept all day but just at night-times.

'You want tae go back to care, do yeh?' She was up then, jabbing a finger at my shoulder, speaking in a fierce, hissing whisper. 'Well, fine, because I'm fuckin' sick of yeh, yeh ungrateful brat. I'll take yeh to social services in the morning an' Tiny too though they'll split yeh up and then I'll finally, FINALLY, get some fuckin' peace!'

I bit my top lip with my bottom teeth and stared at my cornflake cakes looking innocent in the Flora tub, as though they hadn't caused all this, then I looked up at Ma and she grabbed the tub and threw it against the wall.

'In fact, no! I'll take yeh tonight. Go on! Pack yer things . . . I said fuckin' go.'

Tiny had started to cry in her crib and I walked over to her.

'Don't you touch her! I'm warning yeh, I'm the grown-up here. I'm the ma!'

Her lips were white at the edges; she had flecks of spit down her dressing gown.

I ran to my room and stuffed things into my school bag with shaky hands: books, pants, a jumper for when it was winter, the furry one-eyed blob I'd sewn for Tiny. Then I sat on the bed and waited for her to come and take me back to Nell or somewhere else at least.

She knocked on the door, three hard taps, and came and sat next to me.

'Yer all packed then?'

Her voice was soft, jokey even. I said nothing.

'Well, I think they'll have closed now. We'll have tae wait until tomorrow if yeh want to go, though I'd like yeh tae stay. Listen, Janie, I went to the doctor last Monday and he says I'm very depressed. Do yeh know what that means?'

I imagined Ma being squeezed, pressed down by some invisible force, her legs crumpling like paper.

'It means I get really sad an' the doctor gave me some tablets but they take a wee while tae work an' until they do I'm just trying tae get through as best I can fer you an' fer Tiny.' I looked up, saw her take a big gulp. 'In the meantime, will yeh forgive yer sad auld ma?'

Then I saw. Like peeling back sunburned skin I saw the raw red underneath and once I'd started peeling I couldn't stop, even when it started to hurt. I saw the dark smudges under her eyes, the nervous fidgeting fingers and the white sweat rings on her T-shirt.

I kissed her in the space between her hair and the top of her ear and gave her hot back a rub. 'I love yeh, ma, and Tiny too, she loves yeh.'

She gave a small smile then her face turned hard again. 'An',

Janie? Not a word about this tae anyone outside these four walls, do yeh understand? This is private. We're fuckin' lambs to the slaughter without Doug here an' they'd have a field day with us.'

I nodded and cold, white prickles filled my arms and legs. Not because I was scared of what was outside, but because Ma looked filled with horrors and I was scared of what was inside those four walls.

They moved us to the next estate; a straight ten-minute walk away from Craigneuk and there weren't tower blocks but tenements. Outside our ground-floor flat we had a scrap of grass and a concrete square where kids swung from the single, bent goalpost bar.

Ma made me go out and invite those kids to my birthday the following week. She even made me invite the boy with the harelip and when he pulled a box of Roses chocolates from behind his back with a big smile I felt shamed she'd had to force me at all.

Ma started baking in the new flat. She got books from the library and made whatever she could with cheap stuff from the bucket shop.

My favourites were palmiers, two crumbling loops of puff pastry glossy with melted sugar. I thought they looked like a fanny but said butterfly to Ma.

We got some cheap minty-green paint from the supermarket and painted our bedroom but it was the shiny kind and as soon as winter came a long shadow of mould slunk up from the skirting boards and kept rising. It matched the black goo that surrounded the window frames.

The tablets must've worked though, because now Ma never wanted to sleep and stayed up late, a full ashtray by her elbow, watching *Prisoner: Cell Block H*.

School was the same except every day, for an hour, we had

Holy Communion lessons. Me and Martin Hughes weren't being confirmed so we had to sit in the store cupboard with books of Bible stories. In the playground the girls talked about their white dresses and veils, how they would wear their hair in French plaits, the Holy Communion parties and presents they would get, and I begged Ma. 'Please, Ma, please let me have Holy Communion! I promise not tae believe in it but it's not fair I'm being left out!'

Ma was firm and said we didn't have the cash anyway. I told my teacher I felt left out and she tilted her head and said, 'A good soul going to waste.'

Ma visited the school.

There were Orange Parades through the streets sometimes and I'd go out to watch and wave until one of my pals' das caught me and said, 'They'd spit at yeh as quick as look at yeh, Holy Communion or no Holy Communion. Run home now and tell yer ma tae look out fer yeh.'

I looked at the huge arms beating drums and their sweaty, serious faces and did as I was told.

Tiny was not any more. She was really called Tiffany and she had soft rolls of flesh at her joints and a head of wild hair like her da. I still wasn't jealous because twice at Christmas she knocked over the tree by headbutting it, trying to get at the sparkle of the tinsel. She was still a bit simple.

Doug didn't visit that Christmas and I knew full well the selection boxes with 'DADDY' written in black block capitals had been bought by Tiny's Uncle Sammy but I ate the chocolate anyway.

12

The night I gave Ma her heart-shaped card caked with glitter was the night someone fired a gun outside our bedroom window.

In the morning yellow tape struggled against the wind and an angry policeman, without a uniform, came in, drank some tea and turned his nose up at Ma's palmiers. It was a drug shooting, he said, looking around the room. 'Usual sort of thing.'

I stood with the other kids all that day, looking at the dark stain on the grass, wishing I'd seen something to tell the others.

Two nights later Ma said I wasn't going back to school. She'd heard there was work to be had and she was sick of staying cooped up 'in this shitehole'. I didn't ask who'd told her, it was obvious from the whisky on her breath that it came from Sammy. Asking questions was no use because there were two suitcases already packed and at the door. The next morning we were on a National Express headed for North Shields, across the border into England, and another B&B with bunk beds, a griddle pan for cooking and a metered shower, 20p a go. Ma never mentioned the job again.

The B&B was better than Sleathes' but worse than Burton House. Ma said it wasn't a proper B&B, even though it was called the 'Pride of Shields B&B', but a halfway house, and when I asked halfway to what, she told me to 'shut it, smart-arse'.

She wouldn't let us go down and have the English Breakfast even though it was included, because she said everyone gave her the creeps. 'Shovelling it into their gappy-teethed gobs like there was a famine.'

Ma was clever with the griddle pan though, and made a big bag of sausage squares last a whole week. She fried eggs and tinned potato slices to go with them and for afters we'd have Scotch pancakes with Tip Top and strawberry jam.

If I was bored I could go down the office that was really just someone's room, and pick a video from the case and by the time I ran back upstairs it would have popped on the screen because all the tellies were joined up, like magic.

Ma let me watch *Dirty Dancing* nearly every day because she was usually sleeping anyway. I asked her if she could 'do the lift' with me but she'd no energy since the doctor here had given her those pills.

'Fuckin' placebos, the bastard! Thinks I can't tell the difference.'

Tiny cried all night, because of the shouting from downstairs so I'd take her into my bunk with me.

I went to school and the kids called me the Loch Ness Monster and followed me after school to see if I really did live in a homeless shelter, like Kevin Hays said. I would casually walk into the back garden of a nice-looking house with my heart thumping in my mouth and hide behind a bush until they'd gone.

When I ran home to Ma and told her with a hot, shamed face what they'd done to me she just looked more tired than ever and went for a sleep.

One night I had to go out into the street in my knickers and Ma just in her dressing gown with Tiny in a blanket because one of the 'mad auld fuckers' was holding a lighter under the smoke alarm. A fire engine came anyway and I hid behind Ma.

'Janie, no one cares that yer just in yer pants. Be sensible,' though she pulled her dressing gown around herself and shuffled us away from the eyes of the rest of the B&B crowd.

Not long after that night Ma got a housing association man come see us. He had a suit, clipboard and clean white nails. Ma showed him around.

'As yeh can see it's wee fer three of us. You've no idea what having a house would mean.'

He smiled and turned his wedding ring. 'I think I can imagine.'

I didn't look round, it was the bit where Patrick Swayze goes back to take Baby out of the corner, but I piped up, 'An' yeh've tae pay twenty pee fer a shower, and if it's Sunday, then yeh have tae wait until Monday after the benefits book's cashed. An' we've all tae go together in case any of the auld buggers tries peeking. Just fer a shower!'

'Janie!' I didn't need to turn round to know Ma was blushing.

'Well, it's true, Ma. An' it's not even a proper B&B, it's for halfway people.'

The next week the man came in his big silver car and drove us far away from North Shields. He let me read his kids' books in the back seat and even had a car seat for Tiny, but Ma kept saying, 'God, it's far out, isn't it?'

He nodded. 'Lots of countryside for the kiddies though.'

The estate was in a village called Hetton-le-Hole. There were bushes planted high up with walls around them, lines of washing left out that no one pinched and red-brick flats with just two floors.

'It's quiet, but it's safe and family-orientated. I think you'll fit in well.'

He threw Ma a smile and waited, but maybe she didn't see it because she didn't smile back.

*

The last of the mines were closing in Hetton-le-Hole. It was on everybody's lips, a permanent greasy stain. The *Hetton Gazette* had the headline 'THE DEATH OF HETTON?' our first week there.

It was a mining town and without the pits it was just a northern village with no jobs, a French name and lots of angry men. Women stood facing each other in the supermarket aisles; hands knotted, lips bitten, shaking their heads in sympathy and outrage.

Sometimes, on the way to the shops, we'd walk past the mines and I'd see the men, standing in the pale April sunshine, with sunken faces and defeated shoulders drinking from Thermos cups and holding their signs. Ma once gave me a pound to put in the bucket and smiled, embarrassed it was so little, at the man but he just nodded. His grim nod said he understood, God knows he understood.

At school lots of the kids had das who were in the strike. We'd crowd around and they'd tell us about the fights with the scabs and how they were getting a holiday to the sea and a new telly when their da won.

The school was an old-fashioned sort of school. There was country and maypole dancing, a brass band, a netball team and at Easter everyone had to paint an egg and make a bonnet for the competition. I never won because the night before we realised we didn't have any eggs and Ma made my bonnet from old magazine pictures and a shoebox.

'They don't know their arse from their fucking elbow. No originality. They're only interested in flowers and ribbons.'

She seemed more upset than me.

Because there wasn't any uniform at school Ma had taken me to the C&A sale and bought me 'a school outfit'. I got a matching pink jumper and skirt and a shiny black plastic coat.

Ma washed the skirt and jumper every second night but the other kids still called me a tramp. I wore it for two whole weeks before I ran home, up the stairs and took it all off in a pile in front of Ma.

'I'm not wearing it. They say I smell cause I wear the same clothes, Ma. They call me bin liner.'

Ma had been watching *Countdown* while Tiny banged her bread-roll fists on the top of her highchair. 'Janie, hold on, they call you *bin liner?*'

I could see the corners of her mouth twitching like someone was yanking invisible threads.

'Ma! It's no funny. I've no pals, no one'll be my partner fer country dancing. I've tae go with the teacher.'

I could feel the blood raging away in my face as I stood in my pants and vest, every muscle tight with the shame of it. Ma laughed and then laughed harder as my face burned. She bent over trying to struggle out an apology to me but that only made her laugh harder.

I ran to the boiler cupboard and tucked myself inside. She would have to drag me to school if she wanted me to wear that shite again.

The next morning I put on leggings and a T-shirt and Ma didn't say a word, neither did the other kids at school. In the afternoon Simon Dean asked me to be his country-dancing partner and that night Ma bought me a Cadbury's Creme Egg and thanked me for giving her a good laugh for the first time in ages.

I made pals with Lesley who was even scruffier than me and Trisha who was a Jehovah's Witness; I asked her all the time what it meant but she didn't seem to know.

I wore my leggings and T-shirts every day, rolled my almost-white knee socks down to my ankle and practised doing the splits and handstands.

But getting rid of my tramp clothes and bin-liner raincoat wasn't the end of it, the sole started to come away from my left shoe. A hole was so big you could put your hand in and your fingers would come out of the other end, waggling like long toes. We didn't have any glue so Ma, sleep still in her eyes and a face on her that meant she wasn't in the mood, Blu-tacked it up. 'There, good as new. Now get off tae school.'

Through the day I walked pigeon-toed, my feet turned inside for fear of anyone seeing the telltale pale blue line between sole and shoe. I wondered, full of temper, why Lesley, whose da had worked at the mines but didn't even get a payout, had soles and shoes that stayed together and I didn't. The next day Ma let me wear my gym plimsolls and, woken for a while from her wide-eyed dream, said she'd start looking around the second-handers for me. There was a sticky-up bit in the plimsoll where the big toe was trying to get out, they hurt a bit, but there wasn't a bit of Blu-tack in sight.

Ma loved us. She loved the smell of us, our chatter, the feel of our skin. She told us so. She loved Tiny's everyday discoveries and cuddles and my temper, sweet parts and cleverness.

Ma hated Hetton-le-Hole, she told us that too. 'The arsehole of England.'

She hated the estate. 'The fuckin' net-curtain brigade. "Oh, how are you and the children today?" I feel like I'm getting a Spanish Inquisition, yeh take a shite an' everyone knows the colour before yeh've turned round fer a look yerself.'

On Mondays Ma had her drink after the weekly shop. She

would come down with Tiny to pick me up from school, swaying in the wind like a thin tree, staring daggers at the other mas who looked her way. Sometimes she took my teacher aside and complained about whatever had caused umbrage that week; not talking about Nelson Mandela's release, giving me kids' books when as a teacher couldn't she see I was too clever for them? Or sitting me outside for cheek. The teacher shot me panicked glances from the corner, probably getting wasted herself just from the fumes and then gave me an illustrated version of *The Scarlet Letter*.

But it was the Mondays that Ma didn't come that were the worst. The flat would be a tip, the TV blaring and Tiny would be raking her fingers through a tub of marge or pouring shampoo into a box of icing sugar. Ma would sit slumped in her chair, in a stained T-shirt with her flies open and would look up and slur, 'Janie mah lil' angshel, come gi' yer ma a big kish.'

I stayed where I was. 'You're drunk and look at what Tiny's doing.'

I'd march around tidying up, feeling selfless as a nun or nurse and while I walked around with my tight, disapproving face Ma would start in. 'Don't yeh fuckin' lecshure me! I'm the ma. After all the shacrifices I made fer you kids. Stayin' in this dump. I have a treat once a week but Miss Fuckin' Prim here doeshnae want me tae have a treat. Well, fuck you!' I'd carry Tiny out of the room. 'Fuck off then, yeh ungrateful little shites!'

We'd go to the boiler cupboard and play 'The Germans are Coming'. It was an easy game, we just sat there in the dark and then I'd try to surprise myself and whisper, 'The Germans are coming, the Germans are coming!' then I'd stay as quiet as I could, barely breathing with the hot hand of terror clenching at my throat and my heart beating circles in my chest. Sometimes

Tiny got really scared and started to cry but that was better because it was more dangerous hiding a baby from the Germans.

When we played 'The Germans are Coming' it was as if I was Anne Frank, from the telly, being brave for my sister.

The rest of the week Ma slept, watched TV with cups of tea and an overflowing ashtray or sat me down for a 'pep talk'.

Talking back wasn't allowed during 'pep talks'; instead Ma talked in circles with bright eyes. She rolled, smoked and stubbed out endless fags and bent forward to make sure I was listening.

'Yeh see, there's out there an' in here, do yeh understand, Janie? An' in here, Janie, yer safe tae be yerself but out there yeh've tae be an iron fist. An iron fist in a velvet glove, do yeh see now?'

I didn't but I wanted to, it was important, I was scared of getting it wrong.

'Now, say it with me, "An iron fist in a velvet glove." Good girl, an' don't trust anyone, Janie.'

She grabbed my chin. 'Do yeh understand they'd fuck yeh just as quick as look at yeh. The world's an awful place but I brought you kids intae it an' I've tae do my best tae protect yeh.'

She stared beyond me, eyes narrowed, let the roll-up burn down to her fingers, and when the orange tip licked at the skin she jerked. 'Alright, go an' play, but just remember.'

And even for the Mondays, Blu-tacked shoes and name-calling, I knew Ma loved us and so I took everything she said and stored it away in the slots of my ribs and when we lay in the big bed at night tucked into each other, a set of Russian dolls, each protecting the other, I felt like the luckiest girl in Hetton, maybe even all of Northumbria.

13

'Yer Uncle Frankie's coming for a while.'

Ma sat on a grassy patch above us. We were at the new lakes, the ones built on the quarry land, on the first day of sunshine. Already my shoulders had turned soft and sore with sunburn while I helped Tiny move a rock from the muddy bank.

'Fer a holiday?'

She stopped unwrapping the sandwiches from their plastic bag; corned beef and piccalilli, I'd made them myself, even scraping the cold white fat from the side of the meat. I wanted the day to be perfect, just the three of us having a summer picnic, like TV. I'd begged Ma to come out.

'Not really a holiday. Janie, do yeh remember years ago just before we left Aberdeen yeh asked me if yer Uncle Frankie was sick?'

I gave my stick to Tiny. 'You dig around an' I'll come back when it's ready to shift.' I walked up to Ma, covering her in my slight shadow. 'I know what's wrong with Uncle Frankie, Ma.'

'Are yeh sure, Janie?'

'It was on *Grange Hill*, years ago now, but Uncle Frankie's better now? Like Zammo got better? From being an addict?'

'He's not better yet, he's coming here so we can help him get better.'

I rubbed my sore shoulders and thought about how Ma was all folded in on herself in Hetton-le-Hole. How a row in a shop could send her to her bed for the rest of the day or make her sit down full of temper and tell me every detail with white spit gathering at the edges of her mouth.

I kicked the ground. 'An' why isnae Grandma helping him get better?'

Ma made a tight face. 'Same as always, too busy with the bingo an' gossip, but we're not turning our back on him as well. Not when he needs us most.'

The hot air was baking the soft earth, the smell of it laying on the skin, filling up nostrils. Ma unpacked our apples, crisps and Tunnock's Teacakes, flattened to sticky pancakes.

'An' what if we don't want him? Where'll he even sleep?'

She gave me a hard look and I stepped away leaving her blinking in the sunlight. 'What's that face about? I'm ashamed of yeh, Janie, after all yer uncle's done fer us. The least yeh can do is give up yer room fer him.'

I didn't tell her that that face meant I was scared, scared for Frankie and scared for her and us even more. We were a glass family, she was a glass ma and I needed to wrap us up, handle her gently.

Tiny looked up from the bank, in her summer dress and wellies, waving her stick.

'Janie come now!'

I went down to help turn the rock. Underneath, toads no bigger than pebbles kicked themselves free from the warm mud and tried to jump to freedom, but only the fastest escaped Tiny's cupped hands slamming down on top of them.

'Look, Tiny! Yer doing great. Yeh'll have a toad zoo!'

The day was ruined for us but it could still be saved for Tiny.

His skin looked like wet candle wax and there were no presents, only a limp, distracted cuddle each. Ma shielded us from him, took him straight to my room and went down to pay the taxi.

It was like having a wild animal in the next room and I made up a story that he was a werewolf; a kind one, bitten by accident, who we were curing. When Ma opened the door to bring him water, or just to calm him when the shouting got too bad, the smell of diarrhoea, sick and cold sweat wafted through the flat.

At night Ma sat up in the living room, smoking and keeping the TV down low to make sure she could hear if the door went, and by the third day she started looking sick herself with clammy skin, a hard, colourless mouth and roaming eyes.

In bed Tiny would curl herself into me, scared from the moans and pacing in the next room. Our Uncle Frankie made mutant through the thin walls and night-time shadows.

'It's OK, he's not feeling well but soon he'll be better an' he'll stay an' live with us. We're going tae cure him an' then he'll be back to normal an' he'll buy us all big presents. He bought me a rocking horse once.'

On the fourth day Ma caught him on the stairs, his legs given out and kicking away like they wanted to dance, while his face, rolling loose eyeballs and gaping mouth, made him look like he wanted to die. We couldn't carry him so Ma just knelt beside him stroking back the hair matted to his forehead. I took his hand, a piece of dead meat.

'Soon yeh'll be all better, Frankie, we'll cure yeh.'

Then I went and squeezed in with Tiny in the boiler cupboard though I'd grown too much to get the door closed against my legs.

*

It was the smell that woke me, a smell that said the door to his room was wide. I ran to Ma, asleep on the sofa fully clothed, the TV still moaning away in the corner.

Of course he wasn't in the room, his bucket was spilled and sinking into the carpet, sheets rumpled on the floor and a brown stain pooled on the bare mattress.

She was tugging on her trainers, breathing too hard. 'Janie, yer tae stay here an' mind Tiny. If Frankie comes back then you lean out the window an' shout on me, understand? He can't have gotten far in that state.'

Tiny was at the door to the room.

'Stinky!'

'Shush, Tiny, let's go watch the cartoons.'

I waited until I heard the door go and I'd made Tiny a piece and jam.

'Yer tae stay right here, alright, Tiny? Don't move till I'm back.'

She wasn't listening, she was watching *The Raccoons*, bouncing along to the theme music and tucking into her jam sandwich.

I put on my sandals and tried to think where a werewolf would go, if he needed to hide when the sun came. If he was scared, if he didn't want to hurt anyone, especially his sister or nieces.

I ran past the swings and the horses that nipped your fingers if you tried to feed them Polo mints and through the field of tall yellow grass that tiny moths flew out of if you brushed your fingers through it.

The shed on the allotments, it reminded me of the garages from Craigneuk; people who were sick, and werewolves, they liked quiet, dark places where no one else went.

The door was locked but you could squeeze through the slats and into the hot air that smelt of earth and sweat. In the light that spilled through in lines I could see ripped-up magazines with blonde women showing their boobs and fannies, and a bike, on its side with one wheel and no saddle, in the corner. Then I saw my Uncle Frankie, in a ball on his knees, forehead to the floor, bum in the air, like Tiny still did sometimes, a shoelace dangling from a bare leg. His lips dry and pale and his Aberdeen-sky eyes empty.

Ma didn't go to the funeral. We didn't have the money for coach fares and Ma said she wouldn't look 'that woman', Grandma, in the face again. On the day she lit a candle on the windowsill instead, drank a full bottle of vodka and fell into a disturbed, twitchy sleep.

I covered her with a duvet and me and Tiny drew pictures for Uncle Frankie in heaven, a kind werewolf who couldn't be cured after all.

14

In the second week of comprehensive school I came home to hear Ma roaring with laughter. The last year, since Frankie, had left Ma as thin as the skin on a blister and I tried my best to watch for the sharp moments that might leave her raw and sore.

Hearing that laugh made my stomach twist, though I had my own worries resting on my nylon-blazered shoulders. The table had a half-empty whisky bottle, a pouch of Drum tobacco and a *Sun* newspaper on it, and before I saw him I knew he was back.

They looked so cosy, the three of them sitting on the sofa, knees pointed into each other's and Tiny, four now, with a sturdy body a miniature of her da's, sitting on his lap. Stupid Tiny, she didn't even know him. Not as stupid as Ma though, because she did.

'Janie!' She was pissed, words sliding off her tongue like oil. 'Look who's come tae visit an' he got yeh a present!'

She sloshed her glass towards the table where a bright yellow tape player sat.

'I wonder who he stole the money off fer that then?'

I didn't want a visitor. I definitely didn't want Doug. I wanted to disappear into the sea of bottle-green uniforms like all the other kids at comp; just another sloping back and shy bobbing head. I had the proper uniform because there was a special shop to go to and Ma had got vouchers but kids could see the difference. A plain rucksack that said Nick instead of Nike, biros and square rubbers from plastic packets at Somerfield's instead of ones with cartoon characters and rubbers in animal shapes from WH Smith's. I didn't have a charm bracelet, a perm, an anklet of my ma's to borrow and wear over my tights or a tube of pale lip gloss to smear over my lips in the canteen.

Instead, I stood, legs like two pieces of string dangling from my skirt, in my too-big fat fucking 'You'll Grow into Them Shoes' as girls with golden foundation, mascara and friends streaked past nudging my shoulders. Unmade-up, in my pink-plastic-framed NHS specs, I couldn't even read my timetable from behind the blur of tears I held in so as not to mark myself for target practice.

Ma slammed her glass down and Tiny jumped and looked round at us all with her wide blue eyes and a smile like she thought this might be the start of a new game.

'Janie! If yeh can't be civil to a guest in our house yeh can just go to your room.'

But she was talking to my back because I already had my hand on the door ready to give it one of my best slams.

'It's yer choice, Janie. No one is going tae force yeh, but yeh trust me, don't yeh? Yeh know I only want best fer you an' Tiny?'

She was still slurring but you could see she was concentrating on what she was saying. I tucked my skinny knees up my under my chin.

'It's not you I've a problem trusting, Ma. Have yeh forgotten he stole yer purse and left us, "lambs to the slaughter" you said?' I picked at a scab on my heel, let a fat drop of blood balloon and sink into the cracks in my skin. 'An' Tiny? What about him just deserting her?' I didn't say and you, and me.

We were in my room, the room that was once Frankie's. When it was cold the walls got wet and a bit slimy and there was still a stain on the carpet the shape of Italy and a worse one on the bottom side of my mattress but they reminded me of Frankie so I didn't mind too much.

I stared at my New Kids on the Block poster and eyed the battered sausage and chips Ma had brought in.

'Have some.'

She pushed the paper across the sheets and I shoved a chip into my mouth.

'Aw, dinnae cry, Janie.' It was the vinegar but I ate another chip and let her think that I was. 'He's changed. He's been in work fer the last seven months and saving up tae come an' see us with a few bob.'

I grabbed the sausage and took a sharp bite of the end. 'Well, at least yer purse'll be safe. Should I be hiding my jar of five pees?'

Ma gave a laugh then a silent belch, the sweet, boozy smell fought with the vinegar and grease.

'I'm only asking, Janie. Like I say –' she pushed her finger into the mattress with a loose, clumsy hand – 'it's yer choice an' no one, no one, would ever force yeh, but imagine a fresh start and you in a proper Scottish comp, not with these snobby, ignorant bumpkins.'

I thought back to the girls with their dangly earrings and hair glistening and stiff with hairspray.

'An' he's a flat already fer us in Glasgow. The city, Janie! But, like I say, it's yer choice.'

I wiped my greasy fingers down my shins, making them shine in the light of the bulb.

'Janie?' I looked up at her smudged mascara, smeary lipstick; I didn't even know she still had a tube, 'Yeh know I havnae been that happy here, not since even before Frankie? An' Tiny,

Tiny will finally have a da and . . . and you of course if yeh wanted.'

She gave my hair a sloppy stroke. 'Just you have a think an' I'll leave yeh to yer chipper.'

The whisky must have soaked right down to the marrow because her shoulder hit the door frame as her hand slapped the light switch off.

'Ma!'

'Sorry, sorry.'

After the third slap the bulb popped back on. I took a bite of my sausage and looked over at Joey, who had sweet brown eyes and curly hair, my favourite New Kid on the Block.

'Well, some fuckin' choice, eh, Joey?'

A few days later we caught the coach because Ma said we had Doug to help carry everything and we didn't need the furniture since he'd kitted out the new flat for us from Argos.

I carried my school bag and library books, with my school uniform stuffed into the bottom. My New Kids on the Block and Bros posters were rolled together into a tube and held with a hair bobble; I didn't really like Bros that much any more but I thought they might still be popular in Scotland.

I ran around the station hitting Tiny on the arse with Bros and the New Kids while Doug and Ma sat on the seats, the metal kind that you slide right off if you don't watch yourself, especially if you've a whisky hangover like they did. Tiny shrieked and giggled, stomping about on those chubby legs of hers until I missed her arse and caught the back of her legs and she cried out. Then she grabbed the posters in both hands and started twisting.

'Ma! Tiny broke my posters!'

Ma and Doug were nose to nose.

'You said it was Glasgow! I might be cabbage-looking but I'm not fuckin' stupid.'

Doug turned his head and Tiny ran to his side, tugging his sleeve.

'Da, Janie hit me. She started it an' all. Da!'

'Ma!' I held the poster in front of their faces. 'Look at what she did tae my posters.'

'Maybe you'd had too much whisky. I said it was close. One train just. Closer than Airdrie is what I said.'

'I do not believe this! So where? If it's not Glasgow after all, fuckin' where?'

'Da!' Tiny stamped her feet.

'Ma, are yeh no' goin' tae do anythin' about my posters?'

'Right, enough.' Doug grabbed the poster tube from in front of his face and squashed Bros and the New Kids hard into the mouth of the bin next to him.

'Ma!' I grabbed Tiny and gave her a hard slap across the back of her legs. 'Yeh wee fuckin' bitch, that was yer fault.'

Tiny showed her bottom teeth, that was her worst face, and started swinging kicks at my shins with her red wellies. 'I'll get yeh, Janie, yeh fat cow.'

'Doug, don't try an' distract the situation. Where have we uprooted ourselves tae go an' live?' Ma stared at him waiting for an answer, I stared at Ma waiting for intervention and Tiny just kept swinging kicks. He tightened his jaw and closed his eyes.

'A town called Coatbridge. And for the final time, all of yeh, there's no need tae fuckin' swear!'

They called our coach and we walked towards the gate with filthy looks and muttered swear words hanging about us like flies around dog shit. I pulled my posters from the bin and Ma took them.

'Don't you worry. We'll get this straightened out. You just trust yer ma.'

But I'd given up trusting Ma to sort anything out and snatched the posters back.

It was a slow journey back to Scotland even if I did have a packet of Fruit Pastilles, a Curly Wurly, five stolen library books and three trips to throw up to keep me busy.

There were less pensioners in Coatbridge but that just meant the junkies didn't have easy targets for Monday muggings. Syke Side was a tower-block estate and Doug and Ma's fresh start went stale very quickly.

The train from Glasgow was only twenty minutes, and Doug looked hopeful, but then there was the forty-minute bus journey to Syke Side, through the streets of fume-belching factories, and the scramble through the estate to Doug's block because boys on the garage roofs were throwing stones, aimed to hurt, even though Doug said he would 'punch yer teeth so far down yer throat yeh'll have tae shove yer hand up yer arse tae bite yer nails!'

'But look,' Doug said when we stopped to catch our puff by the door of his block, 'it doesnae smell of piss like Buchanan. An' we're only on the fourth floor so we'll never need tae use the lift.'

'Oh joy, it doesnae smell of piss. Whoop-de-fuckin'-doo,' replied Ma through her out-of-breath gasps.

The living room was bare except for a black coffee table and a sticky, black leatherette sofa. Ma opened her mouth and let the air out like she was slowly deflating.

'This isn't going tae work, is it?'

Doug put his hands in his pockets, looked at his belly and shook his head. 'Doesnae look like it, but let's just wait an' see.'

The whole flat smelt of chip fat and roll-ups and Doug, it turned out, had been laid off for a few weeks, 'but only until work picks up again,' he said. That first weekend we stayed indoors watching the telly, eating chips and biting the ends off each other's sentences with narky little ones of our own. I watched Ma carefully but if anything she just seemed glad to have some company. Though it was company from Doug and that should have worried me itself.

Tiny spent hours playing in the bath with washing-up liquid bottles, jam jars or bouncing on her da's knee; holding up his curls, amazed at how they matched. I sulked, complained there was only HP Sauce and tormented Tiny.

'Yeh'll have his nose an' all though.'

That made her cry which was nice for a minute until Ma forced me out to the shop for marge, bread and ketchup so I wouldn't 'sit with a face like a slapped arse making us all more miserable'.

She didn't get it, and I wouldn't tell her, that I was scared shitless of that estate. I told myself it was just like Craigneuk, but when I walked past the empty petrol cans and dog shit, glad the boys weren't on the garage roofs throwing stones, I knew it wasn't the same. I was eleven now and that made everything different.

Doug had pointed the shop out when we got off the bus. It was fifteen minutes' walk through the estate, at the beginning of a piece of scrubby wasteland. I almost took myself and the hot pound coins clamped inside my fist back home when I saw the outside.

The shop was covered in metal boards, the kind you see when a flat's been burnt out and they want to stop the junkies from sneaking in while it's empty. The door was pushed back against the wall and it had 'Open' written in dripping red paint. Inside there was a rectangle of ripped lino and another sheet of metal that made a wall between the girl behind the till and her customers. You couldn't even see the food. Behind a tiny square of thick plastic glass the girl, dark circles under her eyes, gave the tiniest of nods. I looked at the dents in the metal and scrapes on the window.

'You. Are yeh here tae buy somethin'?'

'Aye, um, tub of marge an' a loaf o' white sliced an' ketchup . . . please.'

'It's all sliced white.'

She slammed a metal shutter across the window and then it slammed open again.

'The red sauce – Heinz or Happy Shopper?'

'I, uh, the cheapest?'

'What a fuckin' surprise!' she replied and gave the metal hatch an extra-strong slam.

It was almost October but when I got outside I could feel the sweat drying under the T-shirt I'd borrowed from Ma. Someone was burning a car at the far end of the wasteland. If I had to come here every time I wanted red sauce, I thought, I'll bloody well learn to love HP. I shoved the bread under my armpit and kept walking.

They stood on the corner, in their pink padded bomber jackets, two ready-to-squeeze spots. They looked bored and dangerous and I looked for a way to get past them. They were about my age but their jackets were open to show tight black vests with the tops of white lacy bra cups underneath. They had dark foundation on their faces with a grubby tidemark around it.

One was smoking and singing, that song by the floppy-haired bloke with the funny mole, 'You are the one and only, don't nobody take that away from me. You are the one and only . . .' The other was trying to get a good hock up and was bent, ready for it to drop into the gutter. I looked away too late. The girl stopped singing.

'Who the fuck is she?'

The girl let her mucus-thick spit drip and then splat beside her trainers before looking up. 'Haw! Do yeh want yer hole kicked, hen?'

I stood flat-chested in my ma's stinking T-shirt. I didn't even own a bra never mind a white lacy one and I'd a Mother's Pride stuffed under my armpit. I was dead.

The girl made a show of taking a few steps forward and her mate a show of digging her fingers into her bomber jacket and holding her back.

'She's no' worth it! Think about yer probation.'

I bolted as fast as I could through the estate, my feet slapping down on the cracks of paving stones. The ketchup slipped from my sweaty hand just before I got to the flat.

Later, from Doug's window, you could see the red splat and shards of glass. All that was missing from the picture was the chalk outline of a stupid girl who didn't own a bra and who was dead meat on an estate like Syke Side.

Ma told Doug it definitely wouldn't work. She told him he could have his bachelor pad and see Tiny as often as he liked and that they'd file for divorce for her to be eligible for a place on her own. She waited till they were drunk, and in the middle of the row, Doug came into the bedroom, picked up our portable telly and threw it out the window. To be fair, it didn't hit anyone and he even opened the window first. We'd been there a month, all cooped up. It had got to everyone.

It was the fleas that got to me mostly. They'd come in off the bed that Ma and Doug found in the street though I saw Ma disinfect it myself. At night I felt the fleas jumping all over my legs and tried to kick them off; I'd wake Tiny who would wake up Ma and then none of us could get any sleep for thinking about the fleas. Some nights we just lay under the duvet feeling itchy, scratching our bites and covering the grey sheets with brown flecks of our blood.

'Aren't fleas supposed to go when the winter comes?' I asked into the dark. I could feel Tiny's toenails scratching at my legs and Ma's sharp shoulder under my chin.

'Aye, but these are Scottish mutants, they're a hardy breed.'

'Like Teenage Mutant Ninja Turtles?' Tiny whispered from under the covers where she was giving her ankles a good scratch; I could hear the rasping sound.

'Aye, Tiny.' I pulled up the covers. 'We're bein' eaten alive by teenage mutant ninja fleas.'

'They'll probably outlast us, the little fucks,' Ma added and we had a little laugh and scratched until we were too tired to bother.

Tiny went to the local Protestant school because it was right next to the Catholic one and Ma said she wouldn't have her kids brainwashed like before by praying a hundred times a day. Doug said, 'She's my daughter too.' But he didn't really care so Ma got her way.

About a week into school Ma got called in because Tiny

had been caught with some boys chucking stones over the fence at the Catholic playground.

Tiny was a tough little bugger. When she was two me and Ma got out a tape measure and measured around her head, waist and hips. We kept doing it over and over, making Tiny stay still, but the measurements stayed the same; head thirteen inches, chest thirteen, waist thirteen. Around that time she used to fall forward onto her head a lot and she even fell into a bed of nettles, but she didn't cry, she just blinked her big blue eyes and staggered off again to investigate an empty Coke can.

Almost five now Tiny hadn't grown out of her stocky body and still had chubby legs with dimples at the knees. She had her da's messy hair, though black not blonde like his, and blue eyes with flecks of yellow. Everyone said she'd be a beauty when she'd lost her puppy fat.

After seeing the head teacher Ma took her home and gave her a hard smack on the arse. Doug didn't even look round, just poured another drink and said, 'An' yeh were worried about her being brainwashed?'

I went to a high school in town and there weren't that many Syke Side kids there because most of them got on the coaches to St Mary's each morning.

I fell in with a chubby girl called Trudy, who loved Disney, and Rachel, who already had to wear a B cup and had a brown downy moustache.

We didn't have a lot to talk about but no one would hang about with me and it made them look better to have another person, even if that person was me.

The main thing we talked about was Keanu Reeves. We'd sit on the hidden stairs by the Tech Block sucking on crisps to make them last longer, singing Bon Jovi and swapping Keanu Reeves posters from *Just Seventeen* or *Smash Hits*. Most of the time I had none to swap but sometimes Trudy would give me one that was a bit ripped or had a kidney-shaped greasy crisp stain on Keanu's chin.

At the weekends Trudy and Rachel went to a church group in Motherwell. They told me they were 'saved' but when I asked what that meant they would just share a smile and say, 'You wouldn't understand, Janie.'

When I told Ma, over turkey burgers and Super Noodles, that my new pals were saved, Doug laughed like he did when he listened to *The Archers* and said, 'Well, if yeh didnae want them tae be brainwashed sending them to Proddy schools was genius!' and chuckled away for the rest of the dinner while Ma sat stony-faced.

My trousers were getting shorter, so short you could see an inch of grey sock and three inches of greyer skin when I was sat down. At lunchtimes Trudy and Rachel averted their eyes and that, after giving me the occasional Keanu Reeves poster, was probably the nicest thing they ever did.

'It's just a growth spurt, Janie. What do yeh expect me tae do about it? We're moving an' we've not a tin-opener to our name.' Ma was packing things into our suitcase. There was plenty of room; we'd never had less.

'It was you who said we'd have everything we needed here. What a fuckin' joke.'

'Hey! Enough of the language. Just cause yeh come from fishwives doesnae mean yeh need tae speak like one.' She had a bra swinging from her finger. 'Just be grateful that we've a roof an' four walls of our own an' we can get away from the fuckin' fleas.' Her eyes flooded, she looked down at the bra and added, 'This isnae how things were meant tae turn out, yeh know.'

It wasn't the tears that softened my hard child's heart, they were an everyday thing, it was the washed-out bra with little holes in the grubby nylon lace and the underwire sticking out. I imagined it jabbing at her while she did the weekly shop, her having to poke it back in all the time. That was what made me go kneel behind Ma, put my arms around her shoulders and lay my head on the top of her back.

'We'll be fine, Ma. I'm sorry.'

'An' we've a garden that just the four flats share. Imagine that, Tiny, in the winter or even this winter if we're lucky with a bit of snow!'

Doug pinched a fleck of tobacco from his tongue. It was a tight Sunday, he and Ma were splitting fag ends apart and using the scorched, leftover dross inside to make new roll-ups. We'd had spaghetti and marge and tap water for dinner. I was even looking forward to school dinners the next day.

'Listen, Iris,' Doug spoke quietly, edging around a row, 'I'm no tryin' tae rain on yer parade but Greenend, it's proper cowboy country. If yer face doesnae fit they just wait till yer getting the shopping an' burn the house out an' it's only if yer lucky they wait till yeh go out.'

Our new home was at the end of the corner-shop wasteland where I'd seen the car burnt out on our first weekend. Whoever had named the estate Greenend had clearly never visited that dog-shite- and crisp-packet-peppered scrub of land.

'Tsh!' Ma whistled through her teeth. 'I've been up there myself. It's fine. Now stop scaring the kids.'

'I'm not scared,' I said, though I was.

'Me neither,' added Tiny, though she looked like she had just shat herself.

Ma said she was gasping, went to fill the kettle, though there was just powdered milk to have with used tea bags and Ma said it was like drinking baby sick.

Doug looked at me. 'Listen, Janie. Yer a sensible girl, just make sure yeh keep yer heads down, alright? An try an' keep yer ma's mouth shut fer once.'

I tutted, gave him a slitty-eyed look, stomped to our room and slammed the door because he was probably right, but she was still my ma, mental or not.

15

We settled into Greenend and time passed with the usual land-marks, Uncle Frankie's anniversary, Christmas rows over spilled drinks and the wrong trainers, the birthdays where all I wanted was cash and a snog at the school disco. At school I kept in with Trudy and Rachel, kept on at them; I could understand, I did want more, I was good enough. I wanted to be in their gang and be like them, smiling secretly, telling other kids they wouldn't get it, that they weren't special enough.

So, I pretended I could talk tongues. I spat the nonsense out, plentiful as gobs of grey chewing gum, fell back into strong arms and said the Holy Spirit had filled me. I swallowed down God and Faith like aspirin; safe in its plain, everyday dullness.

There were ice-skating trips and rock concerts where electric guitars and drum solos blasted out Satan.

'Satan, sinners, we're literally going to Rock You Out!'

There were picnics with games in the summer and for New Year's there was a party with a proper DJ. They said the Church was our family now, that God was our true Father, though for most of us he was our only Father. And there was always a good-looking older bloke who would sit down and listen to you, really listen, and give you a hug. There was lots of hugging, and he'd never lecture you, he'd just say, 'Shall we pray about this, Janie?' and we'd bow our heads. At the end he'd tell me I was special and though I knew he meant 'special in God's eyes' it was still fucking brilliant.

They didn't ask for anything back, not even money for the trips; all they wanted was repentance. You might think that with something like repenting or having your soul saved, once would be enough, but maybe every second meeting you had to do it again.

'Please forgive me, a sinner, Lord. I ask for Your forgiveness.'

You had to pray as well, and hold your hands up and shout 'Amen' or 'Praise, we praise You, Father!' during the sermon. I could make myself cry and they said I must be very close to the Spirit.

They were right. I was swilling the spirit down my throat every weekend with my new church pals. Vodka when we could get it, but usually just MD 20/20 or a bottle of cider. The youth outreach workers, 'the God Squad' they called themselves, and there was nothing tongue in cheek about it, targeted the worst estates in Motherwell, so I fitted in with the other recruits; snug and safe as a lucky upside-down fag in a Benson & Hedges packet, with my own kind.

Soon the older Motherwell girls invited me to be in their gang, the Gees, and the lads were all letting me wear their caps and hoodies because everyone knew no one fancied me.

Trudy and Rachel were rank with jealousy, like dried vomit, I suppose because it was only because of them I was even there, and the crisp eating and poster swaps stopped, and the rumours about me being 'a using bitch' started. Which might or might not have been true.

Except for the lonely school lunches, when I took myself and 20p down to the phonebox in town and called Ma, just for something to do, I couldn't have cared less.

'Just fer a natter. Are yeh watching *Neighbours*? What's happening?'

I didn't give a toss about Trudy and Rachel. I might have no mates at my school but I spent every weekend and most nights in Motherwell with my gang and that was enough to keep me going during the week.

Saturday night was 'Youth Alive!' and then we went on to

Paul's, who used to be saved but got kicked out for getting a girl pregnant. We'd have joints with weed or skunk, usually on Paul's credit from the local dealer, and whatever booze we could scrounge up. Once we were tanked enough we'd go out and hang about on the estate's pavements, under the orange lights, at least until the buzz wore off and we started feeling like twats just standing on a street corner with nowhere to go.

The next evening we'd go to Sunday service, fill up on tea and biscuits, soothe our hangover jitters with hugs, and shout, 'Praise, yes, praise him!' I never had the energy to speak in tongues or repent on Sundays though.

'It's bullshite, Janie. Yeh'll have grown out of it in a few years. I mean, do yeh even really believe in God?'

'I suppose yeh don't want me tae be happy then? Just cause it means being a Christian? At least I've mates and go out at the weekends.'

Ma pulled a face and turned back to the dishes. She had her own problems; like not having any mates or anywhere to go any day except Asda. Problems like Tiny finding junkies' needles in the garden and bringing one back to the house; like the loan sharks turning up at our neighbour's door in balaclavas and holding pry bars, and Ma having to go out in her nightie and say she was calling the police. Even though she thought Margaret was a stuck-up bitch. Then there was the girl my age who was raped walking to the shop after school and they still hadn't found who'd done it.

There was nothing in Coatbridge for Ma but plenty of worries, time to sleep, and Doug. Sometimes he'd come up for a few drinks but he always tried to get Ma into bed and when she told him to fuck off he'd try and tap her for a fiver for a drink to 'salve his hurt pride'. Ma knew his game. 'I'll call his bluff.

One time I'm going tae drag him off tae bed, the old bugger.'

'Ma! I dinnae want tae hear it.'

'Well, anyway,' she pulled the pink fleecy dressing gown round her, 'between that an' the hangover, I'm better off by myself.'

School got much worse; Rachel and Trudy told everyone I was a lezzer. I never did work out why they chose that but maybe they were cleverer than they looked because, despite the fat, moustached source, it was juicy enough for everyone to want to believe.

Girls flinched if I stood next to them and made big scared eyes at their mates and lads would stand behind me in the canteen queue and whisper, 'Yeh like the taste then?' They'd ripple their hand in front of my face like an undulating fish. 'What you havin' fer dinner? Furry kebab with a drink from the furry cup?'

'Fuck up, Adam! Your ma's like an ice-cream van – everyone knows she'll give anyone a lick fer ten pee. Yeh twat.'

I asked Ma if I could change to Motherwell High. 'I'd be with my mates an' maybe if I was there the council'd give us transfer. A new start, Ma, fer you an' me an' Tiny, away from Greenend.'

I stayed home the next week, watching Richard and Judy and that dick Fred jumping about on the floating map and by Friday I was enrolled at Motherwell High. That was the thing about Ma; when she really wanted to do something, she could get anything sorted.

They put me in remedial English for the first week. At Coatbridge being with 'the rems' was like turning up to school with a period stain on your skirt but at Motherwell the remedials were the hard kids and the cool ones who hardly ever came to school anyway.

On my first day I got sat with a scrawny girl with a hole in her trousers, smoker's cough and yellow-stained fingers. She had huge brown eyes but almost no eyelashes. I never saw her smile.

'Wha' have yeh done then?'

There was a bit of wheeze to her voice but I knew a challenge when I heard one. 'In English? Well –'

'No, yeh fuckwit, I mean, like, Es, hash, jellies, acid?'

'Oh. Just skunk, but really strong, an' a wee bit of whizz once or twice.'

I didn't know if I had done speed but Kim said she saw the lads put some in our drinks once and I had been a bit hyper that night.

'Do yeh smoke?'

'No.' I saw a shadow cross her face and I shrugged, pushed out my chin. 'I mean, I only want tae smoke if it's getting me wasted. I'd rather spend my money on gear.'

She was drawing big dicks on the top of her worksheet; she was quite an artist, even if the proportion was a little off on the testes.

'Would yeh ever do smack?'

I thought of cold pale lips and Frankie's dead body lying across old porn in that dark shed. 'No, I'll try anything but I wouldnae do smack ever.'

She nodded. 'Good girl, me neither. I've done –' she counted off on her fingers – 'Es, jellies, uppers, whizz, dope and grass.'

'I've done grass an' all. Home-grown. My mate Paul grows it.'

She looked annoyed and carried on with her list. 'An' downers, mushies and acid but I wouldnae do acid again. If yeh want anythin' just go tae the van.'

'The van?'

'Aye, the ice-cream one outside at lunchtime. He's got everythin' but he'll make yeh buy some sweets or crisps an' all. What's yer name?'

'Janie.'

She nodded, her eyes serious. 'I'm Shona.'

She finished her cock with a tight scribble of pubes and I went back to my fill-in-the-words worksheet, feeling like I'd got 8 out of 10 in my first English class.

The next lesson I salt-and-peppered my essay with commas and they behaved like they'd never seen one before and carted me off, there and then, to the top set. I missed Shona, especially compared to the snotty padded hairband and scrunchie brigade who made up top set.

I wasn't sexy skinny; you could count my ribs and I had dirty-blonde hair that stuck up in funny directions from years of cuts with kitchen scissors. I hairsprayed it into a tight ponytail, with a stiff crispy sticking-up wave of a fringe and wore NHS glasses that made my eyes look wide and shocked. For my fourteenth birthday the girls chipped in and got me Collection 2000 make-up and it made me feel a bit better to have the dark-lined eyebrows, eyes and lips.

I'd only kissed one boy and he told everyone it was boring cause I hardly moved my head even though I'd let him feel my tits through my jumper. I didn't need a school uniform on top of it all. Every day I wore my Doctor Martens, fake but you couldn't tell, jeans and my Fruit of the Loom sweatshirt, sometimes a Nike T-shirt, and every day a note got sent home to Ma who couldn't afford the new red jumper for Motherwell High so she just stuffed them down the side of the sofa.

Besides, I only went home once a week, on a Monday night, to get my share of the nice beginning-of-the-week food and some clean knicks. I'd shout into Ma and Tiny's room as I left on a Tuesday morning, 'Ma! If I'm not home fer a few days I'll just be at Kim's!' She didn't reply.

One Monday night she came into the living room during

Neighbours. 'Janie, I'm worried about yeh being out at nights so much. Are yeh drinking? In Motherwell, with this new crowd? I know they're Christians but kids are kids.'

I looked at her face; she looked shattered and I couldn't be fucked lying.

'Aye, Ma, but don't worry, it's just a wee drink of cider. I never get paralytic. An' I'm not smoking or doing any gear or anything stupid.'

Ma nodded and gave a weak smile. What she would have said if I told her I got so pissed I couldn't walk, that we had credit with half the dealers in Motherwell and that Paul had started smoking smack? But I could tell, I knew, that really she didn't want to hear it. She couldn't manage it. I might have told her then I wasn't sure I could either.

'Well, I'm not a hypocrite, I'll not try an' lay down the law about booze, yer a sensible girl, Janie, but promise me yeh'll tell me if yeh get in any trouble? I'm yer ma.'

'Aye, course. Do yeh want a cuppa?'

'Lovely.'

She smiled and her dark bags under her eyes sagged; with the little flecks of grey through her hair she looked like she was turning to dust. I tore myself away from *Neighbours* and filled the kettle. Ma's voice bounced through the door frame; I imagined her tilted back to shout, 'Yeh know I just miss my wee girl? I miss having a good chat.'

'I know, Ma.'

I came home every Monday and left on Tuesday morning with a tenner in my pocket meant for food that I'd eke out on cider, my share of a quarter and the occasional ice pole or battered sausage.

Then I stopped going to school. I'd just go straight to Paul's or sometimes Kenny's. Paul could usually get some dope but Kenny made me cheese toasties and had MTV.

One day neither was home so I bought a bottle of lemonade and a packet of Bourbon biscuits and went to read *To Kill a Mockingbird* in the woods by the sewer stream. It was Scout sticking up for her da at the courthouse that started me crying. I wasn't crying for my da, I hardly thought about him or listened to Ma's stories any more, not really. I cried because none of us was as good as people in books and because there was nothing but sugar, no dope or booze, to blunt the worry slicing my insides.

As though to prove those tears weren't wasted, Doug proved my point that next weekend. He didn't even say goodbye to Tiny, he just left. Ma and Tiny took a walk up to his on the Sunday to see if he had a loan of a few quid and he was gone.

Either he'd left the door wide or it'd been jimmied because someone had shat in the kitchen sink, a thick long curl of a shite, obviously human, and someone else, or maybe the same person, had spray-painted 'Fuck OFF Pakis' on the living-room wall. Maybe they'd got a bit confused. Ma found two tins of beans and one of rice pudding at the back of cupboard so at least it wasn't a completely wasted journey.

At home Ma gave Tiny, doing squares within miserable squares on her Etch A Sketch, a bowl of rice pudding. 'He'll be in touch soon, Tiny, honest. You know yer da, he's a rolling stone!'

Ma tried to give a little laugh but Tiny just stared ahead and took a big spoon of rice pudding. I was hungover and pissed off about being stuck at home, painting my toenails on the sofa, thinking that Tiny should get used to it.

'Aye, at least this time he left us three cans instead of nicking all our money.'

'Shut up, Janie! My da doesn't steal. At least I've got one.'

Half-chewed flecks of Tiny's rice pudding landed on my foot and she was in front of me now, her face purple, chin wobbling.

'Aye, an' I've one too. I just don't know where he is. So that makes us the same. Now eat yer rice pudding an' leave me alone.'

She threw her bowl at me, the rim hit me on the chin and most of the rice pudding slid down inside my top. 'Ma!'

'What now?' Ma came out of the kitchen, saw me and bit back a laugh, 'Well, don't just sit there, Janie. Go wash it off.'

Ma pulled Tiny onto her knee, and as I was walking to the bathroom, the creamy rice sliding over my belly, I could hear Tiny crying in the way that won't let you catch your breath. 'Now I've no da an' no rice pudding.'

We watched *Antiques Roadshow* and I shared my half of rice pudding with Tiny and painted her nails. 'Hey, do yeh know what yer da's gone off tae do?'

Tiny looked up at my face, her eyes small, ready for a row.

'He's gone tae find work so he can buy yeh some nice things.'

She blew her nails, shiny ladybirds, and stared at me.

'So he'll get yeh a nice princess dress an' maybe take yeh to see the sea. He loves yeh so much that he'd leave home tae make sure you could have some nice presents.'

She stopped blowing at her nails. 'Really? He's going tae come back and bring presents like last time? When'll my da be home then?' She was smiling now, had a far-off look, probably imagining her da with a sack of loot like Santa.

'Well, that depends on the presents. What was the last thing yeh asked him for?'

She smudged her nails sitting on her hands and bouncing. 'A pony!'

'Well, he'll be away saving up fer one then. So he might be a bit longer than last time.'

She went skipping off to Ma to tell her her da was bringing back a pony and I picked at the red, scabby smudges she'd left on the carpet. Poor Tiny, it wasn't her fault her da was a fly-by-night purse-stealing joker.

Hiya Girls,

Sorry about the short shrift. Had to get away. In Yarmouth. Lots of work to be had. You should come – I've a place here all ready.

Love to all my girls.
Doug
PS Tiny, there are donkeys on the beach here!

The postcard had a picture of a donkey in a straw hat with a stick of pink rock pushed between the yellow slabs of its teeth. Ma said it made her depressed, I said everything made her depressed even when she took her pills, and Tiny loved the postcard so much she took it to school to show her teacher and told everyone her da was buying her a donkey in a hat and that that was even better than a pony.

It was the week for post, because a few days after the postcard Ma got a letter from the school saying I hadn't attended for a month and would I be re-enrolling after the summer holidays. She made two cups of tea and we sat facing each other on the sofa. I could see the letterhead and knew I was in deep shite and I eyed the hot tea nervously, but Ma was so calm I wondered if she'd overdone her medication.

'I mean, Janie, it makes yeh wonder what sort of school

wouldn't know where its own pupils are fer a month, or fer that matter even think tae find out.' She shook her head sadly and handed me the packet of Hobnobs.

I shrugged. 'Maybe they thought I'd gone back to Coatbridge High.'

'Aye, maybe.' Ma was being vague; she took a sip of her tea. 'It seems yeh've burnt all yer bridges now though. What you need is a new start.'

I choked down my bite of biscuit. 'I'm not moving, Ma. I've mates here.'

'Who said anything about that?'

'I'm not eleven any more. Yeh can't guilt-trip me into coming. I suppose it's Yarmouth yeh want tae cart us off tae? Following Doug again! Cause that's worked out so fuckin' brilliant so far!'

She started losing her calm, put her tea down with a splash. 'I did what I thought was best fer you two an' until yer a single mother with no protection an' no cash yeh can shut it. Yeh can hardly take the high ground when yeh've been truanting an' doing God knows fuckin' what!'

I stood up to shout down at her but she stood up too. 'Bullshit! Yer fuckin' weak! I'm not moving an' yeh won't make me!'

I tried to pull away but she held my wrist tight and got close into my face so I could smell the metallic coat of tea on her tongue. 'You little shite! I'm fuckin' weak, am I? I can't make yeh move? No? You fuckin' watch me.'

I pulled my hand away and ran out the front door. I was halfway down the road before I realised I'd no money for fares and nowhere to go in Coatbridge, so I sneaked back and let myself quietly into my room.

16

She sidled around me. Told me I'd be closer to London and the 'real world', asked me if I really saw myself living in Coatbridge or Motherwell forever and I replied, 'Fuck, no!' She told me it was one big party every night; there were always holidaymakers out for a good time, and I could get a little job and earn some cash.

In the end what she said didn't matter, because I'd felt trapped in a thick box of smoke, of booze, dope and looming dead ends for just long enough to be looking for what might be beyond it, and I groped my way towards that shaft of light at the bottom of the door, and towards Great Yarmouth.

Doug came the following week with a borrowed car. Ma was the first at the window after he tooted the horn.

'What the fuck is that?'

I pulled the curtain back. Doug stood in front of a low thin car, the kind from seventies detective programmes, grinning away like Mr Big Balls himself. The car was a wreck and exactly the same colour as the curtains I used to tangle myself up in at Buchanan Terrace as a kid.

'It's the fuckin' Tango mobile, that's what that is. *You know when you've been Tangoed!* I'm not arriving in that, Ma. Yeh can let me out at the edge of the town an' I'll walk.'

Ma laughed. 'Janie, fer God's sake, are yeh expecting a parade fer yer arrival in Great Yarmouth?'

She went to tell Tiny her da had arrived, but I could already see her barrelling out the door and up into Doug's arms where he spun her round, drew circles with Tiny's ink splash of hair. I knew she would bloody love that car.

It took us two days to get to Great Yarmouth. We were skint because of the car and the petrol and because Ma insisted on paying the gas and electric bills. 'It's folk like us that ends up paying anyway,' though Doug told her not to bother. She asked about the car.

'Eighty quid! Could yeh no get cheaper?'

'Tha's twenty quid a day, here an' back! Any cheaper an' it would be free an' we'd be packin' yer stuff intae fresh air.'

'An what about petrol?'

'About fifty.'

Ma let out an exasperated sigh and went back upstairs. Doug looked at Tiny and shrugged and she shrugged back.

The car was barely big enough for four people, never mind the bin liners and crisp boxes filled with our crap, or Ma and Tiny's excitement that you could practically hear pinging against the tin-can roof.

'It'll save us money in the long run, bringing everything,' said Ma when Doug told her the car wouldn't take it.

I sat in the back, my feet resting on our telly, looking through my knees at the back of Ma and Doug's heads, thinking about my last weekend in Motherwell.

Paul had got 'special skunk spliffs' and four bottles of MD 20/20 that we mixed into big bottles of lemonade. The spliffs got me so wasted that I thought I was paralysed and couldn't move my tongue until Moira gave me a shake and asked if she could borrow my eyeliner. When the booze was done we went to Jenni's, whose parents were away.

I didn't even get through the door before the lad grabbed

me, I hadn't seen him round Jenni's before, and started getting off with me. He looked a bit older and maybe sexy, but my eyelids kept drooping so I couldn't be sure. Still, I kissed back.

I don't remember getting inside Jenni's but I remember asking him to give me a hickey and him giving me a necklace of them, each love bite a perfect circle the size of a ping-pong ball. It looked like I'd taken a Hoover to myself. Next, I was looking at a Transformers quilt and he was naked and I was too. I was sure he'd see I just had downy blonde fluff, dandelion seeds, and not a thick bush of pubes like I was meant to have, and I tried to cover myself.

'C'mon. I'm fuckin' dying here. It's no' like yer a virgin.'

Had I said so? He squeezed my nipples, they were tiny hard Jelly Tots, and kept pushing his knee between my legs to get them wider. I tried to remember why I was pushing him away.

'I dinnae know yer name.'

He kept his hands on my tits, giving them little rough squeezes. 'I'm Pete Malachy, I go to St Patrick's, I'm sixteen. Now c'mon!'

It seemed fair enough, I let him in between my legs, felt his weight on top of me then I wriggled away again.

'What now? Fuck.'

'Protection. Have yeh a condom?'

'I'm a Catholic.'

Even after two 'special spliffs' and a bottle of Kiwi MD 20/20 that sounded fucked to me. 'No condom, no shag.'

It was only thanks to being pissed I was able to say that.

He walked across the room, his cock bobbing like a wood-pecker garden ornament. I watched him rip the packet open and closed my eyes. I felt his weight and then a sharp pain, like using tampons for the first time, and he started pushing away.

It wasn't what I expected but I knew I should be making some noises so I made a few squeaks, kept my eyes closed, my legs wide and hoped it would finish soon.

Afterwards he got up and got dressed and, since I was still lying naked on Jenni's brother's Transformers sheets, he helped me into my miniskirt and vest, threaded my lazy legs through my knickers.

As he was leaving he stuck his head back in the door.

'What's yer name?'

'Janie.'

'Was I yer first?'

I was tired. 'Aye. Thanks an all that.'

His grin spread. 'Fuck! I knew it.'

Then he was gone. I felt like sleeping or crying but then Moira came in and gave me some cider and said, 'He's a fuckin' ride! I wish I'd lost it tae him.'

I shrugged, suddenly felt great and said, 'Well, no need tae sound so fuckin' surprised.'

In the back of the Tango Mobile, I ate my salad-cream sandwich while Tiny slept with her head on my lap. I was fourteen, I wasn't a virgin and I was going to the seaside.

We made it, just. We had to sleep in a lay-by during the night and in the morning we woke with our tempers and our muscles wound tight and ready to ping. One by one we took a piss by the side of the road. I was last and watched the yellow streams run into each other and under the car.

We ran out of loaf and salad cream so we stopped at a BP garage and Ma got us microwave burgers. The car stank, layer upon layer of reek, my feet stewing in my Docs (hormones Ma said), Doug's 'silent but violents', though he delicately lifted one arse cheek when he let one off so it was hardly a secret, onions, lard and our unbrushed teeth thick with stale sugar.

It was roasting too; our tops stuck to our skin and I could feel little drops of sweat scuttling down the backs of my legs like beasties. Ma begged Doug to crack a window but the handle was stuck.

Not including the occasional Christmas shop or Monday taxi, I'd only been in a car about five times in my life, but even I knew that the smoke it was belching out wasn't right. We could all see it, the engine, and Ma were About to Blow.

'Fuckin' do something, Doug. We can't drive this for another four hours.'

Ma peered through the grey smoke, Tiny got up on her knees to watch the black clouds rise from the bonnet and I inched lower in my seat, away from the curious eyes behind other car windows.

'Like wha', Iris? Yeh know yer problem, yeh've no sense o' limitations.'

'Oh, I've plenty of a sense of your limitations!'

Doug beeped the horn with a series of thumps to the steering wheel and we swerved to the side of the motorway. The only blessing was that we couldn't see what might be coming.

We didn't have cash for a mechanic but Doug still walked to a garage and got them to tow us. Me and Tiny sat in the back of the Tango Mobile while they cranked it up, pushing us back against the seat, burger boxes, half-bitten crusts and stringy tissues collecting at our feet.

When we got to the garage Doug and Ma explained about the cash problem and the mechanic, a skinny bloke in his twenties with big pores and a greasy nose, called his boss.

'Boss' was ancient, bow-legged and swollen at his joints; I wondered how he'd got his leg up into his overalls that morning. He looked at us standing in a row, Tiny pulling her knickers out of her arse, the rest of our cheeks burning, nodded and said Ma could leave her family allowance book as security. Ma tried, but he wouldn't take the telly. That was a relief.

Even though Doug let me have my R.E.M. tape on and Ma bought us an ice lolly at the next shop the excitement was gone. That mechanic had a face on him like he'd caught us taking a piss in the street and our dignity was pooled down at our ankles like jeans.

The car managed to limp into Great Yarmouth, past a pasta factory, the empty docks, through a council estate not quite as rough as Greenend, but for the last stretch along the seafront it lurched like a pensioner coughing up something grim and let out a streak of black smoke from its bonnet. The sun was bright, the air smelt of sea and eventually we pulled up opposite the Sea Life Centre.

I knew the shame was bad when Doug got out with a red face; the man who'd press a finger to one side of his nose and propel a gluey missile from the other nostril onto the pavement of Coatbridge High Street was embarrassed by our Tango Mobile, bin liners and crisp boxes stuffed with knickers and laddered tights. He turned to Ma.

'Yer no payin' tha' garage a penny! Phone the social an' tell them yeh lost yer book. The auld bastard.'

He gave the car door a kick with his size eleven boot and one of the windows thumped down. Ma looked at the open window.

'Well, that's fucking typical.'

17

Doug laid down the rules for us staying in his flat. First was no swearing. Second, we weren't to speak to anyone else who lived in the building; he gave my miniskirt a stare. 'Especially you, Janie, yer no' a kid any more.' Third was that we were never to put our hands down behind the sofa cushions.

'Why would we put our hands down the inside of yer minging sofa? I bet you've been down the back of it ages ago for the coppers anyway.'

'Never mind why. Just dinnae, alright? It's fer yer own good; there's probably dirty needles an' all sorts down there.'

The house would have been gorgeous, it was right over the road from the sea, tall and white, just round the corner from the Royal Hotel.

'Charles Dickens wrote *David Copperfield* there.' Doug gave a proud nod towards it as though he had maybe sharpened his pencils for him. But there were stained mattresses piled outside the flat, kids had tagged the front of the house with blue spray paint and the rest of the outside had dirty brown water marks. Royal it was not.

Doug's bedsit was almost as small as the Tango Mobile and smelt only a bit better. I couldn't understand how all six foot two of him could stand it, it was smaller than my bedroom back in Coatbridge. Ma looked around and I could see doubts and worries tugging away at her stiff smile.

'This'll be fine, just fer a few days, till we find our own place, won't it?'

I kept my face blank and watched Ma's smile fight against the muscles in her face that said this was another hopeless move, sea breeze or no sea breeze.

'Aye, Ma, course. You'll find us a place, you always have.'

The next day, a Monday, Ma reported her family allowance book lost, got a crisis loan and we had a walk around town.

There was a marketplace full of flabby, grey-skinned stall-holders, looking as rancid and soft as the fruit and veg they were selling, and a whole row of stands, queues at all of them, selling newspaper cones of chips topped with a greasy dollop of mayonnaise. In fact, there were chip stands everywhere in Yarmouth, and doughnut stands. Pubs, pawn and betting shops. Ways to spend your money and then dodgy ways of finding a bit more.

We went to the beach and Tiny had a paddle and though we couldn't afford a ride we walked around the Pleasure Beach and Ma gave us a pound for the 2p machines in the arcades. I gave Tiny my cup of 2ps and watched from behind a fruit machine as Ma sat on a bench outside, eyes closed and face turned to the sky, a half-smoked rolly in her hand, almost a smile on her face.

On the seafront, white GTIs raced up and down, competing against the grabber machines playing 'Clementine' by blasting jungle or drum and bass from the boots of their cars. It made your cheeks vibrate if you stood too close.

We walked along the beach, around the blankets covered with crisp bags, *Sun* newspapers and slabs of blubbery pink skin in too-tight costumes. Ma shook her short hair in the wind. 'I love the smell of the sea, Janie, reminds me of being a kid again.'

'Me too.'

My arm was up to put round her shoulder but then Tiny was pulling her off by the hand, towards the slow bent-over outline of donkeys far up the beach. I watched them run-slip through the hot sand ahead of me and all the tourists' heads turn as Tiny shouted high enough to fetch stray dogs. 'Donkeeeey! It's my donkeeey!'

Ma turned to roll her eyes at me. 'Tiny, yer yanking my arm off! An' they're tae share, yeh can't have one to yerself.'

That night I lay with Ma and Tiny in the bed, Doug was on the two-seater sofa with his legs swinging over the arm, and heard girls screaming, couples calling each other cunts and the occasional puker. I heard GTIs racing up and down the seafront and the mechanical 'Oh my darling' of the grabber machines. It might have been cheap and tacky, maybe a bit pathetic around the edges, but Tiny had her da, Ma had a sea breeze, and me, I couldn't wait to get out there, and push my face into the colour and chaos of Great Yarmouth.

Ma had found us a place by the end of the next day and Doug wasn't sorry to see us go, though when he hugged Ma his hand slid down to her arse.

Our new place, a few streets behind the seafront, was a B&B but not for tourists, just for long-term lodgers, with nice regular housing benefits thank you very much. I'd never thought of us as reliable. We had two rooms, a bedroom with two beds, and another room with a sofa where we put the telly. We could never get good reception on the telly even though Ma was a dab hand with a bent coat hanger. We shared a kitchen and bathroom and were told, 'never leave your toilet paper in there, it'll grow legs' by Mrs Pritchet, the bulldog-faced landlady with huge knockers.

For the rest of the summer, Ma and Tiny went to the beach every day with a packed lunch in a bread bag and towels rolled under their arms and came back smelling of sea and scorched pavements and I got a job as a waitress and came back stinking of ketchup, my hands sticky with raspberry sauce and Fanta.

I got £1.50 an hour at the seafront cafe and my only job was to serve up the kiddies' meals. The place was pure filth; there was grease there that would survive a nuclear blast. I felt guilty letting the kids eat the food until I apologised to one too many fat mas with signet rings and frizzy perms who stubbed their fags on the plates and didn't tip.

I worked sixty-hour weeks. The owner, Marco, who had a grey ponytail and a belly that hung over his chef's checks, would ask me to get things from the bottom shelf, and even though I didn't fancy him I'd keep my knees straight so he could get a good look up my skirt. I liked the job and I knew how to keep it. It was spilt-shift, and during the break I'd go to the other waitresses' digs and smoke a spliff, or we'd go to a dark bar and they'd buy me halves of Foster's and lime. They all called me 'baby caner', but it was just a laugh.

When I got my first small brown envelope, chunky with soft fivers, my heart thumped inside my throat.

I bought a make-up set for Ma and a box of Milk Tray. Tiny wanted to go to the Sea Life Centre and we stroked the stingrays' rippling bodies, felt starfish pucker on our palms, made ourselves sick on Pick 'n' Mix. I got Tiny a furry dolphin, took her home, and went and spent the rest of my wages buying rounds with the waitresses in the pub. I drank snakebite and black and puked pure neon pink on a car bonnet. One of them had to drag me home and explain to Ma. She stripped my rancid-smelling dress off and took a cold flannel to my face,

'Like mother like daughter, eh? Still, I'm glad you've some pals.'

Ma got a job too, cash in hand, cleaning at a hotel, and Tiny went with her and dusted the telly screens for 10p a room. At home, Tiny built up silver towers around her knees and asked when she'd have enough to buy a donkey.

Ma came home each morning in her pink tabard with a treat; cream cakes, a few scratchcards, maybe a *Woman's Own*. She loved it, you could tell, tucking into that custard doughnut and cup of tea bought with money she earned herself. Even if she kept saying how being in work made her 'nerves' worse.

'But I'm getting there, Janie. Earning my own cash for the first time in years nerves or no'.'

I always took Tiny for a donkey ride and a McDonald's when I got my wages and the rest went on clothes; orange Lycra flares with a chain belt, white miniskirts, lime-green belly tops. I couldn't afford contact lenses and I had no tits but at least I had a flat belly, a nice wee arse and the clothes to show them off in. I got myself a gold chain, hoop earrings so heavy they stretched the skin of my lobes, and transformed myself, better or worse, into a 'proper Yarco'. I didn't sound like everyone else but at least I looked it.

When the summer season was finished so was our money. Yarmouth emptied out like the morning after a heavy party, and all that was left was a few fag-end-filled empty cans, and the dossers who'd got too wankered to get themselves home again.

Ma said Caister High School was the best of a bad bunch even if you did have to catch a bus to get there. I was nervous, begged not to go, but it was easy being the new girl at the start of a new year. Especially a new girl whose ma would buy booze for her and her mates, who'd smoked dope in Glasgow and who had bought her own school uniform from New Look.

I elbowed myself into a group of girls who had space because one of them had started hanging about with the cooler kids in the summer. They still felt a bit jilted though and you could tell they didn't think I was much of a replacement.

We didn't smoke fags and didn't have a dealer. We just shared bottles of cider that my ma bought for us on Friday nights, before going to the roller rink at the Winter Gardens. They were goody-two-shoes, at least at first, but that suited me fine.

I was good at Drama. All you had to do was remember a feeling: being so scared that your blood turned icy (Tony, the Germans); being angry enough that your bones burned up and crumbled to ash (Doug, Ma); loving someone enough to want to stretch your own skin over them to carry them safely inside you (Tiny, Ma, Uncle Frankie).

I was good at English too. We read *Catcher in the Rye* and Sylvia Plath because Mr Price said we were the smartest kids and if we didn't read them now we might not get through our teens alive and we laughed and he joined in and then stopped and said, 'Seriously.' All the girls wanted to shag Mr Price even though he was shorter than most of us in our heels and had a dusty ridge of dandruff on his collar most days.

My mates weren't in my class, it was mostly squares and geeks, so I answered questions and stayed behind after the bell to catch up on coursework. All over again I loved the sweet, bitter liquorice of new words, like at that first library in Canterbury, and even more I loved Mr Price's shining eyes as I talked about Holden's loneliness or Sylvia taking the piss out of herself in *The Bell Jar*; I felt like he was looking through my skin.

I tried to talk to the girls about it but they rolled their eyes at each other and told me to shut it. I laughed. 'Well, anyway, I think Price's going to shag one of the girls in the class before the end of the year; he keeps going on about how he's getting divorced.'

We spent the rest of the lunchtime, arms linked, walking endless circles around the field guessing who it would be. They never mentioned me, they even thought it might be Fat Beth. I thought about Sylvia, how she felt invisible, and then I thought about 'phonies', and then I stopped thinking because I needed to help them decide where Price and Fat Beth might do the dirty deed.

Jenny was the one with the tits, Kate was the stunner with Timotei hair and big blue eyes, and me and Emma were just the other blondes or, if you wanted to be brutal, Specky and Fatty. That was our gang: Tits, Stunner, Specky and Fatty. It wasn't that much fun being Specky but at least I wasn't Fatty.

Jenny and Kate got boyfriends and things turned. The lads lived at a B&B near the seafront. Jenny's boyfriend was twenty-eight, Kate's twenty-five. They claimed they were just hanging around till the summer when they could get jobs, but the B&B was full of blokes like them, with Tupac and Pamela Anderson posters on the grey walls of their rooms, empty lager cans and dirty socks by the dirtier mattresses and not much else to fill the space.

Reggie, Jenny's boyfriend, had a tape player so we'd all pile into his room, hand over our pocket money to get booze, get hammered listening to Coolio and then get off with each other.

Me or Emma usually got stuck with Mark, who was so lazy he'd only go with the girl on top, or Quiet Danny who never wanted anything more than a hand-job, even then with his eyes squeezed shut the whole time, rocking back and forward. I got first pick and Emma got whoever was left. That's another reason why it was better to be Specky than Fatty.

When the lads had enough for a pint we'd go up King Street and the lads would get us into the Brunswick or Club 151. After we'd bought a drink – because the bouncers watched to see if you would – we'd minesweep for the rest of night, and that was fine except for the occasional soggy fag end at the bottom of a bottle that stung the back of your throat.

Me and Emma would race. See how many blokes we could get off with, opening our legs and wiggling our arses against their legs to the music. I usually won, I took my glasses off when we went to clubs. It didn't matter that I couldn't see, the blokes were all the same; warm, blurry shapes, dry-humping me under the disco lights.

I was hammered, absolutely paralytic. I'd sat for ages on the toilet, with my dress pulled up to my waist, thong dangling from one of my heels, and just stared at the plywood doors trying to read the biro graffiti.

Jenny had got a twenty from her dad because he was maybe having an affair and we'd had two bottles of own-brand vodka between us. Emma didn't hang around with us any more.

I was in the toilets on the middle floor. That was where all the pervy old blokes sat, dribbling into their pints of John Smith's with their tongues hanging out.

It was a shit New Year's Eve. Mark was getting off with someone else and at midnight I'd ended up kissing a sweaty fat bloke who breathed through his mouth. Jenny and Kate were dancing with their boyfriends and I'd been wandering around for ages, pretending to look for my mates, having my arse grabbed by the oldies.

I pulled up my knicks and stumbled out. There was a fight outside where the band would play but there wasn't a band tonight. The crowd seemed to be enjoying the fight more anyway. The bouncer looked at me and I bombed it down to the basement before he could ask for ID. They always waited until you'd spent a few quid before they chucked you out.

I'd never been down there before, to 'The Crypt'. Reggie said it was for freaks and remedials. The walls, painted black, shined with the heat off bodies and spilled drinks. Everyone was dancing to Blur wearing skinny T-shirts and Adidas Gazelle trainers. They mostly had the same short floppy hair. The only difference was the lads had jeans and the girls had miniskirts. They were all bouncing, pulling 'ironic' faces at each other, arms framed around their faces, while the goths sipped their drinks and watched from the edges through eyes slitty with eyeliner, waiting for one of their shouty songs to come on.

'Janie Ryan?' It was a girl goth. 'You're fucked! Shouldn't you be upstairs with the blonde brigade dancing to Boombastic?'

I squinted. It was Fat Beth; she was in a few of my classes but we didn't talk. She was the one we thought Mr Price might do.

'Beth!' I gave her a big hug until her spiked choker was digging into me and I realised she wasn't hugging back. She looked back at her mates, a mass of black material dotted with kohl-lined plastic eyes.

R.E.M.'s 'Stand' came on, and with a collective sigh the dance floor cleared.

'I love this song! Come'n dance.' I kicked off my platforms and did my legs-open, hip-grinding dance to R.E.M. while Beth stood smiling in front of me, not moving, except sometimes to look behind her and shake her head at her mates, who might have laughed, if they hadn't been goths.

*

He had mascara, spiked hair and T-shirt that said 'Vacant?'.

'Come on, at least a handjob.'

We were in the same cubicle that I'd sat in earlier. He lifted my hand to his jeans but I could hardly move my head to snog never mind that.

He grabbed my arse and started to do it himself with his other hand.

'Shtop!' I lurched against him.

'What fucking now?'

He sounded posh; he pulled his face away a bit but his hands still worked away, one on his dick, one on my arse; like patting your head and rubbing your tummy – impressive really.

'Don't do it on my dressh. It'sh new.'

'It's a white dress.'

'Oh.' I looked down at his hand working away and my snakebite-stained dress. 'Aye.'

I giggled and slid down the cubicle wall and that was where Jenny and Kate found me at kicking-out time. It was a laugh.

Or I thought it was a laugh. Until Jenny and Kate pinched and poked at me with it when we got back to school and then blurted it out during Biology, their names for me as precise as the scalpels we cut apart our flowers with. They called me a slapper then shared confused, knowing smiles with each other, and limp luke-warm hugs with me before English when they drew tears, seeing they'd cut to the tender parts.

'Don't be so stupid, Janie, it's just a laugh. See you at lunch.'

I decided after English that day. I didn't go to the canteen to sit at our usual table, drink peach fizzy water and share a plate of chips with them. Instead, I walked round to the bit of field behind the Portakabin. Not the bit of grass by the sports shed that was covered in fag ends and ripped-up porn magazines where the cool kids hung out but the dark, damp bit that was colder even in the summer.

They were sat in the shadows, hunched over, looking as though their arses had burrowed into the soggy grass. I saw Beth sharing her earphones with a girl called Nibble. My heels sank into the soggy grass and, until I reached them, until they raised their heads, scared at the sight of another kid, I could have just turned back. I could have gone and applied layers of lip gloss and gossiped about what a slag Sarah Tucker was. But then Beth stood up and turned to me with a half-smile on her face, pulling the earphone from Nibble's ear; she didn't know if I was coming to cause grief or not but she kept smiling anyway, and I knew I would keep walking away from the canteen, towards social suicide.

I don't really know what it was that made me. The thing about Beth was that I never thought she was waiting to stab me in the back, pinch my boyfriend, tell me my arse had got fat, or that I should go squeeze my spot 'cause it's disgusting' like the blonde brigade did.

It was true that if we met outside McDonald's and she got there first she'd shout across the road, 'Oi, fuckface! Slag. Over here!' But there was always a smile with it, showing the roll of fat under her chin and the deep dimple under her right cheek. You wouldn't believe the filth you can say perfectly nicely if you have a dimple.

Beth spent all her time trying to look hard, with her ink-and-compass tattoos, thin purple lips and spiky jewellery, but I never saw her pass a dog, even the rank, wet ones, without burying her face into their fur. She'd always give up her seat on the bright yellow Banana bus for an oldie, though she would offer it with a sharp jerk of her head and then stare ahead when they thanked her, flicking her lip stud in and out with her tongue so the poor old sod didn't know where to look.

Her body gave her away too. She could paint it and dress it, but it didn't matter how many silvery scratches laced her arms or how much black she scraped on the inside of her eyes, her body was soft and warm. Sometimes it moved like she didn't even notice it happening and I'd find a hand laced in mine or her stiff black hair, the smell of hairspray right up my nose, tickling my neck and her head on my shoulder.

I suppose there was something safe about her. She told me secrets in her flat, deep voice, but didn't ask for any back. She had a guinea pig, Gomez, that she brushed every night in her room while her ma and dad rowed downstairs, because that's what the hospital said she should do when she thought of hurting. Her bedroom walls were covered with cut-out pictures from holiday brochures, mainly Greece but there was one of the Canary Islands too. Beth wanted out of Yarmouth to do something better and so did I and I didn't think she would try to fuck me over while we were getting there together.

I didn't have to push anyone out to get to her either. Nibble didn't care I was Beth's new mate. Nibble had a pencil case of nail varnishes and spent the whole school day painting her nails a rainbow of colours and then scraping it off with her long front teeth. She had wide-set, half-closed eyes and a Cheshire cat grin that was always flecked with pink, blue and yellow. We used to joke her boyfriend 'Gay Gordon' must shit multicoloured turds from all the varnish he swallowed while swirling his tongue around her mouth in the playground.

Gordon, with his puff of orange hair and slim wrists. Before he went in for the snog, with his mouth open, tongue visible, he'd always make sure there was a a bit of a crowd, then he'd tense his jaw, screw his eyes and go for gold. Nibble loved the attention, practically dry-humping him on the field while we rolled our eyes. She'd whisper loudly about how they tried every 'Position of the Fortnight' in *More Magazine*, 'his finger and his cock, like right up inside, my legs wide on top'.

She'd pause, take in our blank, unbelieving faces. Sometimes Beth would snap a bubble of chewing gum to show just how boring hearing about Gordon's cock was, and Nibble would raise her voice.

'Two fingers and a cock! It's all about the girth. Don't tell no one – I don't want them thinking I'm some sort of slag.'

Nibble never noticed that all Gordon's pictures in his folder were of the lads in bands and that if there was a football match on the field Gordon stared for ten minutes then disappeared, slightly bent forward, and came back flushed and silent with his hands jiggling deep in his pockets. The deal was we all pretended not to notice either.

There were others who came and went. Either floated to smaller groups or decided they would be more invisible in a corner of the library or taking long, lonely walks around the school corridors at break times. Diana from Romania, taller than any of the lads, who wore a boy's uniform and never said a word, just stood on the edges smiling grimly from under her thick black eyebrows. Or Shane, a fatty whose ma must have been a sadist because he never had a jumper or T-shirt that didn't ride up to show an inch of flab. But it was really the four of us, me, Beth, Nibble and Gordon, sitting on the field, not looking at each other too closely, and not fighting each other's battles if other kids did look too close and didn't like or understand what they saw.

It worked OK though. Beth had the Brunswick gang at the weekends, goths from other schools who travelled down from the little villages like Ormesby on Fridays, and slept on her floor surrounded by shiny pictures of Greek beaches and breakfast buffets, leaving mascara smudges on the carpet and a forest of stubbed fags on the windowsill to remember them by.

So, I knew. I knew when Beth looked up and saw me walking over to them on the field that day that she was chuffed. Even though she lost the smile and just let a long casual drip of spit drop to the grass in front of her and looked up at me. 'You sitting? Fuck's sake, Nibbs! Stop grinding his leg and shove up.' I sat down, Beth showed me that dimple and asked what I was wearing to the Brunswick that week. As easy as that, I made everything so much better and so much harder.

18

It was unthinkable, unforgivable. Demoting myself was like pulling the wrong toothpick from Kerplunk or making a clumsy grab for the lasso in Buckaroo; it left people scrambling for a sense of order, leaving everyone who was following the rules scrabbling for marbles and plastic bits of cowboy tackle under the furniture.

I left a group of almost-popular blondes and started hanging out with the freaks and geeks who sang 'Green Day' on the school field at lunch. I gave myself a compass tattoo, took off my gold and replaced it with penny-sweet coloured necklaces and twenty black rubber bracelets up each arm.

We were fifteen, we were always changing: no tits to double-Ds, fatty to fuckable, virgin then pregnant. It wasn't that I'd changed, but that I'd upset the natural order. I had pulled myself backwards and that was deemed punishable.

Jenny and Kate started the ball rolling and the rumours frothed through the school canteen behind it.

'Janie Ryan shagged a bloke while Jenny and her boyfriend were in the same bed.'

'Janie Ryan has crabs/Aids/herpes.'

'Janie Ryan sucked a bloke off in the Brunswick toilets. She swallows.'

I tried to laugh it off in the hope it would die, but they didn't want a laugh or a smart-arse reply, they didn't want it to die down, they were after blood.

'Aye, so fuckin' what?' is what I said to everything; it was only just over a month till the holidays, I could manage. I kept my head up and my mouth tight while they stabbed me in the back with pencils and compasses in lessons, smeared dog shit on my denim jacket and sprayed me with body spray.

'What? You should say *thank you*, it's Impulse. You stink of cum.'

I was on my own. Beth, Nibbs, poor fucking Gay Gordon had their own battles to fight and so did the teachers who looked on it all with bored mouths and rolling eyes. 'Yes, yes, all very funny. Now back to Mussolini.'

I didn't tell Ma though she could probably tell. 'How did yeh fall in dog shit again, Janie?' She seemed worn thin, just getting by enough to do the week's shop and tame Tiny's hair into a ponytail in the mornings. I wouldn't be the something else that broke her completely.

Beth could see for herself what was happening, but like the thin scabs up her arms, she picked around the edges but never gouged deep. 'Forget them, they're dicks. C'mon, let's make a plan, if we were catching a plane where would we go? Fuck's sake, don't cry.'

I bit the insides of my cheeks till I tasted metal and waited for the bell to go each day, and when it got too bad, when my heart thumped against my chest and my bladder felt so loose I didn't know what I'd do if there was another small, careful cruelty that day, then I'd bunk off and go to the library.

The library in town was attached to the social. There was always a line of pale-looking girls with grimy buggies and thin blokes in torn Kappa jackets outside, holding their numbered tickets in one hand and roll-ups in the other. I could tell who was really hard up from the way their expressions got pinched up like Ma's used to.

The social reminded me of the squat, blocky buildings filled with bullet holes that they showed on *Blue Peter* when they were doing Bring and Buy Sales for Romanian Orphans. They probably didn't even go out there for the footage, just sent a film crew to stand outside the Yarmouth library, waited until one of the snotty-nosed, blank-eyed kids threw themselves down on the pavement having a paddy and zoomed the camera in close.

On the days when it was too much, and I'd bit my lip and picked my cuticles bloody trying not to cry, I'd catch the bus to town, take off my tie and button up my denim jacket and try to breathe past the panic filling my fingers and between the slots of my bones until I got far enough away from school. If the librarians thought I was a skiver they never said a word. Maybe they realised I learned more those afternoons than I ever did sitting in Home Economics or RE listening to people whisper that I was a smelly cunt.

The library was always roasting and completely dead. Sometimes there was a batty old woman in a headscarf, smelling of pee and jumble sales, her arms full of Mary Higgins Clark books, or a knackered-looking ma and her kids, but mostly it was just me and the books and the quiet soupy air.

I walked the aisles, trailing my fingers across the spines. I understood that name 'spine' because it was the same bumpy feeling as tracing your fingers up and down someone's skinny back.

I'd spend ages choosing my books; the library was a bubble, outside didn't exist. I chose names, looked at the cover, traced my finger across the black letters that made the first lines and tempted myself with the last page before slamming the book shut just as my eyes fell on the words.

There were two librarians, though God only knew what

they did except drink tea. One had a hollow beehive of wispy grey hair, as though it might be a home for a small animal, and breasts pushed into twin cone shapes, I imagined they'd fire bullets if you returned your books overdue. The other, an older bloke, had red flaking hands and dandruff that shook free from his scalp with every forceful thud of the stamp and collected in the creases of his bow tie. All the tea made their breath smell like soft turnips but they had a kind way of laying their eyes somewhere else when I brought my stack of books to the counter with swollen, tear-filled eyes. I liked to think they were a couple. Once I saw him inch the tip of his shoe over to meet the toe of her maroon espadrille and they stood side by side at the counter, legs gently splayed, toe to toe, supping tea and banging stamps as usual.

I don't know why I got teary. Sad to leave maybe, or glad I could be there. Glad I had some words to take away, stories from everywhere, not just made in Great Yarmouth. Not just lies about me.

Ma could see what those books meant to me.

'Yer so smart. It must be from yer da, he loved poetry.'

'And drinking.'

'And drinking, aye, but you're smart enough tae take the good bits and leave the rest, Janie.'

But I never knew if I was, and except for Ma, those librarians were the only ones who knew how much hope was snagged in those books.

I lasted until the very last day of school. I got one of the Flying Banana hopper buses with my blood fizzing for six weeks of working and drinking and they got on the bus the stop after me. A gang of five: four girls and one of their boyfriends, Danny, who used to joke with me, before I was a freak.

They sat behind me and my muscles turned solid. They had too much energy to spend; you could feel it buckling the windows, melting the plastic seat covers. A twist of marker-pen smell got up my nose and I could hear it squeaking on the window.

'Did you hear about that girl?' It was Sarah, her chatty, loud voice full of taunt.

'Who? Janie, that minger? The slag who everyone hated?' Heidi replied.

'Yeah, the one who stank of fish and always had her legs open. She's dead.'

I tried to keep my shoulders still, made my eyes stay on the same spot of window though I could see their grins reflected.

'Oh yeah.' It was Danny, the bastard, shouting over the girls and squeaking away with his marker pen. When we were mates he'd once asked me if I could smell onion on his breath after a bag of crisps. He'd breathed his soft cheesy breath all over my face. 'She was stabbed. Down the seafront.'

Sweat prickled under my shirt, I felt drops popping on my upper lip but couldn't reach up to wipe it. The bus was full. Everyone knew it was me they were talking about.

A pensioner with her tartan trolley stood in the aisle giving them a sour-faced stare; she couldn't have known it would make it worse, that they'd suck up the attention.

'Yeah,' Sarah again, 'she was raped.'

They giggled, high-pitched, forced sounds that slapped me about the back of the head.

'No, no! He was going to rape her but he took one look at her minging face and crabby pubes and stabbed her instead.'

They laughed louder; people turned to stare.

'She was too ugly to live!'

The laughter wasn't forced any more, they caught it from each other and threw it back and forth, wheezing, gasping for breath. The audience tutted, shook their heads at each other and the laughter got louder.

One of the girls, probably Heidi, kept poking me in the back. 'Hey, hey.'

My face was hot. My ears were probably beaming. 'Just fuck off.'

So quiet they couldn't have heard. The poking turned to sharp little slaps to the back of my head. 'Just fuck off!' I shouted and turned my head just an inch but an inch was enough.

'Aw, look! She's crying.'

Danny made a baby voice and stuck out his bottom lip. My tears blistered to the surface. I pushed past the woman with her tartan trolley and tumbled off at the next stop.

I was sobbing before the bus left, I couldn't help it. They grinned down at me and pointed to the back window that said 'Janie Ryan takes it up the arse' in big bubble writing. The e was round the wrong way, stupid fucks. I walked the rest of the way home wiping mascara smudges off my cheeks and thanked God for the six-week holiday.

I saw more of Ma in the holidays. I mean, I spent more time with her and there was more of her to see as well. We went around the Oxfam and Spastics Society shops and I bought myself a bottle-green velvet jacket, vomit-patterned polyester seventies shirts that soaked up the sweat, flares that gave static shocks when you ran for the bus. With my glasses I thought I looked like a sexier Jarvis Cocker, though I had to admit we probably had the same sized boobs. I was an indie kid, I was never going to be a goth; I just wasn't miserable enough. I carried around

Melody Maker and swapped my platforms for Gazelles. Recreating myself was really just in the details.

Ma seemed chuffed with the change, glad I didn't look like the other girls from the estate, I suppose.

'I was a trendsetter too, yeh know, in Aberdeen. I brought back all the fashion from Portobello Road.'

'When you were with Da? What did he wear? Were you hippies?'

'No, he was too old tae be a hippy, forty-odd when I met him. He was stylish though, and I was intae the flares an' long floaty skirts. I had an amazing see-through gold dress, I'd wear it with no bra, no one could take their eyes off me. You wouldn't think it now but . . .'

She trailed off, I wasn't listening, I was flicking through the channels looking for *Friends*, imagining me blonde and tanned if I found my da and he let me stay with him. Ma put her feet up over my lap, and lit a fag.

'A stunner I was, just like you. Especially now you look less like one of those Yarco slappers.'

'Ma! I never looked like one of them. I'm half American an' I think it shows an' all.'

Ma gave a short laugh. 'Yer right, Janie, yer better than the lot of them an' don't you forget it. Now give my feet a rub, will yeh?'

So we sat drinking our tea, having a laugh, watching young Americans drinking coffee, having a laugh. I was in a good mood so I gave her her foot rub, used my thumbs to squeeze the soles of her feet, they smelt a bit yeasty but not bad, and Ma leaned her head right back, closed her eyes and let the canned laughter seep into her lugholes.

She was right about no one ever guessing she'd been a

stunner. She'd started wearing tracksuits from the market, baby blue and pink so they picked up stains and were always grubby at the sleeves.

'They were cheap. An' who cares what I wear anyway?'

That's what she said, a disappointed look on her face, when I rolled my eyes at her new buys. I could have gouged them out when I saw the way all her excitement at her bargain disappeared, sometimes I forgot we were on the same side, but she wore them anyway.

Her face was sagging and heavy now, no sign of the sharp cheekbones and googly black-rimmed eyes I remembered from my childhood. Her body was probably sagging and heavy too but it was hard to tell under the sweatshirt. I'd long since reclaimed the make-up set I bought her though sometimes she let me put a bit of blusher on her, before we went up town.

Ma didn't care what she wore though, she just looked more and more like a Yarmouth ma every day. A few bulging Iceland bags and she'd fit in perfect.

'Ma, why don't yeh have a look in the lonely hearts an' all?'

She was looking in the *Advertiser* for jobs for the summer season, while Tiny coloured and the *Antiques Roadshow* blared in the corner.

'As if, Janie.' She didn't look up, just worried the biro between her teeth then swapped it for a puff of her roll-up.

'I mean, Ma, yer still young, well, no old anyway, an' we could do yeh up an' yeh might meet someone nice. Just cause my da bolted, Tony was a psycho an' Doug was a waster –'

'Janie! Can yeh just shut it?' She gave the paper a flick.

'Come on, look, I'll read and you just say, "Aye" or, "In yer fucking dreams".'

She rolled her eyes and passed the paper over. Tiny abandoned her crayons and pivoted herself on her chubby little belly to get a better view.

'Right. "Man of mature years seeks GSOH." What does that mean?'

'Good sense o' humour. Anyway, no "man of mature years", I'm only thirty-odd.'

'Fine, what about "Seeking open-minded bubbly lady fer –"'

'Bubbly? Jesus.'

'Alright, fair enough. Here's one . . .'

Ma and Tiny's eyes were on me now. I traced my finger past the 'good clean couple' and 'beautiful buxom' . . .

Tiny wriggled forwards a few inches and put her chin between Ma's knees so she was staring up at us, a big-eyed seal. 'Are yeh getting a new boyfriend from the paper? Yeh could just go out with my da?'

Ma smoothed her hair a bit. 'No, Tiny, yer sister's just being daft. Too much imagination is her problem.'

I rustled the paper. 'That's a good thing by the way, Tiny. Anyway, listen to this. "Gentle, intelligent 40-year-old man seeks interesting companion for nights of food, music, friendship and possibly more".'

Ma craned her neck over. 'Where's that one then?'

'Here: "Men seeking Men".'

'Aye, very fuckin' funny, Janie. I'm glad yer ma's just a big joke to you. Anyway, I'm better off by myself.'

'No yer no', Ma, you should meet someone or get out a bit.'

She shifted her knees from under Tiny's head now and had turned away from me towards the ashtray; shoulders tight, she made herself another roll-up, pulled the paper back and covered her face. 'Yer a kid, Janie, yeh've no idea about things.'

'I'm just saying. Or yeh could make some pals an' go out an' maybe get something better than cleaning this season. The Flamingo Arcade are looking fer cashiers. You could get a haircut, maybe a perm, an' go on Slimfast an' –'

Ma slammed down the paper. 'Is it not enough that I'm going out to work cleanin' other people's toilets an' that this place is tidy an' there's food in the fridge? I don't need a lecture from my teenage daughter thank you very much.'

'Well, someone needs tae cause yeh hardly leave the house now, except fer shoppin' an' work. An', Ma, it's true, yer getting huge an' no amount of elastic waistbands is going tae be able tae hide it soon.'

Tiny stood up. 'Yer not huge, Ma! Janie's a stupid bitch.'

Tiny reached across and patted Ma's belly and Ma turned her face towards the telly in the corner; it was always on, an extra person to turn to when we got sick of the sight of each other. I couldn't see the hurt on her face but I saw her suck in her stomach. 'Sorry, Ma, I just want yeh tae be happy. What are yeh goin' tae do when we move out? It would be nice then, if yeh had someone.'

Ma turned and took a quick puff of her roll-up to smooth out her wounded expression. 'Janie, I stay out of your business an' you need tae stay out of mine. That's how this works.'

I said nothing, took back the *Advertiser* and flipped to the jobs. No one asked her to stay out of my business. In fact, sometimes I wished she'd stick her nose right in it.

'Right, I'm going for a sleep. Wake me when *Corrie* starts, an' put the Fray Bentos and chips in twenty minutes before that.'

She gave the top of my head a kiss, I smelt her roll-ups and sweat smell, then she shuffled off to the bedroom in her slippers and trackies to close out the last three hours of golden afternoon sun.

Circling ads for Waitresses Wanted, I realised that Ma's days of bouncing back were done, she was happy just to roll along till she came to a stop. Then I thought I might be able to make it as a miserable goth after all, until Tiny climbed up beside me. 'Yer no' really a bitch.'

She tucked her head under my arm, started quietly singing 'Three Lions'.

The Greeks owned most of the seafront cafes. They all had names like the 'Olympia Grill' and 'Athena's Chip Shack'.

I went to work at the Acropolis Cafe, a proper waitress with an apron and a pad of my own and my wages went up to £2 an hour plus tips. It was good working for the Greeks, they didn't tax you, but everyone knew that if you pissed one off you'd never work for another, and they had tempers on them that would have given the Ryan Temper a run for its money.

I worked with two Romanian sisters. One was tall, beautiful and a bitch about sharing tips, and the other was a short dumpling, as soft and sweet as butter icing. We'd often catch the tall, bitchy one pocketing a tower of coppers from a table, muttering to herself, 'I have a first-class university degree.'

After work, Beth, who worked on the dart stall on Britannia Pier, would come and meet me and we'd change in the toilets, banging our knees against the sink trying to get our high heels on and spraying Impulse up our skirts. We'd down a few shots of sambuca in whatever club was likely to have a few tourists in it, get us caught up. We'd dance all night, maybe pull a bloke or two, then stagger back to mine at 3 a.m. ready for a few hours sleep and the next day's fourteen-hour shift.

When I had a day off and I was too hung-over to make it in to town, I'd lie on the sofa all day and read or watch *My So-Called Life* or *X Files*. I'd remind myself that I was different from everyone else in Yarmouth; an American, I could go and live there any time I wanted, go on dates, hang out in diners, get my first ever tan instead of blistering bright pink skin. Sometimes it worked and I felt the walls crumbling away from around me. I got transported to places where anyone could do anything and good things happened to kind people. But sometimes it was just like my books, and it really was just words and stories and when I tried to get back that electric, excited feeling I just felt a bit empty; like I needed a few shots or a good ride. Still, those programmes and books were a bruise I had to keep pressing and I went back again and again to them over the summer. No matter how off the rails I got, whatever stranger I had let shag me, or however hammered I'd been the night before, I always found myself back turning those pages, or flitting through channels, and hoping. And on the days when it didn't feel like magic, I let that empty feeling sink into my bones and it scared the shit out of me.

Ma finally got a council place that summer and we moved to the Barracks Estate; it was so close to the Pleasure Beach that you could smell when they were frying a fresh batch of onions and hear the roller-coaster screams when you were having a shite.

I got my own room to cover with Oasis posters and Ma got herself a garden with a sad, lopsided pampas grass in the middle. Ma seemed happy enough just to stay in the sunny garden while I worked and Tiny ran with the estate kids or visited Doug in his bedsit a few roads up. I'd hoped Ma might make a few pals but then I remembered Pam next door, who was so fat she went to the offie in an electric wheelchair and came back with carrier bags of bottles clanking from its handles, and I thought Ma was probably best off by herself, even if Pam had been friendly, and she hadn't.

Sometimes me and Beth got a day off together.

'We're like family now, you an' me. Yeh know me better than my ma an' me you. I sometimes wish we could stay on the beach together an' never go home at night,' I told her.

Beth, drawing moustaches on a picture of Sophie Ellis Bextor, gave me a hard look through her eyeliner and drew a speech bubble next to Sophie's mouth that said. 'More twat, vicar?'

Beth didn't go in for smushy stuff but I knew she was sad the days were getting colder too. She knew that that summer we were closer to each other than our own families and the beach was more familiar than our own homes.

We used the beach for eating ice creams and cones of chips, for sunbathing slicked in baby oil. We met the other freaks there, and went under Britannia Pier for sloppy, pissed-up sex with tourists who'd be on a coach home the next day while we were laughing about their wonky cocks or weird sex noises.

During those six weeks we got to know everything about each other without even meaning to. By the end of the summer I'd a red stripe down my nose that foundation couldn't cover and Beth had morning sickness.

We both knew we'd never have a summer like that one again.

19

They got embarrassed teenage mums to come and talk to us. They stood in shapeless jumpers of no particular colour and mumbled about how much they wished they'd used protection/waited for someone special/finished their GCSEs, but they all finished by saying that their Marky/Chantal/Moira was the best thing that ever happened to them.

The following week a nurse showed us how to put a condom on a banana while blindfolded. They really went to town on sex education but it was a bit like bringing out a fire extinguisher after the place has been torched by estate kids; we'd all been 'sexually active' for at least two years, and that was just the slow ones.

Beth wasn't the only one to come back with more than a suntan from the holidays. No one could believe the number of girls wearing their boyfriends' school jumpers and complaining of backaches and cravings. People thought it was an epidemic or something to do with the tides, 'so many careless girls in one year'. Not one word about the careless lads.

'I bet the head's having a fit.' I was sitting with Beth behind the music rooms pretending to hang out but really just hiding in the shadowy steps.

'How's that?'

'Well, half the girls in Year Eleven are up the duff, it doesn't look good on the school.'

'What the fuck's that supposed to mean?' She'd been really touchy since she'd found out. After we'd done the test in

McDonald's toilets I'd bought her a Happy Meal. She ate her nuggets without a word until I offered her my toy to save for the baby.

'What's he going to want a My Little Pony for?'

'Might be a little girl. Do you know whose it is?'

'What's it matter? It's mine now, like it or fucking not.' She ran out of McDonald's crying, and when I tried to go after she shouted at me to piss off. No one looked up from their Big Macs, they heard worse from the kids' parties.

Now, sitting on the steps, I thought she might do the same again. 'Jesus, no offence.' I saw little dark spots on her school blouse. 'Are you cutting again?'

She shrugged, tugged at her sleeve with chipped black varnished nails. 'Are you trying to deliberately piss me off today?'

I ignored her, snapped the elastic of my necklace against my neck. 'Have you decided yet?'

'Keep it, I suppose.' I looked at her with her blood spots on her blouse and bitten nails. She was going to be someone's ma. She met my eyes and gave a tap-water smile. 'Since all the cool girls are having one.'

She laughed, a sharp, heavy laugh that dropped to the pavement between us. When the bell rang I was even glad to go to Maths.

We lived for the weekends. I put up with all the shit, that hadn't stopped after the summer, it just stopped being new, and lived for Friday nights down the Brunswick.

All week we'd talk about what happened last Friday, who we'd get off with, who was a bitch who deserved a slap and what we'd wear; though for Beth that meant baggy and black and for me, same as always, that meant short and sexy.

After a week of being squeezed tight, flattening myself down, trying to merge into walls and disappear myself into carpets, I could go out to the Brunswick and not give a fuck. Be seen, be looked at and give as good as I got.

Shots burned down my throat and I kept drinking until I was on my back. Passed out or with someone on top, it didn't matter. The point was to smash apart the weekdays.

That Friday I was pissed as usual but not hammered, walking ahead through Market Square with the lads from the band, Toe Jam, trying to impress them by saying how old school Jo Whiley was, and then I was flat on my arse. The skinny drummer helped me up and I was pissed enough, and chuffed enough to be on my way to my first lock-in, that I just gave a bow to the lamp post as Gordon and Beth clapped and cheered behind me. 'That's what I call a Glasgow kiss!'

At every lamp post that we passed on our way down the docks they shouted, 'Watch it, Janie!' The docks were deserted by day, except for a weightlifting gym above a tyre yard, and by night the only movement was the ripped red canopy of the bar, flapping in the distance, signalling us in.

Gordon hung back, hands in his pockets.

'You're sure this is alright? I mean, it's cool for us just to turn up?'

The singer turned his head an inch or two but kept his eyes on Beth's boobs, just like he had all through his set. 'Yeah, I told you, Trevor the owner's sound, I get him gear sometimes. Come on.'

He dragged Beth by the hand and started running and we all followed, our whoops and laughs echoing off long empty shells of buildings. By the time we were knocking on the thick metal door of Dick Van Dykes, Great Yarmouth's only and not-so-premier gay bar, we were tangled up for the night with each other, breathless from a shared joke, reckless from our sprint through the deserted docks, excited by the blacked-out windows and an actual metal slat that opened to see who was asking to get in. The singer from the band pushed his way forward. 'Trevor, we alright for a drink? They're cool, they're with me.' He grinned round at Beth and easy as that the door clunked open.

I don't know what we were expecting, maybe more mirrors, sex swings and feather boas. What we got was three old bald blokes at the bar, two younger ones in vests dancing up at the end of the room to a mini-disco machine throwing out weak primary colour strobes, a smelly grey carpet, aluminium chairs and tables and eighties posters of bare-chested, bare-arsed blokes across the walls. Gordon spoke first, staring around. 'Fuck, this is . . . weird?'

We got our drinks in while the singer had a chat with Trevor, middle-aged and neat in stonewashed jeans and polo neck. Gordon's Jack and Coke came with little penis ice cubes floating in it. He wasn't pissed enough not to look nervous and he kept looking over at the lads dancing, pulling his bony hands in and out of his pockets, tugging at his Bush T-shirt, staring down at the tinkling penises in his glass.

'Can I get some dick an' all please?'

The singer rolled his eyes as I sloshed my half of snakebite across the counter towards Trevor who put his hands on the high waist of his jeans and looked at Gordon shuffling over to a dark corner table.

'Darling, cock is just for the boys here.'

By the time I walked back to the table, ready to complain of my lack of cock, everyone was watching Beth do a tiny blow job on one of Gordon's ice cubes. You could hardly tell she was pregnant cause she'd always been a big girl, but you could just see the lads in the band thought she was sexy. It was her boobs and that dimple, the lucky bitch.

'Aye, very impressive, Beth. Let's dance.'

After a while the oldies at the bar headed off and the band left to score some dope and never came back. The drummer hadn't even given me a goodnight snog. By 4 a.m. it was just us and the two younger lads, pals of Trevor's down from Diss.

'Yarmouth's a shithole but it's better than Diss and I like you. You're not a country bumpkin. What's the scene like in Scotland?'

He had hold of my hips, was shouting boozy breath into my ear, but I could tell he was looking over my shoulder at Gordon, sat at the table staring at his glass, the dance floor and then back to his glass.

'D'yeh like him then?'

'Beggars can't be choosers, love.'

He pushed by me and started trying to chat him up, but Gordon just kept staring at the other lad vogueing on a table while Beth pretended to stick notes in his invisible G-string and blew him kisses.

I was by myself now, sat alone in the only gay bar in town, watching Gordon's arms twitch and his Adam's apple bob, his eyes avoid contact as the lad laid his hand on his leg. Gordon didn't move it though. Watching Beth shake her arse and her three-month foetus to Ace of Base, pressing at my lamp-post swollen face with my fingertips.

Trevor walked over to me. 'Here. Special occasion. For that eye.'

He slid a pint glass across the counter to me, filled with glistening penises just starting to melt. I held one to my eye and crunched through the rest of them, bouncing away to the music, until my teeth were screaming, my tongue was numb and Gordon was scared off by a hand up inside his shirt.

When Trevor let us out, I gave him a kiss on each cheek like I'd seen on TV. The light was starting to bleed into the oil slick of the sea.

'Did yeh have a good time then?'

I took Gordon's slim hand in mine, Beth's soft, sweaty one in the other; they held on but didn't reply. We walked, three in a line, towards the centre of town, the cold lying on our grimy skin, all the things we could be talking about gathering up in our mouths.

Beth waded in first. 'He was such a good dancer. If I'm having a boy I hope he's queer. I'd love going out clubbing with him.'

'Aye, but you'd keep trying to cop off with his blokes.'

'Only if they were fit.'

Gordon stopped walking, pulling us back. His eyes, lashes so pale you could barely see them, were red-rimmed with tiredness, maybe something else.

'You two –' He looked bent over, all bony shoulders, hair madder than ever, his hand hot in mine. 'You two won't talk about this? At school or anything?'

I squeezed his hand and looked at Beth who gave a small shake of her head. 'Naw, but I am going to tell everyone you mugged me for my kebab to explain the black eye.'

He shrugged. 'Fair enough. Cheers for tonight, it was . . .'

Seagulls were starting their long daily circling now, cawing to each other and the deserted streets below.

'A laugh?'

'Yeah, it was cool.'

He said his goodbyes to me, Beth, baby Beth. Still hand in hand me and her stood and watched him walk away till his hair was just an orange dot on the grey of the street.

Beth spoke first. 'He's alright, isn't he?'

I put my head on her shoulder and she must've been tired because she didn't shake it off.

'We all are.'

Ma pissed herself at my eye in the morning, after she threatened to murder someone, until she'd got the facts right.

'Did someone do that to you?'

'Aye, Ma, a lamp post. I'm a drunken twat.'

Then she put down her fag and got off the sofa to come and have a closer look, checked there was no blood in the eye, that it was just a good ripe bruise, and got me a bag of onion rings from the freezer. I lay down on the carpet in front of the fire in my nightie, the bag of onion rings over the top half of my face and then she pissed herself. I couldn't just hear her laughing, I heard the springs of the sofa straining as she rolled about.

'Where'd you get to last night? Was it just you an' Beth?'

'An' Gordon.'

'Gordon? Poor lad. No Nibble?'

'They'd rowed, she's a nutter. We were cheering him up. Just us and some lads from the band that was on at the Brunswick. Singer fancied Beth. It was good night. Is my eye that bad? '

Ma hoisted herself off the sofa, lifted the bag and made a face. 'It was a good night, was it?'

'It was aye.'

'Well then.'

The eye was bad though, bad enough to earn sympathetic

smiles from women on the street for a week to come, but it was worth it. Worth it to see Gordon not stooped and shy, to feel his hand warm and relaxed in mine, even just for the night.

Before Christmas a careers guidance counsellor came and installed himself in a Portakabin in the playground. Rumours whizzed through the cold, bored air: he was a pervert; he worked for the benefit fraud people and was collecting evidence about parents. The best story was that he was a talent scout for a music company.

'Aye, he's going tae say what did yeh get in yer mock exams an', by the way, would yeh mind beltin' us out some Spice Girls an' all?'

Some of the rumours had a sharp glint about them though. He told girls to think about training as a nurse or about a GNVQ in childcare. Unless they were pregnant, in which case he told them about the benefits they could get.

I walked in wanting to teach him a lesson but he had bags under his eyes and sweat patches the size of two oranges though it was freezing. He looked tired, a bit confused and I was half-hearted.

'So what are your interests?'

'Oh, I think I'm suited tae oral work mainly.'

His eyes flicked over my laddered tights and then back down to his hands on his folder. I leaned forward; I'd taken off my bra in the girls' toilets.

'Oh, you mean like maybe a call centre or something?'

'You mean like chat lines? 0890 numbers? Aye, maybe.' Forget sad, I thought, he was a bastard, sitting there being condescending to us. Encouraging us to aim for the gutter. 'But I'm really, really good with my hands an' all? What do you think I should do?'

'Well, nursing's a good steady job, and tell me, do you like children?'

The sweat patches were the size of melons. No, it was sad I decided. He sat in a Portakabin all day with a little fan heater and us lot for company. I sat back up straight, pulled my skirt down a few inches and dropped the tease from my voice. 'Listen, I don't mind children but not fer a job and I'm not interested in nursing neither before yeh say it. I was thinking about studying tae be a lawyer.'

'A solicitor.'

'Aye, what's the difference? I could do legal aid, help people not able tae afford a proper lawyer. An' –'

He gave a grim laugh then straightened his face. 'Well, if that's what you think. Maybe the Citizens' Advice Bureau would be the sort of thing –'

'Why would I not just go to uni an' study law? It's free, isn't it? So everyone can have a go.'

I felt a prickle of tears, a bit of something lacing through my words, hurt or maybe anger: pathetic. He leaned forward and spoke slowly, a suppressed laugh dancing at the corners of his mouth but not reaching his eyes.

'You're from the Barracks Estate, am I right?' He was acting like the Big I Am now.

'Aye. So?'

He nodded and leaned back, putting his hands behind his head. Those sweat patches could have been seen from space. 'So. So, let's just say that you'd be one of the first and probably the last.'

'Aye, but I'm in the top set fer English an' I read all the time. If I get good marks I can go to college. What yer going to be hasn't anything to do with how much money yeh've got. Just cause I'm from the Barracks, why not?'

He stood and walked round to my side of the desk, put his hand on my shoulder and looked out of the window. 'OK, well, let's say I'm Tom Cruise, why not, OK? And I go home to Nicole Kidman each night and have a nice Porsche sitting outside to drive to the pub. My job is guidance, Janie, and that means I've got to get students to be realistic as well.'

I thought wet was sinking into my shirt from his palm but I didn't shake it off, I was concentrating on not kicking him in the balls.

'Take a look around you when you get home, have a think about it and ask yourself, "What's realistic for me? How will I make a living?" I'm sorry if it's –' he raised his arms so his fingers could make little marks in the air – '"harsh" but my job is managing expectations.'

I bit down on my tongue.

'That'll have to do for now.' He opened the folder in front of him, ready for the next kid. 'Have a think about what I've said and I'll see you before your exams for a follow-up. Just remember –'

'Aye, I've got it thanks, I'll be realistic.' I turned and left the Portakabin. 'Yeh fuckin' sweaty dick.'

I had a cider hangover, the kind that lies thick on your tongue and heavy in your guts. I knew I must've had chips the night before because of the crusty smudge of ketchup under my chin that stung when I scratched it off. There was something sticking into my arse as well, *The L-Shaped Room*, large print and hardback because it was all I could get from the library, but it was Ma shouting up the stairs that woke me. Got me to open my sticky eyelids like peeling the skin off a not ripe enough satsuma.

'Janie, get down here! Janie!'

'What is it?'

'Just get down here.'

I put on a pair of trackies under my minidress and thumped down the stairs, putting a hand against the cold white wall to push away the spin in my head and sick feeling floating just behind my ribs.

Ma was at the living-room door, eyes bright. 'Janie –'

'Will yeh give me a minute? I'm dying for a pee.'

'But –'

'Hold on, Ma, I'm dying.'

She thudded down on the sofa. 'Right, go then.'

There was a bit of sting to my piss, it smelt a bit like cider and that made my stomach turn again. I leaned over my thighs and let my hair flop down over my shins so the sound of the yellow hitting the bowl and water filled my ears.

'I had a win.'

I looked up at the door, my chin digging into my knees. 'Ma! I'm having a piss. Have yeh never heard of privacy?!'

'Fine, I won't share it with yeh then, smart-arse.'

Back in the living room, I looked at her right forefinger, at the line of dark grey under the fingernail, and started to get a bit excited. 'Tell me then.'

She was flushed, her arms itchy with a secret as she smoked her roll-up in tight little puffs, gave a happy shrug. 'I thought you didn't want tae know.'

'Ma, come on. I was bursting, sorry, just tell me. What was yer win?'

She stood up, walked back towards the kitchen.

'Sure yeh don't want tae go for a shite an' all? You look a right state.'

'Ma! Fuck's sake, just tell me.'

'I only won 174 fucking quid on a scratchie!' She grabbed hold of my elbows and did clumsy celebration jumps made more sloppy by her big slip-on slippers like someone on an advert for scratchcards. Instead of a real ma in a real grotty kitchen with a hung-over teenage daughter. 'A hunner and seventy-four, Janie!'

'When did yeh find out? Have yeh got the money? Let me see the card.'

I couldn't stand it, the thought of her red cheeks and excited elbow-clutching being a mistake; besides, I was already counting up what my share might be. She wouldn't be rushed though.

'I'd just dropped Tiny off at Doug's an' then got it from that wee Spar by his, the one with the miserable bitch of an assistant. An' yeh know I wouldn't shame myself in front of her sour mug usually but I just had a feeling, Janie.' She was filling the kettle, moving her quick, energy-filled hands towards the tea bags. 'In my waters. I even sat on the seafront tae scratch it. Yeh know I'll usually wait till I'm home and do my scratchie with my cuppa and a rolly. Anyway, I checked an' checked again, I wouldnae give her the pleasure of refusing me, and then I marched back. Yeh should have seen the face on her. "Your lucky day," she said with a face like a slapped arse!'

'So you got the cash?'

'Aye, crisp twenties. There's your share.'

She jerked her head to the four pound coins on the sink draining board and handed me the tea. I blew the steam away, my tongue itching to get the liquid in me.

'Aye, very funny. What you going to get then?'

Ma put two slices of Mother's Pride under the grill. 'Janie, yeh might be out all hours flashing yer belly button an' fuck knows what else, but I'm still yer ma an' know yeh back tae front. What you mean is what are *you* going tae get.'

I shrugged and laughed, then she did too, the orange light of the grill across her eyes like a mask. 'Aye, alright, what am I going tae get? And don't go saying four measly quid.'

And even though it made me not want my toast I did a few clumsy jumps of my own across the sticky lino.

It was freezing but Ma said she wanted to sit by the sea. The salty wind licked at her hair and made the ends curly. It showed up the silver strands more and the side of her face crinkled as she dug between her back teeth with a ripped-off piece of her Rizla packet. Probably trying to gouge out the slivers of fatty bacon like I was with the tip of my tongue.

'Isn't it funny, Ma?'

'Hngh?'

She had two fingers inside her mouth, really having a good root, looking out to the beach from our little bench on the prom.

'How we know each other. I knew you were going to rip off a little square of your Rizla packet after yer bacon bap.'

She made a sucking sound with her tongue on her teeth and I could practically feel the raw bit of gum free of the scrap of bacon, the way it would taste metallic at the tip of her tongue. I huddled into her, away from the cold.

'Aye, we're peas in a pod alright Janie.' She gave me a look, put a nervous hand on my back; I couldn't feel it through my coat and two jumpers. 'I wouldn't have done anything different, yeh know, having you. Even though I was just a kid really.'

'But yeh say all the time when we row that yeh gave up everything for us.'

'Yeh know I've a temper, Janie, but we're a good team, you an' me.'

I shrugged her off, squeezed a bit of bread roll into a doughy ball. I hated it when she tried to act like my mate, like it was fine for me to be out every night because that's what she was used to.

'Do yeh want me to end up like that then? Like you?'

A chip wrapper tumbled over Ma's feet; she looked down and kicked it off, brushed crumbs from the front of her jumper, turned away to open the clasp of her bag and then closed it again.

'Ma, I asked you something.'

She looked dead straight at me, her face too young to be as tired as it was, sadder than it might have been too. She took a strand of my hair and tucked it behind my ear, gave my earlobe a little tug and shook her head. 'Aye an' no. I wouldn't know what to do without you an' Tiny. I just want the best for you two, Janie, I'm just never sure how tae give it.'

'Then you wouldn't want me tae stay here then, would yeh? Be miserable an' lonely an' never travel or have a decent job?'

'I went tae London, an' had good pals and nights out.'

'Aye, but that was –'

She balled up the paper bag on her lap in a quick, angry movement, scrunching it tight. 'Fine, Janie, fine. Just like yer da.'

'How? How am I just like him?'

She whispered. Those words should have been lost in the noise of the seafront, but I didn't hear those noises any more, I'd heard them so often. 'Full of yerself.'

Behind her head I saw the grey murk of the sea push towards Great Yarmouth and then draw back again, frothing at the effort of just doing that because it had no choice. I felt the soreness in my throat but it didn't come out in my voice that was too loud. 'Ma, I –'

'I'm sorry, Janie, forget that, I'm being daft. Now come on!

Enough of this. We've had our feed, let's go spend some of this lovely cashola on my girls!'

And with a quick nudge in my ribs, Ma turned herself away from me to undo and redo the clasp on her bag again, pointlessly.

We bought Tiny a make-up set and four pairs of Tammy Girl leggings patterned the colours of tropical fish. In Boots, Ma let me smudge blue eyeshadow onto her brownish waxy eyelid with my finger and I let her spray some perfumes onto my wrists and rub them together. We went to Prism Records and she got me and Beth tickets to see Rocket from the Crypt at the Waterfront.

'Ma, it's almost fifty quid, I'll just get a few tops from New Look.' I wanted the tickets, and to see Beth's face when I pulled them out on Monday, but I didn't want the rich feeling to go. Or Ma's cheerfulness, her new fast walk and purse flourishing. I really didn't want the sums on the backs of envelopes to come back or Ma's hard disappointed face when she had to say no to Tiny or me. But Ma wanted this day and she wouldn't have listened if I'd told her to slow down, to maybe save a bit. All the winnings were for me and Tiny and getting to treat us was worth more than money to her.

'Janie, I'm getting yeh a treat an' that's that. When it's gone it's gone!'

That's what she said when we had chocolate biscuits too.

We only had one row that day. I saw her looking at a cream blouse with brown flowers, rubbing the silky cloth between her fingers and then turning the price tag, dropping the blouse limp again.

'Ma, treat yourself, honest, it'll be nice tae see yeh in something new. I'll make yeh up, do yer hair.'

She looked embarrassed to be caught looking, shamed. 'I don't need it.'

'That's not the point. It's a treat, not needing it is the whole point.'

Her body was as limp as though her own hanger had been taken from inside, and her mouth drooped. 'Naw it's fer you two this windfall.'

'Why do yeh make everything so hard fer yourself? When it's gone it's gone, Ma, and –'

And there were the tears, a film of oil on the brown penny of her iris, ready to spill down cheeks. 'This money's fer you two, fer a treat. It's rare enough I can give yeh both one. Just leave it, Janie.' Then quieter, stepping backwards from the blouse, 'Leave it.'

We went and got Tiny, who danced around our bodies, arms reaching high, grabbing at the shiny, crackling Boots and Tammy Girl bags held over her head. Ma gave Doug a half of whisky and a peck on the cheek. Just like it was Christmas.

Tiny rode facing us, on the front of the trolley in Iceland, almost tipping the whole thing, as me and Ma piled it high with big bags of crisps, frozen pizzas and Viennettas in every flavour. Ma made zigzags on the shiny orange floor with the trolley and hummed, 'We're in the money, we're in the money,' the three of us laughing, in our three different voices over the hum of the chest freezers, the waft of all the perfume Boots had on display that day chasing us as we went.

'Ma, have I ever blamed you fer needing yer sleeps or not working full-time even when we were really skint?'

'An' what's that supposed to have to do with anything?'

'Because I'm telling yeh, I can't do another day at Caister

High! Not with Beth gone. Yeh don't understand what it's like.'

'I'm stuck in this house surrounded by inbreeds like her next door eating herself tae death. So don't you tell me I don't know what it's like! An' do yeh see me giving up? Just chucking it all in?'

We'd been having a nice night, sleepy from a big dinner, cosied up with cups of tea and old magazines with *Catchphrase* humming away in the background.

I'd thought it was a good time to tell her I wouldn't go back. So she could get used to it. Now we were face to face and I could tell that there was no edging back from a full-on slanging match. I didn't really want to edge back anyway.

Tiny turned from the carpet, where she had been watching the telly, an annoyed look on her face. Roy Walker was telling us to 'Just say what you see. Say what you see.'

'Aye, actually, Ma, that's exactly it. You're only in yer thirties an' you just sit around all day filling yer face with Findus pancakes and bags of frozen Iceland eclairs. You barely even notice what yer own kids are gettin' into because yeh've given up on yerself. And when yeh do notice yeh don't have the guts to stop it.'

I stood up and she did too. I was an inch, maybe two, taller than her, even barefoot, but she got right up into my face, pushing her head forward into the space between us so she was shouting into my mouth. 'Do you know what I've done fer you two? What I've been through? Yeh've no idea! I sacrificed my whole life so you an' Tiny could have a good start. So don't call me a bad ma.'

She was screaming now, jabbing my chest to make her point, and I butted back into it knowing there'd be a bruise tomorrow to make her feel guilty.

Tiny stood up but she didn't speak. She still had the same empty look on her face she'd had while she was watching the squares reveal Mr Chips 'making his bed and lying in it'.

'I didn't ask yeh to sacrifice anything an' it doesnae need tae be yer whole life. Yer not even old for God's sake! Go out an' have some life and fun and stop using us as yer excuse cause yer too scared.'

'I'm allowed to go out an' have some fun, am I? Oh, well, thank you, Janie. How generous! Are yeh finished using me then? You ungrateful little fuck. Yer nothin' but a slapper even after all I did tae bring yeh up decent.'

'Yeh don't own me an' yeh can't keep me here because I won't make the same mistakes as you.'

'Yeh already are an' I gave yeh the best start I could, even though I was almost as young as you are now.'

Spit landed on my face, and I felt tears rising, blood surged through my arms willing me to slap her; just one hard slap to watch her flabby body crumple onto the sofa in shock.

'Oh aye, Ma, thanks fer that great start. What with all the homeless hostels an' council estates an' moonlit fuckin' flits it's no wonder I'm turning out so well. Oh aye! An' let's not forget yer drinking, an' crying, an' sleeping all the time. Thanks so much for my ideal childhood. It was really worth the sacrifice. You should have left me in the care home or with Da's wife.'

She gripped my wrists, pushed me against the wall and used her weight to pin me there. I was shaking and my legs felt floppy under me, like strips of paper. Tiny ran two steps and grabbed Ma's arm. 'Stop it, stop fighting.'

But we were in too deep to pay attention to Tiny's thin arms trying to push us apart.

'Bitch. Yeh're not my daughter, do yeh hear me? Yeh fuckin' nasty, spiteful little bitch.'

She slammed me against the wall with every word. All three of us moved, tangled in each other, the Russian dolls turned into a three-headed monster.

'I hate yeh. Get off me.'

I pushed Ma off and she turned to the kitchen slamming the door behind her. I went to the sofa, took some breaths to get rid of the white static I could see and wiped the snot from my lips while Tiny stared at me, her belly of puppy fat shaking under her Spice Girls T-shirt.

'I hate you both!'

'Tiny, stay out of it.'

'Why do yeh have to ruin everything and argue all the time?' She ran from the living room and I heard the thump of her feet on the stairs and a door slam. Poor Tiny.

'I'm getting out of here.' There was no one to hear but saying it made it real. I stood on shaky feet, found my trainers and started looking for my purse. I could her Ma throwing things out of the kitchen cupboards then she threw the kitchen door wide and came in with her old red handbag.

I looked at her face, tight and frantic.

'Leave me alone, I'm going out. Just leave me alone.'

The words tumbled out but she already had my wrist and pulled my face to hers. 'You're going nowhere!'

I snatched my hand away, my heart was thumping, a hysterical trapped kid, and I started pulling up sofa cushions and moving empty crisp bags to find my purse. Ma put her hand in the bag and brought out a photo of me.

'What's this then, eh? If I'm such a bad mother?' It was me on a birthday morning in rag curlers and vest and pants, a party tooter in my mouth. Ma crumpled it and threw it at me as I moved around the room.

'An' this, bitch! What's this then?' The only baby picture Ma had of me, naked on a changing mat with orange flowers. She ripped it into small squares, threw them at me and they fluttered to the floor pathetically.

I moved to the kitchen and she followed. I felt like my windpipe was crushed or something was lodged there, stopping me from shouting back. She pulled out more photos. 'An this! An this? An this! Yeh little fuck!'

She pushed them up into my face and ripped them in half. She could barely breathe between her screamed words.

'Leave me alone.'

I saw my purse under an Asda bag, grabbed it and ran for the door, pulling my coat off the bottom stairs. The last words I heard before the door slammed were, 'Yer no daughter of mine, yeh ungrateful little cunt.'

I ran into the street and the cold air, but I only got a few doors down before I knelt and puked into the gutter and for some reason the only thing on my mind was the Tango Mobile and its last painful lurch along the sunny seafront a year and a half ago.

20

It burned at me like I'd been at my scalp with peroxide. The house was stale, choked with fag ash and empty words from the telly. I felt sick all the time. It didn't seem to matter if I starved myself or ate so much I almost choked. I had some bad, black days but mostly it was just a tugging in my stomach and a cold, flat feeling as though I was watching all this on ITV after the watershed.

Ma wouldn't listen and Tiny sat at the edges of it all watching us with sharp, disapproving eyes, building towers of coins on the carpet, knocking them down to start again and see if she had enough for a donkey.

I kept trying to tell Ma I'd go to college and get my GCSEs, or I'd travel, maybe work abroad, I wasn't going to spend my life living for a two-month summer season and self-medicating with the cheapest booze to get me through the other ten.

I wasn't going to let the Yarmouth filth clog me up and stop me moving. I knew there was more out there, I just had to find a way to get to it. But Ma wouldn't, maybe couldn't, listen; she turned the telly up, rolled another fag, walked to the fridge.

'Ma? Are yeh listening? What are yeh even looking for?'

'Just something.' She turned and I saw her face flat and numb in the cold light of the fridge. 'Something tae fill the hole.'

She would have listened, been gentle if I'd told her what she'd probably already guessed. Then told her how. She just wanted to keep me there. I thought she might even have been glad. But I knew that if I gave her the secret I might as well have given her everything. A little mass of cells, a growth. Not cancer but feeling like it. The Lump, sucking away and getting fat on all of my plans and dreams and future. I looked at Ma sitting with her tea in front of *Coronation Street* and pushed it deeper.

But of course she'd know; for all the things she pretended not to or couldn't handle seeing, she saw it all. When I'd done the test in the bus-station toilet I hadn't been sure myself, they had those blue lights in there so junkies can't see their veins, or maybe so girls in school uniform can't see if they're fucked or just having an irregular cycle. I had to open the door a chink and there it was, in a thin line of daylight, two little blue lines cutting right through my future. I dumped my unmagic wand in the tampon bin, and the first thing I did was promise myself not to tell Ma; the second thing was to not think about it for as long as it took me to get shit-faced.

In February I took a job selling hot dogs in a little booth attached to an arcade. All day I listened to rattling coins and laser-gun sounds and the tinny 'Oh My Darling Clementine' played over and over, watching bright cars streak along the seafront, smears of paint on a grey sky.

Soon enough the sizzling fat and sweet onions nagged at my stomach and I had to leave. I didn't give any notice, just tucked the thirty pounds I'd earned into my jeans pocket and carried home a jumbo box of hamburgers that Ma and Tiny would still be eating now if she hadn't thrown them out as soon as I brought them in. We had mangy dogs sniffing outside the gate for days.

I found another job; I still looked reliable and sweet on the outside. I pierced ears at a jeweller's on Regent Road. On a Saturday I could do fifty pairs of ears and twenty noses with the little golden gun. There was always a pause when the metal hit the gristle of the earlobe, and it felt good to give the trigger that extra squeeze.

I liked it there, gallons of tea and never-ending fig rolls, except for when you'd see a woman with her dirty, snotty-nosed kids come in trying to sell her ring, or an ugly necklace that said #1MUM like the one I'd once got Ma. I'd go and sit in the toilet so I wouldn't see the shame hovering at the edges of her eyes. One less witness to the quick way she pocketed the cash like she was scared someone would take it back again.

The stocktaking was good too. That's what I did at nights. After the jeweller's I'd go and have a Fat Boy All-day Breakfast, hoping I wouldn't see it again that night, then went to the Toy Market across the road and helped them with their big before-season stocktake. I spent hours counting piles of Slinkies, whoopee cushions and cheap baby dolls with staring eyes and faces that would crumple in on themselves if you left them too close to a fire. I took one of those dolls home and hid my wages in the head; a sick joke. I didn't need to hide the money but I got used to hiding everything. I squashed the doll between my mattress and bed frame. Like Ma would say, out of sight, out of mind. But I couldn't ignore it and, of course, Ma wouldn't either.

I couldn't think while I was stocktaking, ticking the print-outs, and that was good too. That, as well as the sickness, was why the hot-dog stand was no good because there's too much time to think while all you have to do is move the sausages a centimetre this way and a centimetre back. It's then that the thoughts that are carefully plugged like a blocked drain, clogged with slimy hair, start reeking.

Behind all that, right at the back, trapped where the little flies buzzed, there the Lump was. It tried to make me listen, plagued me with a craving for fizzy penny sweets, and punished me with stringy bile and dry heaves if I didn't give in, and punished me again with cola-cube-coloured sick if I did.

Every morning, and then when it started in the night-time too, Ma would be standing outside the bathroom door for me with a mug of tap water. She'd put her head to one side, pull her concerned, knowing face.

'What's it this time then, Janie?'

And I'd take a gulp of the steely water to get rid of the taste, shrug and walk past her. 'Hangover. What else?

It was a battle, it was war, and I might have been occupied but I wasn't defenceless.

'Are you sure you want to do this?'

She was Irish, the auburn curls of her tight perm stiff and shiny. The little gold cross she wore swung just above my eyeline, a point of light. Her eyes were too dark for her pale face like uncooked pastry, two dried currants staring blackly into mine.

I wondered if she'd believe that I was once considered 'close to the spirit'. Should I respond in the nonsense tongue spasms that meant God was talking through me? But it's hard to be defiant when you're on your back and you have on a robe that shows your rainbow knickers if you stand up. I stared at the raisins.

'I've already said yes twice. Why is twice not enough times for me to say it? I'm sure. Give me the jab.'

She pushed me over and gave me a sharp jab just below the red piping of my knickers that meant I couldn't get pregnant again for three months, no cotton wool or swab, then walked back through the ward like she was trying to slice the air.

I stared at the ceiling with its brown, finger-shaped stain

and a daddy-long-legs taking refuge from the bleach smell. The woman next to me lay on her side, her body going in and out, a squeeze box of sobs.

I wondered if it was deliberate. Why else wouldn't they close her curtain or mine? There was a woman across the ward reading a *Woman's Own*, flicking through, licking her middle finger as she went. She looked like she was at a spa and I thought that she must be getting her tubes tied. We were all in for our tubes in one way or another.

You could taste it on your tongue, after the pinprick, before you felt it sneaking away up your arm like metal. The anaesthetist kept saying, 'Count backwards, Janie, from twenty . . . nineteen . . .' and while I counted backwards and felt the drug filling up my vein I had a little daydream that we would get married. I couldn't see much over the mask but he had soft eyes and gentle hands and didn't seem to hate me for taking up his time with my Yarco slapper shite. He held my hand gently and the needle hardly hurt at all going in.

My nose itched and the Beautiful South played in the background. I had that tape, I listened to it when I was in the bath and sung along. The first thing I said after they vacuumed me out was, 'I know all the words to this.'

They wheeled me from the room with the lights and tables of other sleeping patients and back to my ward filled with grey afternoon light. The squeeze-box woman was on her other side, facing me. She looked older, at least thirty, and she wasn't shuddering any more, just staring with wet leaking from her pale brown eyes. I thought she might shout or attack me but she didn't even seem to see me.

They brought round lunch and said I had to eat before I could go. I ate the hard little pot of green jelly. I felt empty, though I knew that was just a trick because they hadn't taken anything but a lump.

I've always liked jelly, the way you can gulp it down without using your teeth. That's what green jelly reminds me of now, pale brown leaking eyes, the same colour as the saline stains splashed up my thighs, and the currant-eyed nurse staring at me from the nurses' station probably thinking to herself, 'Oh! She's eating her pudding. Lord help us if a murderer can sit here and enjoy a pudding at the NHS's expense.'

You wouldn't think I'd eat green jelly any more but I do. It's important to remember.

I caught the Banana bus home. They didn't check that someone was there to get me, I just signed the form and walked out, the giant NHS sanitary pad like a whole toilet roll jammed between my legs.

Ma was having a sleep when I got in and Tiny was at school. I lay in the bath that turned a pale brown from the saline and whatever was still inside of me and then lay on the sofa under a pale yellow candlewick and ate some rice pudding from the tin while watching *Neighbours*. Ma came in and sat at the end of the sofa on my feet.

'How was Beth?' She scratched at a spot on her chin. I stared at the telly.

'Fine. Her bump's already huge.'

She looked at me, her eyes squinting with leftover sleep and impatience. 'You alright?'

'Aye, just a bad hangover.'

She nodded, a heavy movement like she expected nothing less, but she leaned over and tucked the blanket under me, her fingers flat between my body and the sofa. I was worried she'd smell the hospital on me, or maybe feel I was just a pinch of flesh lighter.

'Well, yeh'll get no sympathy from me. The way yeh carry on with shots of this an' that, with pints of snakebite. And keeping Beth out all hours when yeh know it's no way fer a girl in her condition to be behaving. Yer asking fer it.'

You could say I was asking for it. I'm sure they would say that. A girl my age drinking by herself in the Garibaldi, chugging back Orange Breezers at the bar for everyone to see. Wearing that little vest, her belly showing.

And if I could defend myself? I'd say I was only by myself because my best mate was pregnant and that I'd only picked the Gari because it was for oldies and I didn't want to see anyone. I'd tell them that I was drinking Breezers because they were on special and that I needed a drink after another day when I was called a cunt and a whore at school and then had another screaming match with my ma. That I didn't think to change when I left the house, didn't think that jeans and a vest were a come-on.

I'd tell them that I only took the oldie's drink because he put it in front of me without asking if I wanted it and it was a vodka and Coke and I was sick of fizzy, sweet Breezers and that when I drank it down in one I was waiting for him to say, 'Easy there, sweetheart, there's more where that came from,' or maybe, 'I'm not made of money, you know,' when instead he just watched my throat as I emptied the glass in two deep gulps.

But what would be the point? Because after that there's nothing, just a black hole with a scared, sick feeling around the edges. Then, when I'd say I couldn't remember, they'd say it again, 'You see? Hammered. Asking for it.'

But I didn't ask to wake up frozen on the beach in a dark, damp circle of my own piss. I didn't ask for my knickers to be ripped or the bruises up each thigh, a yellow-and-pink finger painting that wouldn't fade fast enough. Or for the pain, outside and in, when I sat down for a week afterwards.

And after I dragged myself home reeking and ashamed and not knowing why, and I forced myself to push that night down to the bottom of me and sanded off the sharp edges with more booze, I didn't ask for my period to abandon me after our four short years together.

It is true I asked for a lot back then: my belly button pierced, red Converse, Glastonbury tickets, a valentine card from a lad I fancied, for Beth not to be pregnant, for a future away from Yarmouth. But I didn't ask for my mouth to fill with spit or my gullet with bile when I felt sand on my skin, or to find myself panting for air if a lad so much as whistled at me. I never asked for the thwack, thwack, thwacking that echoed in my limbs or the feeling of filth right up inside me.

You might think that I'd be angry. At them I mean, at those that thought a girl like me would ask for it, a girl who'd go out and do that every weekend with some stranger anyway. A tart from the estate, who'd be pushing a buggy by the time she was seventeen. Who dressed to be looked at, who, you could just tell, from the way she walked, her head held high, swinging her arse, thought that sex was as predictable and pointlessly unprofitable as the penny machines in the arcades. It was no wonder that those pennies cascaded over and pinned her down, filled her up with the taste of other people's pockets and hands. They would laugh and say, 'The penny dropped for her alright,' or, 'I heard she spent a penny all over herself.' They would roar together at the girl who was asking for it and got it given.

But I wasn't angry. I thought those things myself, plucking at my eyelashes and eyebrows with my fingers, teeth ripping at my cuticles, as though I was getting rid of myself one tiny piece at a time. Start gouging out little bits with my nails, then chunks with a bread knife and finish the job with a cheese grater or maybe the pumice stone that Ma kept on the edge of the bath.

I thought, what was the difference? What did it matter whether I chose to give it to some stranger whose name I wouldn't remember or had it taken? Hadn't I spent enough time in the shadows of that pier holding my legs wide anyway? I thought everything they would have thought myself. Asking for it. Deserved it. Welcomed it. And it would have been easier to keep thinking that way but it wouldn't stick. What did stick was the steely taste in my mouth, the feeling of someone else inside of me and his dirty fingers in my mouth. A person who hadn't checked first whether or what I was prepared to give. So I'd tell them, the reason I knew I wasn't asking for it is because, if I did ask for anything back then, though maybe it was asking for too much, the thing I always asked for was a condom.

21

I only meant to go for an afternoon sleep, like Ma did. The day after the hospital I went to lie upstairs in Ma's pink fleecy dressing gown with that plastic doll tucked in the space between my legs and empty belly. I didn't think I'd bleed for a long time or feel that trick of feeling hollow but I did. In the end I stopped trying to fill it up with piles of toast and cans of rice pudding and cradled the emptiness.

I slept. Sleeps like army blankets; dark, heavy and itchy, that I woke from dazed and numb until I felt the empty space inside, and then I popped the doll's head off, counted the notes and promised myself, tomorrow, I'd get myself back to the land of the living.

I stayed in bed for over three months. I got up once a day, when I heard the door shut. I ate whatever was in the oven covered with a plate, and went upstairs with one of the books that Ma left on the table and read until the words blurred off the page.

Ma tried to talk me out. 'We've all got our problems, Janie. But we've not the luxury of wallowing. That's what yer doing while I'm trying tae manage.'

Then drag me out. 'Now get up an' stop leeching off this family. Get up! I'll have yeh fuckin' sectioned! Is that what yeh'd like? Electric shock therapy? Pumped full of pills?' She screamed, ranted and went round the room stuffing things into bin liners and I watched and waited until she exhausted herself, and went off for a cry and a long sleep herself.

'Please, Janie.' She was on the edge of the bed. 'I can't cope.

I need yeh tae be strong fer me. Think about Tiny. What's it doing tae her tae see her big sister like this?'

But Tiny was fine. We argued less. She would sometimes come in after school, sit behind me on the pillow, French-plait my hair and tell me about *Neighbours*. When I couldn't sit up, when I felt like my tongue was an animal that had crawled into my mouth to die, then she'd just come and sit, turn the pages of my books and try to read the words or rock the doll in her arms.

Solid little Tiny, Tiffany now, who learned not to expect too much back for everything she gave. Tiny, with her wide face, sturdy runner's legs and quick, hair-plaiting fingers, that's what got me out of bed. Plus I owed something now, I had a debt and the first instalment was just me getting up.

So it was Tiny that got me to shower, put on some clothes and get out of the house and up to the shopping centre, head down and shaking the whole way, to buy a little toy pram. Tiny got me to sit and eat Victoria sponge and slices of block ice cream with the pink candle still sticking out of it. Because even if she didn't expect it, didn't ask for me to be good to her, it didn't mean she didn't deserve it.

At four and a half months empty, when I would have been six and a half with a swollen belly, I kept the curtains open and let the evening spill onto the pages of my book and the words stopped sliding off the bottom. I felt the bubbles in my blood and the walls didn't seemed so closed in. I took the notes from the doll's head and gave the empty doll to Tiny to push around in her little pram.

'Be careful an' don't leave it too close tae the fire. The head's flimsy on that make.'

'Aye, just like us,' I thought I heard her say as she wheeled the squeaky pram down the road, but it might have just been one of those hollow-feeling tricks.

We took our chances without coats to get the last of the sun, even though the chilly breeze made the hairs of your arms bristle. It was a bit of a walk to the big Asda, through town, towards the train station and the bit of swampy wasteland that got the best of the town's sunsets. As we walked across the old wooden bridge the mirrored walls of the superstore were pink and orange, absorbing the light; it looked like a casino, or a fancy hotel, not the next step up from Lidl's in the cheap-food chain.

I'd promised Ma I'd come to help her back with the bags, but we hardly said a word, just walked side by side enjoying the view, the skin of our arms skimming each other's, our hands bumping.

'That's a good one.' Ma nodded her head to the bleed of colour dissolving into the plastic-bag and bottle-strewn marshes.

'Aye, it's pretty.' I walked on, my eyes dead on the horizon, letting the light sink right into my pupils, so when we got inside I almost walked straight into the old bloke with his saucer-sized badge saying 'Welcome! Ask Me Anything!' Ma steered me towards the cafe as I blinked away the flashes and pops in front of my eyes.

'Let's have a cuppa and then get the shop in.'

I'd been properly out of bed for weeks now but it still made my teeth hurt a bit, walking through the cafe; my heart beat louder every second beat, and I felt a scorching lick of heat up each of my arms, little twitches in my lips and eyes.

Ma turned round and caught me just standing there in the aisle of the cafe, a pair of grans looking up from their teacakes to give each other a look. She took my arm and sat me at the nearest table, still piled high with dirty plates, a chicken nugget with little teeth marks leaving a greasy smear.

'Just stay there an' I'll get us some grub in.'

I nodded and kept myself staring at the little crescents in the nugget, imagined the little sweetcorn-sized teeth that had made them, then pushed it with a swipe onto the floor, squashed it down with my trainer and kept my eyes on the table. It helped me to think that no one was looking. I knew they weren't really, not in Asda where there were all sorts. I just needed a minute for my heartbeat to stop shouting, my skin to stop burning.

Ma set the tray down. 'I thought we could do with a treat. We never do this any more.' The tray had a pot of tea, two shiny-looking scones, little plastic pots of jam and cream. Ma stuck her knife through her scone. 'Dig in then.'

And so I did. I concentrated on making a scone with the perfect thickness of jam and an even dollop of cream, sandwiched the halves of scone together and filled my gob with it. When I looked up Ma had a dollop of cream down her chin and I knew I had crumbs all down my front, but I did feel better.

'Gorgeous.' Ma poured our cups of tea, just a bit too dark, a bit tepid, but I gulped mine down.

'Aye, thanks, Ma, this is lovely.' I waited until Ma was using a licked finger to chase the crumbs of her plate, craning her neck for a nearby ashtray. 'Ma –' I brushed the crumbs from my front – 'do I look . . . weird now?'

Ma stopped chasing crumbs and looked up, her shoulders dropping. 'Weird? No, Janie, don't be daft. Yeh turn heads, yeh must be able tae see that.'

'Do I seem, yeh know, different, strange?'

Ma pushed aside the tray. 'Let me just get an ashtray.'

I watched her walk over and get one from the wonky tower of them by the trays, She took a pre-rolled rolly from her tin that had magic mushrooms on the front that I got her on Mother's

Day. Lit it up and took a long puff. Her face was hard and I wished I'd never asked.

'Janie, there's nothing strange about yeh. I know yeh've been feeling . . . upset. Are all the things that yeh were upset about over an' done with now?'

What could I reply? She made it sound like it was a pissed-up row with Beth or a lad breaking up with me. But it wasn't her fault, I didn't want to share it then and I still wouldn't. I shrugged. 'Aye, I mean, I suppose. I've stuff tae sort out.'

'Well, yeh seem better and I was thinking . . .' She put down her fag and rummaged in her bag. 'Look, I was thinking about a course.'

She spread the glossy booklet in front of us; she had pages marked already. 'I was thinking catering, or maybe some GCSEs just fer a start, like.'

I looked up from the prospectus. She looked chuffed, kept giving the shiny paper little rubs with the tips of her fingers. 'That's a brilliant idea, Ma, you should maybe do the catering cause then yeh've a job at the end of it an –'

'This isn't fer me, Janie. It's coming up to starting time but I've had a chat with the college an' they said under special circumstances they can do you a late enrolment.'

I took the book now, filled with shiny-haired, white-toothed, book-carrying students in Gap jumpers. Were they bollocks Great Yarmouth College students. She'd turned down the pages, GSCEs, Performing Arts, Foundation Studies Animal Care.

'Animal Care, Ma? Listen, I –'

'Well, it's just a suggestion. The point is this summer's over an' done with. Yer feeling better, yeh said so yerself, and now it's time tae get on with things.' She pushed the book forward a bit so it nudged my chest.

'No. No way. I've been making plans myself.'

She stubbed out her fag and pulled the book back across the table, smacked the open pages shut. She stared at the table arms folded, like she'd known all along I wasn't going to college but wanted to hear me say no. Give her the upper hand. 'What's the plan then?'

I was blushing in front of my own ma, but I'd almost been a ma myself and that meant I couldn't be a kid any more, even though she made me feel like one. 'London maybe. I've saved cash. I thought about looking fer my da maybe or getting a job in one of the hotels. Live-in.'

'Look fer yer da? Is this because of our rows? Come on, Janie, you know me, it's just the Ryan Temper. Yeh know yer ma loves yeh. You're as bad as me fer it.'

'It's not the rows or you, Ma. It's this place, you know what it's like. You were my age when you left home.'

'Aye, an I was a kid. I ended up in a right state.' She'd raised her voice and one of the nans looked over, with an unimpressed set to her false teeth. Who were we to spoil her Monday teacake?

'Ma?' I reached across and put my hand on the sleeve of her sweatshirt, wormed my fingers into the sleeve like I would have if I was a kid. 'It'll be different for me.'

'That's exactly what I said. Now come on, I want tae get home fer *Ready Steady Cook*.' She shook my hand off and walked a few steps ahead, then she stopped and offered her arm and I linked mine through it as we walked to the trolleys.

I waited until I'd unpacked everything with Ma before I took my shower. Her head was half in and half out the freezer's mist when she saw me with that morning's still damp towels.

'Another shower, Janie? We're no made of money, yeh know; it's not just the gas, water costs a bomb an' all.'

'I've my period.'

I got in and made the water as hot as it would go, so it felt like my skin would come off like scraps of wet tissue. I hadn't lied to Ma, except the lady at the Brook Family Planning Centre said it was called spotting, probably the end of an infection, and that I should have come earlier. She was nice enough, just like the one that had booked the appointment with a not-too-happy not-too-sad smile, but spotting was a cute misleading name for having your period all the time.

My wrists stung a bit in the water, I guessed from holding the frozen bags of veg and chips across them while Ma loaded the freezer, but it was a sweet sort of soreness. I washed my hair twice, left my conditioner in and let the water thump down on my chest, imagining the sounds it made behind my ribs. I soaped my hands and ran them all over my skin, all over my changed body, a body with a little pot belly and shyer shoulders. My constant reminder, as if I needed one.

Ma was on the sofa watching *Holiday* when I came out in my towels. I sat in front of her on the carpet so I could stretch my legs in front of the fire.

'Look at that, a thousand quid for a week in Argentina learning to tango. I'd love tae do that. She's a great tan.'

'And boobs.' Ma took the towel off my shoulders and started giving my hair a rough dry, getting her fingers right into the scalp, pulling at the roots a bit. 'Ma, a bit softer maybe?'

'Sorry.'

After she'd finished, and I felt like I had whiplash, she went to get the brush. I leaned back against her knees and she spread my hair across her legs and started brushing the ends out, each stroke snagging a tangle. My legs were burning a bit now but I didn't move.

'Janie, yeh know you going will break my heart.'

'Ma, I've told yeh –'

She put her hand on my shoulder to stop me from turning round. 'Shh, Janie, calm down. I'm just telling yeh so yeh'll know I'll miss yeh.' Her knees pushed me forward a bit while she rummaged for something and then there was a roll of paper in front of my face. 'This is just a wee something.'

I unrolled it, an address for Jennifer Furlong, a twenty, two tenners. 'Listen, Ma, I've saved tons this summer an' as for finding Da that was just –'

'It's just an early present, what I was putting by for yer big birthday. An' the address might not even be any good but I thought it might get yeh started. I thought I'd give it to yeh now. In case yeh don't get a chance to say goodbye. Like I said, it'll break my heart but yer a good girl, Janie. You'll do brilliant.'

I scrunched the paper and notes in my fist, let the fire keep burning my legs. Ma took my hair in both hands and put it over my shoulder. I bit the insides of my cheeks, waited for the pain behind my eyes to go and reached up and touched her bony knuckles, just for as long as she'd let me, just for a second. We sat quiet for a while then. Watched some presenter's fat cycling-shorted Lycra arse tour the South of France on a bicycle until Tiny burst in, out of breath, bringing the smell of night-time and sweat with her.

'Ma, I stepped in dog shite and they were all laughing at me!'

Her chest heaved, nose streamed, her face was bright red: she was ready to blow. We were both glad to get up and deal with Tiny's dog-shite emergency. Ma with a fork kept for the purpose under the kitchen sink, and me with a choc ice and a promise to put the shitters up anyone who made my little sister cry.

*

'Jack Frost Cider?'

Beth shrugged.

'It was on special and if you don't like it you buy the booze next time.'

'An' what's with the jumper apart from the fact that it's September.' I plucked at the nubby wool of her pink jumper, her black bra visible through the loose knit.

'Black shows the baby sick.'

'Well, at least yer underwear's still gothic.'

'And my tits are huge now, probably the only thing about this I'd recommend.'

'Ta, but I'll go fer silicone.'

We were sat on the beach a few yards from where Beth conceived Jade. It was either there or the car park behind Asda, and Beth chose the beach, said it was more romantic.

The bottle passed between us while Beth rocked her buggy back and forth with her left arm like she'd had a piston installed in her shoulder while she was pregnant. Her eyeliner was wonky and her lip gloss went over the edges.

'Are yeh going tae the blind school for make-up classes now then?'

'Yeah, they said they saw you there the other week looking for a boyfriend.'

Our laughs were swallowed by the waves and the squeak of the buggy wheels.

'I always knew you'd get out, Janie, I just thought I'd be coming with you.'

'I'm sorry about everything.'

'Don't worry, if you'd got yourself pregnant and were reduced to wearing pink jumpers, I'd be on a coach quicker than it takes Michael Simpson to cum as well.'

'I don't just mean that. I know I just disappeared on yeh when yeh needed me.'

A football flew over our heads, hit the side of the pram and set Jade wailing.

'Stupid twats, can't you tell the difference between a baby and a goal?'

'Aye, fuck off an' play somewhere else, dickheads!'

Beth lifted Jade from the buggy and cradled her on her shoulder. Jade was three months old but Beth looked like she'd been a ma forever.

'Look, I'm just trying tae say I'm really sorry an' just cause I'm going away doesnae mean I'm not still yer best mate.'

She took another swig, her head turned away from Jade. 'I know. I'm coming soon too. I'll get a council place and I'll let you stay if you do all the nappy changes and babysit while I go out clubbing with fit London lads and then we'll go on holiday to Greece, or maybe the Canaries.'

Even though she was a goth Beth was never one to hold a grudge. I leaned over and kissed the side of her hair. It smelt of baby sick and cider, a good smell.

'Fuck, you aren't turning lezzer on me?'

'Well, if I was I wouldn't go for a someone in a pink jumper with wonky make-up, though you do have even more massive boobs now.'

She shifted Jade to the shoulder nearest me. 'You won't even hold her? Now, Jade, why won't grumpy Auntie Janie give you a cuddle?'

I looked away and pasted on a smile as wonky as Beth's lip gloss. 'Naw, I'd drop her on her head.'

'So? I do it all the time. That's why we're drinking on the beach.'

I took Jade's soft sleepy body in my stiff arms and she stared into my eyes, in a vague, disinterested way, blue on blue. She was perfect and for a minute I thought my insides were shattering. But just for a minute.

'Aye, well, that was lovely but yeh can take her back now. That's enough for me for the moment.'

Beth laughed and we swapped, baby for cider bottle. I cradled it in my arms. 'You've your bairn an' I've mine, an' look, I'm a natural.'

We hugged and I thought I saw tears but Beth said it was just a bit of sand.

'I got you a present.'

'Early?'

She threw the box to me. Mates: Extra thick for maximum protection.

'Mates from my mate. Beth, I'm touched.'

The wind had picked up, hair blew into my mouth.

'Just remember those instructions, extra thick is the condom not the blokes you're shagging.'

We said goodbye on a laugh.

The first thing I did was buy the pills. £2.74 for twelve pale blue robin's eggs in their little blister pack. It was as simple as that. I bought the ticket from a woman with a tight blue rinse, the same colour as my pills.

She had a packet of Werther's Originals on the counter next to her and had ripped off the paper in a long spiral of brown and cream. In a square of sunshine, behind the glass, they looked like art.

'Return?'

I looked up from the packet and smiled. 'Naw, just a single.'

She raised her eyebrows but wrote me out the ticket and handed me the waxy paper ticket along with a Werther's Original squeaking in its plastic wrapper.

I waited outside the gates of Tiny's school. She'd started wearing her hair in thin plaits with beads at the ends and I heard her clicking towards me before I could pick her out from the sea of red sweatshirts.

We walked along the deserted pier and swung our legs off the edge, drinking cans of Coke and eating Smarties. We talked about her project on the Vikings; she showed me her Paddington Bear book. I tucked thirty pounds into the pages; I kept one of Ma's tens to buy myself her present, and said she should take Ma to the pictures and for a fish-and-chip supper.

'It's our secret for today, alright? Now yer so big yeh can keep a secret.'

'You'll be back though, Christmas an' that?'

I didn't answer, just rippled my fingers through her braids to hear them click, which made her giggle and give me a sticky kiss on my cheek.

That night I crept in and curled myself around Ma's back, tucked my knees up in the bend of hers. Tiny came in in the morning, still soft and stupefied with sleep, and made herself into a little ball pushed into Ma's front. There we lay; Tiny, Ma, me. Ryan Women, with filthy tempers, filthy mouths and big bruised muscles for hearts.

I didn't want another row, or more bitter words and names to swallow, so I left a note. She'd said herself she thought I might not get the chance to say goodbye. Still, it was a cowardly note, telling Ma not to worry, that I loved her and to look after Tiny.

Inside the envelope I put the Sellotaped glossy squares of the baby picture, but it wasn't the same, if you looked closely you could see the rips.

I took two of the robin's eggs pills and got settled down in the familiar chemical air and scratchy chairs of the coach. It was the first time I ever got off a coach without the taste of vomit in my mouth and all for the bargain price of £2.74.

The Victoria Line spat me out at Oxford Circus. A sea of people moved around me in the dirt and heat of the evening. I thought the man in a blue T-shirt, skinny and sunburned with yellow hair, was selling something till I heard him shout into his megaphone.

'Sinners, all of you sinners, put down your shopping bags. They're empty! Empty like your life. Turn to the Lord and ask to be saved sinners!'

I suppose he was selling something. People rolled their eyes while he paced, picking people out of the crowd who looked more sinful than the others.

'*Standard*! Get your *Standard*!'

I pushed through and stood on one of the corners of the crossroads. I had my school bag, still with Tipp-Ex hearts and skulls, over my shoulder, and a soft roll of twenties getting damp inside my left bra cup; just to be safe.

I smelt frying onions and someone's breath, bitter with stale coffee, just over my shoulder and pushed forward. I didn't want to start this new life pushing through but it seemed to be expected.

Beyond the crush I started walking, looking in shop windows and at people grey with tiredness. Was this what I'd come for? Red buses and black cabs and new-wave punks spitting on the pavement? It didn't feel any better than Great Yarmouth except it was just me, without Ma or Tiny or Beth.

I walked towards a building towering up ahead with its sad fountains, which no one was looking at, gushing murky water. My mouth was dry from the tablets and I lumbered myself up onto the wall of the fountain. I just needed a minute. I'd make a plan.

'Alright?' He wore a leather jacket and a band T-shirt. His Vans were ripped along the edges. I looked at his squinting eyes, brown and green mixed together and his floppy almost ginger fringe. 'What's your name?'

He smiled and his teeth had a sharp, yellowish look about them. I said nothing, pulled my rucksack against my stomach and fought the urge to bring my hand to my left breast.

'Listen, you look a bit lost. Do you need something?' Still smiling, he kicked his wrecked Vans against the wall, fingering whatever little bags he had inside those leather pockets.

The 37 bus went past, and I imagined it winding through the streets to tall white houses with fat, furry cats and pale porridge-coloured rooms. I looked back at him and considered the something he had for me in his pockets.

'My name's Jane Ryan and no, I don't need anything. Thanks though.'

My mother's daughter, I had a plan. I hopped down from the wall and got on the 37, just for a bed for the night, for a catch-up, maybe a few answers.

The rain started through the last of the pale autumn light and the road unfurled ahead of me, a shining grey ribbon full of possibility as each new twist revealed itself.

THE BEGINNING

ACKNOWLEDGEMENTS

First and foremost my thanks go to my wonderful agent Juliet Pickering at AP Watt and my brilliant editor Becky Hardie at Chatto & Windus. Both championed the book from the first and I am enormously grateful to them for making the publication of this book an absolute pleasure from submission to shelf.

Thank you also to: Fiona Murphy, Vicki Watson and the rest of the Chatto team, Clare Elliot, Judi Bennett, Helen Rosner, Suzie Ostrove and my beautiful godson Xander.